Moose Pond Lodge

Gini,
thank you so
much for supporting
this! I hope you
enjoy the story;

Karri
Moser

Karri L. Moser

ISBN 978-0-692-99222-7

Printed in the U.S.A.

First Edition

Cover photograph taken at Mi-Te-Jo Campground, Milton, New Hampshire.

This novel is dedicated to Alyssa--A force of nature from the beginning

"Someday when the pages of my life end,

I know that you will be one of its

most beautiful chapters"

--Unknown--

Chapter 1

The mountains are calling and I must go—John Muir

As Molly drove the winding road, a flood of memories engulfed her. She didn't need to see the sign, *Moose Pond Lodge 10 miles*, to know where she was. The towering white pines on either side blended into each other as they flashed by the windows. The last time she saw those trees, she was twenty-three and heading the other way. At that time, she swore to God she'd never return to Maine. Molly was still shell-shocked that she was driving back more than ten years later, with a daughter in the back seat, and a soon-to-be ex-husband left in the rear-view mirror. As she rounded the last turn, the green and white fence came into view. Molly fought the urge to turn around and forget she ever got that phone call.

"Wake up, kid. We're almost there. Just another mile up this road." Molly said as she glanced around, wondering how time could leave a place so untouched. "Almost there." Emerson squirmed a little and rubbed her eyes. She had been asleep since Connecticut.

Once forgotten childhood memories distracted her as the car found its way that last mile. She saw herself as a 12-year-old kid running up the road to get back before dinner, or before she had to help clean the dining hall for the afternoon show. Molly remembered the sense of accomplishment the first time she climbed the stool to run a credit card. She also remembered the taste of success the first time she used her girlish charms to convince a guest to pre-book his favorite cabin for the next summer. Molly shook her head, absorbing the fact that her daughter was the same age. She was amazed thinking back on the responsibilities that had fallen on her tiny, twelve-year-old shoulders after her mother died including making menu decisions for the nightly dinners and signing delivery orders.

Once the grief from her mother's death dissipated like morning fog from Moose Pond Lodge, it was time to get back to work. That work became more difficult for the teen as her father descended into depression. Molly had no choice but to step up to keep the place going. She had nothing else to do as the only child of Mason and Rosemary Bordeaux growing up at a summer resort.

Moose Pond Lodge had belonged to Rosemary's parents and was the premiere resort outside of Great Pines, Maine. Over one hundred acres contained the mountain hide-away that crept to the sandy shores of Moose Pond. There were 12 small cabins peppered in the clearing down a trail from the main lodge. Each was complete with either a full bed or two twin beds. Each had a small kitchenette, a bathroom with a clawfoot tub, a desk, and a closet filled with extra quilts handmade by Molly's mom. Some of the more expensive cabins, including the honeymoon cabin, had fireplaces, a loveseat, and a small front porch flanked by two rocking chairs.

Molly's parents devoted all their energy to keeping the clientele Rosemary's parents had acquired. As other resorts cropped up between the White Mountains and the coast, it became harder to make the small resort stand out. Entertainment became the key. On weekend nights, the dining room was cleared of the long tables. Folding chairs would be lined up. Mason made a make-shift stage and Rosemary sewed a curtain. Local musicians, singers, dance groups, and comedians would perform for a small amount of money, or free drinks and food. As the entertainment became a source of enticement, Mason built a small bar area off the main lobby. "The Bordeaux Lounge" was the nightspot for parents after kids fell asleep in the cabins and where Molly learned how to make the perfect highball. It was the also the place that gripped her father as his depression meshed with alcoholism after her mother died.

Despite her dad telling her when she left that he'd leave her nothing, Molly knew when Mason's lawyer called her two weeks ago that the responsibilities of Moose Pond Lodge were hers once again. Mason had died, alone and bourbon-soaked. His long-time lawyer and friend, Mr. Castille, was waiting for Molly to return to Maine and sell the resort.

The green and white fencing ended as the pines parted and revealed the main lodge directly in front of Molly. She gasped as it came into full view. The paint was peeling, the porch looked lopsided, and the bushes looked as if no one trimmed a branch since she left. She realized her father had gone downhill over the last few years, but she never imagined he'd let the resort go downhill, too. Guilt bubbled up in Molly's gut. She could taste it as she parked the car in front of the porch. No, she told herself. It wasn't her fault he let everything go after her mother died. It wasn't her fault he chose to drink instead of fly out and see her and Emerson at Christmas. It wasn't her fault he died in a pool of his own vomit on the lounge floor and went undiscovered for two days. It wasn't her fault he never called a gardener, a painter, or anyone else to help him maintain the place in between seasons. As Mr. Castille opened the door and stepped onto the porch, Molly realized it wasn't his fault either.

Molly unstrapped her seat belt and opened the door slowly with her foot. The pine air hit her hard. It made her head spin. She adjusted her sunglasses and stepped out.

"Hello there, Mr. Castille. It's been awhile, huh?" Molly said.

"Mr. Castille? Hell, girl, you've known me since you were in diapers. Cut the formalities and shit. Get up here and give Uncle Bob a hug." He said as he walked closer to the steps. He got around slower than Molly remembered. She wondered how her father had gotten around the last few years. Molly closed the car door and smiled as she raced to meet Bob.

"It's so good to see you. I've missed you so much, kid. Where's that girl of yours? I've seen a thousand pictures." Bob said. "I've missed you, too. I'm sorry I didn't make it back sooner. I had some personal stuff to take care of before leaving Nashville. I hope all of Great Pines doesn't hate me for not making it back for his funeral." Molly said. While she didn't care what anyone in Great Pines thought, she still cared what Bob Castille thought. "Emerson?" She called out behind her shoulder. The car door opened and Emerson slowly walked up to the porch. She extended a hand to Mr. Castille.

"Mr. Castille, it's nice to meet you. I'm Emerson Watts." She said. He reached and hugged her. She resisted for a moment and kept her arms by her side.

"I've heard so much about you, kiddo. It's nice to meet you in person. You look like your mom when she was that age," he said. "Come on, let's go inside. There's a ton papers to sign."

Molly started to step forward toward the screen door when her legs froze. Every memory of her childhood involved that place. The thought of reentering that world and revisiting all that had happened there paralyzed her. She drew in a deep breath and reached for Emerson's hand. Molly hesitated. She wasn't just walking back into her past; Molly was dragging her daughter into it also. But, entering that past was the only way she and Emerson would have a future, a future free of her soon-to-be ex-husband.

As she followed Mr. Castille, the smells and sights enveloped her. She coughed. Her throat started to close as the memories wrapped around her tighter and the musty smell settled in her nose. Nothing much had changed inside. The entryway of the main lodge still rivaled the grandest ski lodges in New England. The floor to ceiling stone fireplace dissected the main lodge in two. One side had been the lobby and social hour area, with plush sofas, antique chairs, and books shelves. The other side was still the main dining hall where dinner was served for up to twenty-five guests at a time. The moose antlers high above the fireplace anchored the entire building, even though cobwebs were woven from one end to the other. That set of antlers was the subject of more pictures than Molly dared to count. The same quilts hung over the chairs by the door. The guest book was in the same spot on the counter. The stool was next to it. The couches were new, however. Mr. Castille walked around the fireplace into the dining area. As Molly followed, the sounds of shows, the smell of bacon, and the clicks of high heels tapping on the floor filled her ears. There was a stack of papers on the table next to a briefcase.

"Molly, you okay?" Mr. Castille said as he dragged chairs to the table.

"Yeah, I'm good. It's just a lot to take in, you know? It's been so long, and it's like nothing has changed. I'm just a little overwhelmed." She said. Molly's eyes darted all around the large room. Her voice echoed. She squeezed Emerson's hand tighter. Emerson rubbed her eyes and squeezed her mom's hand.

"I understand. He didn't change much. You're right about that. You know your dad. He didn't see the need to change anything as long business was still good." He said as he sat. "Listen, we don't have to worry about all this stuff right now. I can go over these tomorrow after you've gotten settled. I take it you're staying here?" Mr. Castille said.

"Yeah, we've got nowhere else to stay. Technically, this place is all I've got."

Since leaving Emerson's father months earlier, she and the ten-year-old had been staying with friends. Tying up loose ends with Kenny the Philanderer and getting court permission to take Emerson from Tennessee took up nearly every spare moment Molly had since she got the call about her father. She hadn't thought a day past pulling in and signing papers to sell the resort. A quick sale would mean a nice chunk of money for her to start over. But, she didn't know where exactly that fresh start would unfold. Now that she was standing in the dining room and saw the condition of the place, Molly suddenly wasn't sure a quick sale could happen or if selling right away was in her best interest. She didn't expect walking into Moose Pond Lodge to lure her back into a Maine mindset. But, without warning and without permission, it did just that.

Molly tucked Emerson into bed in her old room after getting her somewhat settled. She could see in her daughter's eyes that the lodge was less than impressive. Then again, Molly knew uprooting Emerson just months after leaving her father wouldn't be a smooth transition for the kid. Molly then said goodbye to Mr. Castille for the night. He'd return in the morning to discuss the fate of the resort. As he pulled away, Molly let the quiet sink in as she wandered around the main lodge. Part of her wanted the childhood memories to suck her in and fill her soul. Part of her wanted to wake Emerson, throw her in the car, and just keep driving. Once the swirls of memories slowed, Molly's eyes grew heavy. She knew going into her parents' bedroom was the inevitable next step after a long couple of days of driving and avoidance. She retrieved her suitcase from the couch in the main lodge and walked down the pine-laden hallway that led to the 'personal quarters' of the resort. The last door at the end of the hall was her parents' bedroom and sanctuary. Molly slowly pressed on the door with her luggage, and it opened with the long creak her father always vowed to fix. She flipped on the light with her free hand.

There were boxes along the side wall. Mr. Castille had packed some of her father's clothes and belongings. Her mother's quilts still flanked the edge of the bed. She lowered the suitcase to the floor and drew the quilt to her face. Her long blonde hair fell over the sides as she dropped her head to inhale the scent. It smelled like him, the dad she loved as an only child. She remembered running into his arms after falling off the fence post at the end of the drive. She remembered running into his strong arms after her mother died in a car accident in town. Each time he embraced her, Molly inhaled as she nuzzled the crook of his neck. His scent took away all fear, chaos, and pain that ever touched her as a kid. That scent was in the quilt. She let tears fall openly as she struggled to inhale more of the only thing she had left of her father. She drew the quilt to her mouth to muffle the cry so

Emerson wouldn't hear. She cried for her father, her mother, all they created and left behind for her. Molly cried for the pain of the last few months and broken vows that led her to leave Kenny the Philanderer. She cried for Emerson, the life she had taken her from and the uncertainty of the life that would unfold before them. Everything about their lives had changed in a blink. All her plans, her hopes, her certainties had all fallen to the wayside. Somehow it had all unraveled, and she found herself, once again, inhaling her dad's scent and hoping that would fix it all. Only this time, it was just a lingering scent on a quilt, nothing more.

Chapter 2

Keep your sense of proportion by regularly, preferably daily, visiting the natural world—Catlin Matthews

Molly stirred in her parents' bed as she saw the early spring sun rise. She rubbed her eyes and drew in a long breath. Remnants of her dreams still floated in her mind. She dreamt of her childhood and could taste the lobster rolls by the bonfires. She heard her mother's laugh for the first time in years. Molly smiled and wondered if the photo albums were still on the shelves somewhere. She pulled back the quilt and rose. She wanted to be sure Emerson could find her. As she wandered down the hall, she heard clanking the kitchen. Emerson was already awake and riffling through cupboards.

"There's not a lot here, Mom, but I found some cereal." Emerson said while perched on the counter.

"Well, the milk is definitely bad. Better check before you get your hopes up." Molly said. She turned her head when she heard a car door slam. Molly looked out the main lodge window to see Mr. Castille walking up the stairs with an arm-load of groceries. She ran to open the door.

"Bob, you didn't have to do that. We're fine, really." Molly said.

"I know, I know. I just wanted to bring a few things over for you. I know how kids can be." He said with a smile and wink. Molly couldn't help but smile back at him.

Molly showered and got dressed for the day as Emerson picked Mr. Castille's brain about all things Maine, Great Pines, and the lodge in its heyday. As she walked back out to the main lodge where they were splayed on the couch, she saw the stacks of paper on the end table.

"I guess it's time to get down to business, huh?" Molly said as she sunk into the leather chair closest to the fireplace.

"Yeah, it is, if you want. But I gotta tell you; it's a little more complicated than signing to accept the property and then throwing a for sale sign out front," he said as he reached for more papers from his messenger bag.

"Why's that? I don't mind a short sale, really. I just need enough to make a fresh start for Emerson and myself. I'm not looking to get anything major out of this place. Trust me, if I wanted more money, I'd really go after Kenny the Philanderer instead of just taking what I need for Em." Molly said. "I'm sorry, Em. I swore I'd never be one of 'those parents' who talk crap about an ex in front of her kids."

"It's okay, Mom," Emerson said without looking up from the photo album Bob found on the shelf. Molly saw Emerson roll her eyes before turning the page.

"Well, Molly. I had an inspector come out when I packed up some your dad's stuff. I figured getting a jump on that would help you out and save you some trouble once you got home. It's not up to code in many ways. Things here need to be fixed before you can sell, that's if you want a decent offer. Now, you can always assign a trustee, like me, to oversee all that so you can just walk away, sit tight somewhere, and sell when it's ready. You can also still walk away completely, leave it up to the state, or whatever if you want to just wipe your hands clean of this place," Mr. Castille said. "Or, you can sign to have it all in your name, take a few months to get it fixed up and ready to open for the season, sell, and move on like you said. Or, one option you have is to do what your father intended."

"What my father intended?" Molly said as she drew up her legs underneath her.

"You know, fix it and keep it. It was all for you anyway. He wanted you to run this place. That's why he left it to you." Mr. Castille said.

Molly's eyes darted all around from the dusty wood floors, up the stone fireplace, and to the tips of the moose antlers. Keep it? That was one option that never entered her mind.

"Me, run this place? Jesus, Bob, it was hard enough for my mom and dad both to run it each year, even with my help after she died and until the day I left. I can't take this on and run it. That wasn't the plan. You said I needed to come back and take care of the finalities, sign some papers, and be on my way." Molly said. Her eyes welled up. "I never...I never thought about coming back here to run this place. That wasn't in the cards, Bob."

"What was then, Molly? What was in the cards? As far as I know, none of this was in the cards. Your mom passing away like she did when you were just twelve, your dad drinking her away each night and letting this place slip away, too, and you, you and this kid needing a place, a home, after getting away from Kenny the Philanderer, was any of that in the cards?" He said. "Sorry, kid, I don't even know your dad."

"It's okay," Emerson said, again without looking up from the album.

Molly shifted more in the chair. The fight or flight response gurgled in her gut. She fidgeted with her hands. Bob reached over and tapped her knee.

"Listen. You don't have to decide all this right now. Hell, you don't have to decide anything for sure now, except signing the ownership papers. You've got time to figure out the rest. How about this. You sign the papers then we find someone to come fix the things that absolutely need to be done before you sell or reopen, or whatever." He scooted closer to her. "Stay here in the meantime. Rest up, plan, get yourself on track and figure out your next step. I know a lot happened down there in Nashville. Take time here to regroup, you and the kid. What do you say?" Mr. Castille said.

Molly let one tear fall. She squeezed her eyes to make the others retreat as she swooped her hair behind her ears. Time to regroup was something Molly knew she needed, but didn't want to slow down long enough to do it. She looked at Emerson. Molly needed to enroll her in school somewhere soon. She told the Nashville courts she'd have her in school within two weeks of leaving. She assumed a short sale would mean some quick cash and the ability to drive back and buy her own house there or somewhere else. Molly was notorious for realizing the details mattered long after the details needed to matter. When she drove away from Great Pines 12 years earlier to join Kenny, whom she dated all through college, she didn't have a plan other than to be with him each night. An unexpected pregnancy dictated the rest and her father's alcoholism cemented her reasons for not coming back.

"How long do you think it'll take to get this place fixed up?" Molly said. The word regroup suddenly sounded like the best option she had.

"Not sure. Two months, maybe. It's already getting warmer out since we've had an early thaw. I'd say it can all get done and sold maybe before tourist season starts Memorial Day, or shortly after. That's my best guess at this point." Mr. Castille said.

Molly stood up and walked over to the book shelves as she listened to Emerson giggle at the pictures on the album pages. Molly knew without looking which pictures her daughter had discovered. She ran her fingers along the spines of the other albums and her father's old books. There were old farmer's almanacs, Maine tourism books, and regional short story collections dating back to her childhood. She looked out the large picture window, which was clouded with streaks as the sun shone through. The trees were starting to bud early as the last few piles of dirty snow melted into the corners of the driveway.

"Okay, Bob. I'll stay here, enroll Emerson in school, and do what I can inside while others get the outside up to code. Then, hopefully by the time it's all done and ready to sell, I'll know where the hell I want to go next." Molly said. She folded her arms. Hopefully leaving after a sale would be as easy as leaving the first time. "I guess we better call Kenny the Philan—I mean, your dad, and have him send more of your stuff." She shook her head as she broke her vow once again.

Mr. Castille showed Molly where to sign as he went through one stack of papers. Her work at a Nashville law firm meant she was more than familiar with the jargon. He tucked the rest away as he outlined who he knew to complete the work that was needed. The list seemed endless—the support beams under the lodge were rotting, porches needed new railings, doorways in some cabins were not up to new codes, parking spaces in the delivery zone needed to be wider, trails needed cleared, and every inch of the place needed a good cleaning. As the gravity of the situation became clearer with each item on Mr. Castille's list, Molly realized there wouldn't be much time for regrouping. As a means of pushing it all aside, she told Emerson a trip to town was in order. Emerson groaned.

"Come on, kid. We gotta get some supplies and proper groceries. Plus, we'll stop and see about enrolling you in school. Can't avoid that unless you want to go back to Nashville and live with Kenny the—your dad." Molly said. She rolled her eyes. How did she become 'that parent' in such a short amount of time, she wondered?

Driving the eight miles to Great Pines was like riding a bike, an old rusty bike she thought she'd never see again. Nothing had changed, or so it seemed. She knew her Tennessee license plate would stand out like a sore thumb during the off-season. She pulled into the only grocery store in town. Weekly trips with her mom suddenly resurfaced, and she could smell her mom's perfume. It was a musky scent, not floral and light like Molly liked. It was deep and complicated, like her mother.

As the two went up and down the few aisles, Molly couldn't help but smile seeing several foods and brands she never realized she missed. There were just certain things that set New England apart. It never occurred to her until that moment that she ran from more than the Moose Pond Lodge. Once she forced the cart into the checkout aisle, getting the wheels caught on the end cap, she looked up to see a familiar face. It was Maxine Frost. She had been Molly's partner in crime all through school. Even though they grew apart when she left for college, Molly left Great Pines with fond memories of her adventures with Maxine.

"Molls! Oh my God!" Maxine said, alerting the entire store of Molly's return. She dropped her scanning gun and ran around the register to grab Molly before Molly even had a chance to meet her half-way.

"Maxine. My lord, you look incredible. You work here now?" Molly said as the two embraced. Maxine's brown bun vibrated back and forth as she pulled Molly tight and rocked her.

"Yeah, yeah, I do. Josh and I bought it a few years back. We're short-handed and I just run register until the kids get out of school and they get here to work. I married Josh Frost a few years back, but you probably knew that from your dad. Oh, honey, that's why you're here, huh? Your dad? I'm so sorry. Josh and I sent flowers to Heathrow's when we heard." Maxine said as she let Molly go and rubbed her arms. Molly forgot how nurturing and affectionate Maxine was.

"Thank you, Max. Yeah, I knew you married Josh. Dad did manage to pass along some town news when he wasn't, you know. Anyways, Yes, I'm in town to fix up the place. I guess." Molly said.

"Oh, my daughter. Emerson, this is my old bestie from way back, Maxine. Maxine, this is Emerson. She's ten." Molly reached behind her to pull Emerson forward. Maxine grabbed the girl's arm and pulled her from the aisle. She hugged Emerson like a long-lost daughter.

"My God, Mol, she looks just like you did at that age. I bet you hear that a lot?" Maxine said. Molly nodded yes. "Hey, come on over for dinner soon? Like the weekend, maybe? Josh and I would love to have you, and Emerson, too, of course." Maxine said as she made her way back to the register.

"Max, I'd love that. I'm not sure who the hell else I still know around here besides you." Molly said. Maxine made her way back around to the register and started to ring up the groceries, giving them a few minutes to catch up. As soon as Molly said she was staying at the lodge until it was ready to sell and she could move on, Maxine's face dropped.

"Sell? But then what? You never come back to Great Pines? But, this is your home, Mol." Maxine said. A despair crossed over her face and pangs of guilt fluttered inside Molly. She hadn't thought of or considered Great Pines her home in years. To Maxine, there was no other home out there. Molly explained her divorce and need to start over fresh somewhere.

"Why can't you get a fresh start here?" Maxine asked.

"I just…I just never planned to stay, that's all. I didn't even plan to stay longer than a few days until Mr. Castille, Dad's lawyer, told me selling wouldn't be possible without this crazy list of repairs." Molly said as she and Emerson placed the bags in the cart.

"Oh, I see. You were just coming to sign papers, collect a check, and take off without saying anything to anyone? Including me?" Maxine said. Suddenly, those pangs of guilt festered even deeper. It began to burn as Molly could taste the hurt she caused Maxine. She walked around from the cart and wrapped her arms around her old friend.

"I'm sorry, Maxine. Please don't be hurt. I've had a ton of upheaval lately, with Kenny the Philanderer and my dad dying. I'm all out of sorts. Quite frankly, I have no idea what I'm doing or what I will do." Molly said. Even though it didn't excuse returning all these years later and not planning to let anyone know, Molly knew her words were true. She hoped it provided some salve to the cut she inflicted on the kindest person she had ever known.

"Saturday night. You guys come out for dinner, and that'll make up for all. Okay?" Maxine said as she jotted her address on the back of the receipt. Molly promised they'd be there as she pushed the cart toward the door. School registration was the next stop.

As she unpacked groceries, Molly found a note on a legal pad on the counter. It was a detailed list of who would be out to the resort to start work. Bob had lined up a contractor, grounds crew, plumber, and an electrician to start the basics. He also arranged for payment of the life insurance to ensure the financial backing for the repairs. Bob had taken on so much, and Molly realized she had done nothing but push back in the twenty-four hours she had been back in Great Pines. She made a mental note to thank him and take a more active role in what was happening and what needed done. After all, it was her responsibility, not his.

Molly found comfort watching Emerson explore the resort even though resentment oozed from Emerson with every apathetic shoulder shrug. Molly reminded herself Emerson's brooding was only natural considering all the changes. She watched Emerson rummage through the books, albums, and tons of 'thank you' cards and pictures sent by guests. Notes of appreciation and praise for the grandfather she barely knew filled the lobby wall.

Molly always sent her father tickets to fly out for holidays. Occasionally, he did visit. Those rare visits always ended with some regrettable incident initiated by drunken rants or mishaps. Despite the inevitable tension and escalating fury, Molly still sent tickets year after year. The tension it caused between her and Kenny was palpable. Molly simply wanted her father to have a relationship with Emerson, to be the grandfather she deserved, to be the man Molly grew up with and turned to for protection. At least through the hanging thank you notes and letters of adoration, Molly knew Emerson was absorbing a bit of who he was and who she wanted Emerson to know.

As Molly wandered the resort buildings with a list of to-dos, she found herself immersed in some of those letters that acted as wallpaper in the lobby and lounge. The ones hung with tape had yellowed. Others, pinned with tacks, curled up at the bottom. She read the lines--the exclamations of the best fishing, most relaxing days on the beach, best desserts, funniest shows at the end of the week, personal attention to every request, and the best staff. She also came across a few comments regarding the cute antics of a young Molly. The newest letters and postcards weren't much different, minus the references to Molly. Amazement filled her eyes as she realized that even though the lodge and cabins were plagued with neglect, and shrubs and trails overgrown, her father had still made the guests feel welcomed and special. Somehow, in the grips of the alcoholism that drove her from Moose Pond Lodge, he still managed to attract guests and keep up the traditions that she, her mother, and the countless guests loved about that place.

Molly's trip down memory lane needed to be put on hold as she made her way to the office phone to call Kenny regarding school for Emerson. Molly looked in the mirror and tied up her hair. She took a tissue from her pocket and wiped under her eyes. Even though it was just a phone call, Molly needed to feel put together before daring to dial his cell. She figured if she looked the part, her voice might sound it, too. She noticed her hands were grimy from running her hands along bed frames in the cabins. With a contained blonde mane and no more smudged eye liner, Molly decided she was ready to hear his voice and stand her ground, dirty hands and all.

The annoyance in his voice was evident before he finished his 'hello, Mol'. Molly drew in a deep breath and hoisted her feet up on the desk. She leaned back in her father's chair and let Kenny know about the school enrollment, what forms to fax, plans to fix the resort the next few months, and plans to sell so she could buy a place for her and Emerson, a place closer to him so he could see Emerson whenever he wanted. While he may have been Kenny the Philanderer to her, he was a devoted father to Emerson. Molly could never disparage him as a parent, even if she was falling into the trap of disparaging him as a person more frequently than she cared to admit.

"Well, I want to fly her down for a long weekend, at least. And I mean soon, Mol. I'm not waiting until summer to see her and the judge never agreed to you taking her that long either." Kenny said. He sounded hurried. She could tell by the crackles in the connection that Kenny was entering the parking garage at work. She glanced at the clock and realized he was late.

"Why are you so late?" Molly said.

"What? Well, that's none of your business anymore, now is it." He snapped. As soon as she heard those words, she knew he was right and regretted the question. Old habits were dying hard. "Summer, Molly. By summer you need that place sold and get back to Tennessee with Emerson. Listen, I met with a realtor, too. I'm going to sell the condo and look for something closer to the hospital. So, that'll give us both some extra money to work with, hopefully. With the upgrades we made to the kitchen last year and all, we should be good selling it now." He said.

"Sell the condo? You love that condo, Ken." Molly said. Then again, she thought he once loved the life they had together in that condo.

"Yeah, well, a lot's changed, you know? I'll let you know about any offers. Put Em on the phone. I wanna say 'hi' before I go in," Kenny said.

"Sure. I'll get her. Em!" Molly yelled while still cradling the phone.

"Jesus, Molly," Kenny said.

"Sorry. So, where you going to staying in the meantime? Which one is it this time? The ICU nurse from last year or the intern from last month? I'm not sending Em anywhere near Tennessee if I don't know who you're living with or where." Molly said. Yep, she thought, she had most definitely become *that* woman.

"Dammit, Molly. Just get Emerson. I'm not doing this right now. You left. You up and left. I was willing to try again and do my part to fix this. But you, you threw in the towel. Your dad's death was just the perfect excuse you needed to give up on us." Kenny said.

"Give up on us? You threw us away when you started screwing around with Susie-whats-her-face the anesthesiologist with the stupid butterfly tattoo on her left boob four years ago and—" Molly said as Emerson walked in the office. She kicked the desk and pushed her chair all the way back to the wall. "Em, your dad is on the phone." She held out the receiver to her daughter and brushed past her as she took it.

Molly pivoted her body on the other side of the door frame. She was only five feet from the phone, yet out of breath as if she had run a mile. Molly folded her arms and let out a long, deep breath. Her cheeks were hot. She reached up and released the hair tie. There was no need to look or feel put together for another second. It was painfully obvious that she neither looked or sounded the part to anyone. She looked up at the ceiling as she overheard Emerson tell Kenny she missed him, too. Emerson started to tell Kenny about the lodge, which he had only been to a few times when they dated. Once they finished college and Kenny got the job at the hospital in Nashville, they never looked back.

Emerson started to cry and told her dad to visit. She had never been away from him for more than a week before. Molly's heart raced and she started to sweat. Hearing Emerson break into tears made her gut seize. She peered around the door frame to see Emerson standing there, behind the desk, with tears streaming down her face. Molly bit her bottom lip as she saw her daughter's heartache in living color. Nothing made sense anymore. Maybe Kenny was right. Maybe she used her father's death as an excuse to flee instead of trying harder. Maybe she was tearing her daughter's life apart for no reason other than resentment of Kenny. Even if she was justified in leaving him, was she justified in taking Emerson so far? The determination that filled her veins during the days of driving from Tennessee to Maine and the determination she had felt just an hour ago making a detailed list of repairs all fell away and laid at her feet. She not only doubted why she was doing what she was doing, but now Molly doubted if she could do it at all, or if she should. All her life, Molly realized, her parents made the decisions, then Kenny did. She went along for the ride and relished in their successes. She relied on them to make the big plans, big moves, and navigate the roads she found herself traveling. Now, she was alone with Emerson in tow and no one to guide or stabilize the world around her. It was all her choice now, and she had no idea whether she was making the right one or not.

"Honey, tell Dad you have to go," Molly said, with a vague attempt at once again sounding put together.

Emerson groaned. She wiped her eyes with her free hand and tucked her long brown hair behind her other ear.

"Mom says I gotta go." She said. She then nodded in accordance with the instructions of behaving and doing her best in school, staying strong, and everything else Molly knew Kenny was rattling off to the ten-year-old. "I love you, too," Emerson muttered and she put the receiver back on the black phone, a phone that was as old as Molly. Emerson walked up to Molly. She wrapped her arms around Emerson, only to get a half-hearted hug in return. Emerson slinked from her grasp and made her way back down the hall to the grand lodge lobby. Molly leaned back on the door frame and let out another long breath. She looked up as if the skies would open and a roadmap would appear. "My God, Molly, what the hell are you doing?" She said to herself.

After a hurriedly made dinner of grilled cheese and soup for her and Emerson, Molly found herself cleaning up the large cook's kitchen just as she helped to do as a child. The deep stainless steel sink and pull down faucet were some of her favorite toys. Molly loved the hot water and used to test how hot her hands could handle. She did it once again, watching the red spread from the tops of her hand to her fingers. She winced.

Mr. Castille texted the times a few workers would arrive in the morning to discuss plans and estimates for work. Molly grabbed a bucket from under the sink and filled it with some of the cleaning supplies she bought. Without any other adult around to distract her and a deafening level of silence, Molly decided she would begin to clean the walls and counter in the lounge once night fell. The floors needed scrubbed, and the bar was still sticky from her dad's last nightly binge.

When Molly walked into the lounge, which was only half the size of the main lobby, the lingering smell of booze filled her lungs. That smell had permeated every nook and cranny, every knot in the wooden bar. She emptied the bucket and filled it with hot water and soap, wincing as her hands turned to fire once again. As she ran the soapy rag over the bar and down the sides, yellow stickiness trickled down to the floor. The true hue of the wood started to pierce through. "Jeez, Dad. Did you ever clean this place?" She said as she went over the same area again and again. She heard rain drops hit the roof and the humidity level start to spike. While nowhere near as hot as Nashville could get in the spring, Maine was experiencing an early warm-up. Sweat was dripping from her pores as she worked. As the lounge grew hotter, Molly took off her flannel shirt and wrapped it around her waist. She started on the walls as the bar dried. She thought to herself that it was probably the cleanest it had been since she moved away. Emerson peaked in from the doorway.

"Mom, I'm going to watch a movie in your room and go to bed, okay?" She said. She shuffled in and Molly wrapped her tired arms around her daughter.

"Okay. I'm going to clean this up some more; then I'll be in to bed. Just get comfy and find me if you need anything, sweetie. And, lock the main door when you go back, please." Molly said.

Emerson released her goodnight grasp and shuffled out of the lounge just as sluggishly as she shuffled in. Molly could still hear the conversation between Emerson and Kenny. Molly knew she was laying a lot at the feet of a ten-year-old. She had upended the kid's entire existence and landed back in Great Pines in the process. As much as she seethed at the thought of Kenny being anywhere near, she knew Emerson needed him. The side of himself Kenny offered Emerson was something Molly didn't want to tarnish for the girl even though Kenny had burned an image of himself into her mind, an image no ten-year-old wanted. With each passing hour, it was growing increasingly difficult to honor that bond and keep her own sense of sanity. His years of deceit slowly wore her down. His lies slowly eroded her sense of right and wrong, her trust in her own gut. His constant need for affection from every woman in the room chipped away at her sense of self-worth. She no longer felt like the beautiful, young, funny, and vibrant girl who enthusiastically followed him to Nashville. She thought she was following a rock-star med student who was going change the way medicine was practiced. She thought they'd rise together and she'd go to law school while he slaved away at the hospital. Only, that's not the way any of it unfolded for either of them. He gave up on being a surgeon, and she got pregnant. Even though he still had a more than respectable career as a physician's assistant, he blamed the pregnancy for his inability to keep up with the harsh reality of life as an intern. She started to blame his job and the pregnancy for her inability to start law school. It was only a year after Emerson was born that Molly grew suspicious of one of his co-workers. By the time Emerson was in kindergarten, she knew her suspicions were spot on, and it wasn't just one co-worker. They played the blame game. The forgiveness and 'let's start over' games would follow each time. The resentment and anger would pulsate in Molly's veins for months. Then, he would break through somehow. He'd thaw that resentment, and she'd see her role in why he strayed. She'd want a reset as much as he claimed he did, too. Only, she came to realize the last two years, it wasn't a reset of her life with him that she wanted. It was a reset of her life in general.

The last straw came two months before her father died. Molly was working as a secretary in a law firm downtown. It was a total waste of her skills and talent, but it was steady pay and she could leave as soon as Emerson was finished with the school day. She got a call Emerson was sick and needed picked up. As she walked a feverish ten-year-old up the stairs to their condo, Molly heard rustling and something fall in their unit. She rushed to open the locked door, unsure who or what could be inside. The door flew open, and Kenny was standing there in all his naked glory barely holding on to the wall as a nurse he worked with was on her knees in front of him. He had knocked over the end table and lamp as she took him to climax. He was staring Molly and Emerson right in the eyes and unable to pull himself away from the nurse. Molly didn't see horror in his eyes, horror over the fact that his daughter had seen him like that. She didn't see regret or even shame. Kenny looked at Molly and their daughter with complete and unabashed anger that they had ruined a perfectly good blow job by opening the door. He managed to yell, "Get out!" as his eyes rolled back. The nurse on her knees didn't even stop and look behind her. Molly shook herself from the paralysis of the moment and grabbed the door. She swung it closed with a force that surely cracked the frame. That was the exact moment when she knew she needed to get out, for her and Emerson. That was the end of the beautiful, adventurous, vibrant young couple ready to set Nashville on fire. That was the slow, prolonged death of all Molly thought she had accomplished or even would accomplish with him by her side.

Weeks of couch surfing while apartment hunting ended with the call from Mr. Castille. News of her father's death was the death of her past. It became a bookend to match the death of her future. Molly, without trying, had entered an odd sense of purgatory, a limbo between who she was and who she expected to be, or who she even would be in a year. Somehow, that purgatory was to be spent in the lodge. Maybe, she thought, by doing her time to clean it up, fix what needed to be repaired in the lodge, she'd fix herself, too. Maybe she'd wash away the grime, the neglect, and uncover her real hue, too. Maybe, she'd find a new life for that place and herself. Or, perhaps her worst fear, all that cleaning and fixing would result in no new answers and no clearer path than what she had in mind when she swung that door shut.

Molly rung out the rag again and noticed the water needed to be changed. It had grown too murky to be effective. Her eyes met an opened bottle of bourbon behind the counter. It wasn't on the shelf with the others. It was strategically placed next to the stack of ash trays and extra towels out of sight. A small glass was next to it. It was her father's bottle and glass. She picked up the glass and held it to the light. It was murky and sticky on the bottom. He apparently never saw the need to rinse it out after a night of drinking. The outside of the bottle was sticky. She rinsed the glass and wiped it out with a fresh towel. She rescued the bottle from its dark enclave and let the sour mash see the light. Molly poured a shot into the glass and grabbed two ice cubes from the freezer. The clink was a familiar sound. It elicited a sense of both dread and safety. She let the scent rise slowly and pass through her. It was sweet, pungent, and romantic as it danced around her. Molly smiled as the ice cube slid around the curves of the glass and the colors danced under the light above the bar. She slowly rose the glass to her lips. It had been awhile since Molly had bourbon. Wine was her go-to when things got dicey with Kenny or when she was all alone as he "worked" late. Molly let the drink flow past her lips and felt the slight burn and tingle as it hit the inside of her cheeks. She let it slide down her throat. The warmth flowed down, and the burn subsided, leaving a refreshing and clean feeling behind. Molly smiled. She sipped more. She exhaled and let the depth of the bourbon escape with her breath. She sipped some more. Molly then reached for the bottle and poured more into the glass. Her mind lightened, and her cheeks flushed. Molly forgot how quickly bourbon takes hold. She felt warm all over, a feeling she missed. It was like being hugged. She wondered if that's how her father felt each night in the lounge. One hug might be warming. Comforting. But, Molly wondered at what point did it become stifling and debilitating for her father. Molly suddenly found the sensation both soothing and scary.

Molly sat on a stool on the other side of the bar and reached for the bottle. She pulled it across the bar and drew it into her arms with her free hand. Her glass was still in her other. The ice clinked again as it became smaller, breaking the silence in the room. The warmth that filled Molly's throat and stomach spread to her head. She was light-headed as the bourbon's grasp embraced her. She glanced around and noticed the spot on the floor where her father died. The area was lighter than the rest of the worn wood floor. Mr. Castille had scrubbed it cleaned, revealing a level of flooring that hadn't seen the light of day for years. Molly wondered if it would've looked less obvious if he had let it go. From what she was told, her father had laid on the floor for at least two days. His bloated body stretched from the bottom corner of the bar to underneath the table by the door. He had either fallen off the stool, the very stool she sat on, or had tripped and hit his head on the table. To Molly, the details were irrelevant. All that mattered was that he died, alone and drunk, in a pool of vomit. As much as the image of his demise was burning through her as she sat inches from where he died, other images floated into her tired, bourbon-soaked, mind. She drew in a deep breath and exhaled the scent of bourbon once again. Molly slowly brought the glass to her lips again and let her childhood flash through her mind. The sound of her parents laughing in the lounge as she ran through chasing her dog enveloped her. Molly remembered the thrill of getting tips as she carried a tray of drinks from the lounge to the lobby couches where guest sat in front of the fire in the fall. She smiled at the memory of sneaking out the front lodge door as her parents entertained guests. She wondered if they ever knew how much she snuck out during high school, especially the summer between her junior and senior year. Molly found it hard to process the thought that Emerson would be that age in just a few short years. The last ten years had flown by as it was. She sipped some more. The ice was completely gone. She lost track of how many times she poured more bourbon into the glass.

Molly got up and walked across the lounge to the door. She flipped on the outside light and pressed her nose against the glass. Her eyes were drawn to the trail that led to the cabins. So many hours of her childhood were spent cleaning the bathrooms, making the beds, laying out fresh towels, and taking immense pride in how each one looked as the guest checked in and made their way down the trail. She remembered blushing as she put champagne and flowers in the cabins reserved for guests on honeymoons. Moose Pond Lodge was the quintessential destination for adventurous newlyweds in the 80's and 90's. As she peered down that dimly lit path through the lounge door, Molly thought of her own honeymoon. The last thing she wanted was an outdoor adventure when she had just escaped the clutches of Moose Pond Lodge. She and Kenny the Philanderer opted for a hotel in the city, looking down music row and absorbing the sights, smells, and sounds of downtown Nashville.

Her father was disappointed that they had the wedding there instead of Great Pines, but she was eager to start their life far away from Maine. His feelings were just collateral damage on the fast track to her dreams, at least the dream life she thought they were creating. The honeymoon and first two years were the happiest times for them. Molly wondered how many of those couples who walked that path to the secluded cabins were still married, or at least still happy. The weddings at the lodge seemed so romantic and exciting at the time—the flowers and drinks, the candles and matches on the tables by the tub, the giddiness as those couples walked arm in arm to the cabins, while her father followed with arm loads of luggage. In fact, her entire childhood seemed foggy with a romantic sense of adventure. She met people from all over the world. The accents, the cars and license plates, the parties and bonfires at the end of the week, the comics telling dirty jokes on stage, jokes she was never supposed to hear. Most of all, the drinks. The drinks flowed freely, and the guests grew louder as the summer nights wore on. They seemed encrusted in happiness and newness. They were all on vacation. It made Molly's childhood, her life, feel like a never-ending vacation, too. Only it wasn't. The guests would all go home after a week or two and new ones would arrive. It was a revolving door and she was stuck in it, spinning around for 18 years.

The fog of her bourbon breath created a circle around the window. She leaned back and sipped some more. This time, the bourbon went down easier, smoother, and without a burn. She swayed back and forth thinking of dancing in the hotel in Nashville. Kenny the Philanderer held her so tight. His hands ran up and down her back and behind the night of their wedding. He kissed her neck as they swayed to the bed. They didn't even bother to close the curtains or turn out the lights. It was bourbon that warmed her that night, too, along with his touch. As much as the last few years and the sight of him at the condo scarred her and filled her heart with rage, she missed him. She missed the Kenny he was that night and for many nights in the beginning, before their lost dreams and reality weighed on their shoulders. She wanted to go back to that revolving door of her childhood. She wanted to believe each cabin or hotel room decorated with flowers and champagne was all that was needed to create the perfect marriage and life. Molly felt the tears well up. Ordinarily, she would push them aside as she had so many times the last month. But that night, in the lounge, Molly didn't have the energy or sobriety needed to squeeze them back and bury inside again. She sipped more and let them trickle down her face. The tears and bourbon on her lips became one. Molly let failure and heartache creep into her soul and accepted both as her reality. It wasn't the reality she wanted, but the one she accepted that night. She let more ice cubes fall into the glass to cut the burn of the bourbon and the burn of what had become of her life.

Chapter 3

Of all the paths you take in life, make sure a few of them are dirt—John Muir

The sun pierced the open curtain and stung as an alarm bounced around her mind. The light and warmth both sent a sharp pain from Molly's eyes to her the back of her head. She felt her temples throb as she tried to open her eyes and confront the day. It was Emerson's first day at school, and a bevy of workers would be arriving to start work on the lodge. Molly wanted the world to stop. She hadn't had a hangover in a while and was sure this one was the worst ever. As Emerson stirred next to her and rubbed her eyes, Molly pried open her dry mouth and let her tongue smack against the roof. The slightest movement of her head sent her world spinning. She caught a whiff of bourbon. Molly didn't know if it was her breath or on her clothes from the night before. Emerson groaned, and Molly realized her cell phone alarm was still going off.

"Mom, turn it off. I'm up. I swear." The girl said from under the blanket.

"Okay, kid. Come on. It's your first day. Go hop in the shower." Molly said.

She tried her best to sound official and mom-like, not like the hungover fool she felt like inside. Her head started to throb more as she rubbed her eyes and gingerly slid up from the blankets. Never again, she told herself, again. Emerson slithered out of bed and made her way down the hall to the bathroom. Once Molly heard the water start, she attempted to stand. Her head throbbed even more. Never again. She pulled her shirt up over her head. A good whiff of bourbon went up her nose. Molly reached in the suitcase on the floor and pulled out a fresh sweatshirt. She pulled off her jeans and slid on sweatpants. Molly stood in front of the mirror attached to her mother's old dresser. 'Hot mess' were the only words that formed in her mind. She ran a brush through her long, blonde hair. Her head throbbed more as she tied it up to look somewhat normal. Molly made her way to the kitchen to retrieve some sort of pain reliever. As she poured water into a clean glass and popped the pill in her mouth, a loud honk, then a series of honks, reverberated through the lodge. At first, Molly thought maybe it was in her throbbing head. But, as she swallowed, she realized the workers were probably pulling in.

"Shit. I forgot they'd be here early." Molly muttered as Emerson came up and hugged her from behind. Molly swung around to look down at the girl. "First day, lady. You look lovely. Where're your glasses?"

"On the counter with my backpack. Do I really have to go?" Emerson asked. She pulled down at her sweater and pulled up at her jeans. She was growing like a weed and outgrowing clothes faster than Molly and Kenny could buy them.

"Yes, you do. This weekend, we'll go shopping for more new stuff, and your dad is sending a few things, too. Now, get your glasses and I'll bring you breakfast. Cereal alright?" Molly said. She tried to block out the throbbing and focus on getting Emerson outside in time. The ticking of the large clock in the kitchen echoed in her head, along with every other noise. She grabbed a bowl, milk, and cereal to take out to the dining room. Molly couldn't help but smile when she saw Emerson sitting there. She looked so grown up compared to the girl who had started fourth grade in Nashville.

Five minutes before the bus was to pull up to the end of the lane, Molly scrambled to gather paperwork and lunch money as Emerson hunted for her shoes. Together, they opened the front doors of the lodge and started to follow the fence down to the mailbox. Memories of running down that drive to catch her bus washed over Molly. They walked past four work trucks lined up in the driveway. Molly told herself she'd speak with them once Emerson was on the bus. The lights flashed as that bus slowed and Molly noticed Emerson fidget with her glasses. She squeezed her shoulder and leaned down to kiss her head.

"It'll be fine, kid. They'll love you. Just be yourself, and I'll see you in a few hours, okay?" Molly said as the bus screeched to a stop. Emerson bit her bottom lip and nodded. She drew in a deep breath and started up the bus steps. Once seated, Emerson looked down at Molly from the window and shrugged her shoulders. Molly fought back the tears as she blamed herself for putting Emerson in this situation. She loved her old school, teachers, and friends. She shook her head as she started back up the driveway. "Nope. Her father did this to us. Dammit Kenny." Molly said to herself as she got to the trucks.

"What's that, miss?" A voice asked from the back of a truck.

"Nothing. Sorry, just talking to myself. I'm Mol...Zack? Zack Preston?" Molly uncrossed her arms as her eyes met those of the stranger at the back of the landscaping truck. He flashed a smile. "What? What are you doing here?" Molly asked. Her heart fluttered.

"Yep, it's me. Molly, right? I forgot your dad owned this place till I saw you walk past. Was that your kid?" Zack said. He wiped his hands on his pant legs. They were grass-stained.

"Yeah, she's ten. I just got back here a few days ago. My dad died a few weeks ago. I'm here to fix this place up before selling it, hopefully. You helping your dad with landscaping? I thought you got a big football scholarship and left this place years ago?" Molly said. She suddenly remembered she was in sweats, hair tied up, and suffering from the worst hangover. She tried to readjust her messy mane. He looked insanely more muscular than when they were in high school.

"Yeah, I know about your dad. I'm sorry. And yep, I had a full ride to Boston College. But two blown out knees my sophomore year kinda killed that dream. I stayed for a bit, but then came home. I run the landscaping company now. It's a good gig around here, especially with all the resorts cropping up the last ten years." Zack said. "So, who hired us to clean up this place for you?"

"Oh, that was Mr. Castille. My dad's lawyer. The sooner I can get the work done, the sooner I can get the hell out of here, again." Molly said. She wanted to take those words back. She knew she sounded like a stuck-up snot when she said things like that to people in Great Pines.

"Well, I guess that's why I'm here. I'm taking the mowers down the path to the cabins and start in the back. I'll be working my way up to the main lodge the next two weeks or so, depending on rain or not." Zack said. He laid ramps on the edge of the truck bed. Molly watched his muscles peak from his shirt sleeves.

"Oh, yeah. I'm sorry if I'm keeping you. If you need anything, I'll be inside cleaning up. Or, maybe in one of the cabins fixing those up, too." Molly said. She stood still, staring at his eyes. Every memory of those eyes escaped her pounding head and flowed through her entire body.

"Okay, then. I'm gonna get these mowers back there. Good to see you though." Zack said. He hopped up into the bed of the truck.

Molly nodded and started to walk toward the steps to the lodge. She exhaled and wondered how much he remembered about her. Molly suddenly went from being a thirty-five-year-old woman trying to fix up a treasured resort to being a fifteen-year-old girl worried that she'd trip over her own feet walking up the school steps in front of the cutest football player in existence. She made her way to the bathroom to start to put her hungover self together. Molly gasped once she caught a glimpse of herself in the mirror. She not only felt desperately hungover inside, she looked it too—with a dash of homelessness thrown in, too. Her make-up from last night was smudged. The circles under her eyes rivaled that of a rabid raccoon. Her hair was a tangled mess, and she still smelled like bourbon. Poor Emerson had to board a new bus with a hot mess of a mother standing there in sweats. She couldn't believe the first glimpse Zack Preston had of her in well over a decade was this version of herself.

Molly turned on the shower and slowly crawled in as she wished for a time machine to redo the last hour of her life. While the water felt good, her hangover still made every cell of her body scream with the sound and sensation of the water. Standing under the hot water, in the shower she used her whole childhood, her new reality sunk into her pores. While the prospect of sitting in the lounge each night drinking away her reality was surprisingly appealing, so was facing the demons and misguided decisions that led her right back where she started. Sure, it would be easy to sit and get bourbon-soaked, cry over Kenny the Philanderer, and drag her hungover butt out of bed each morning to get her daughter off to school, all the while renovating the very place she ran from. But, suddenly the realization that she could end up like her father washed over just as the soap did. Today, it was only one hangover to get over the hump of one night of self-pity and self-loathing. However, one night could easily slip into dozens, then hundreds. Molly could easily be a hungover hot mess watching Emerson drive away from Moose Pond Lodge, just as she had done years earlier. Of course, she knew she wasn't destined to be an alcoholic who would drown her sorrows each night. But Molly also knew, her father never set out to be one either.

Molly rinsed her hair and let the water pour over her body, even though all she wanted was to crawl back into bed and sleep off the bourbon that was still in her veins. She stood taller than she had in a while. Today would be a new start. It had to be. She knew she had a choice to step forward and shoulder the responsibilities she agreed to take on, or wallow and stay stuck in a pattern that would lead nowhere. Molly turned off the water and grabbed a towel. While the pounding in her head still lingered and her body still ached, she had a rush of ideas flood her mind. Once the bubble of self-pity burst in her head, it was as if there was suddenly room for something else, something more. She caught a glimpse of herself in the mirror as she dried off. Molly smirked. She may have felt like a burgeoning rock star on the inside, but even after a shower, she looked like a hot mess on the outside. One step at a time, she told herself as she slid on clean clothes.

Her stomach finally allowed for the thought of food, and she ramped up hydration efforts before going back outside to meet the other workers and hopefully, get a second chance to talk with Zack. As Molly strolled out the front door, the sun reminded her hangovers don't go away because confidence suddenly crept into her soul. She squinted just as she approached the top step. Molly stepped on her shoelace and started to stumble. She reached for the railing and only her pinky made contact. As it bent back and Molly felt a splinter ram through her skin, her foot twisted from the trapped shoelace. Molly yelled out just as her body lurched forward and she pummeled down the front steps of the Lodge. Molly's hands hit first and then she felt the dirt of the driveway in her mouth. Her freshly washed face and body, and her newly found confidence was now just a puddle of splinter-laden dirt. She moved her tongue and felt the grit of the Earth in her mouth. Molly coughed and instantly felt a sharp pain pierced through her ankle and to her calf. As she drew up her hands to lift her body from the dirt, an arm reached around her and helped her to her feet. It was Zack.

"You alright? That was one hell of a fall. I heard the thud from the other side of the truck." Zack said. He brushed dirt off her shoulder. Molly tried to stand upright. "No, don't put pressure on it. Here, sit on the bumper." He lifted her by the hips and helped her sit down.

"My God, my ankle," Molly said as she winced. "This is a bit more than embarrassing. I can't believe I fell like that. You must think I'm an idiot."

"Nah, I see grown adults trip from untied shoelaces all the time," Zack said with a smile. He winked at her. She relaxed her shoulders and smiled back. Molly realized she still had dirt in her mouth and let out a hacking cough. Zack drew back a little.

"I'm sorry. I have dirt in my mouth." Molly said as she hacked some more.

She was wondering why she ever got out of bed or tried to come back outside and impress him at all. She glanced down at her shoes. How could she forget to tie her shoes? She thought, what kind of woman holds her head up high, lets confidence drip from her fingertips, then immediately trips down the steps because she forgot to tie her shoes? Molly slouched even further while adjusting her butt on the bumper.

"Your ankle. Is it okay? Can you stand?" Zack said. He took a cloth out of his back pocket and wiped dirt off Molly's forehead.

"I don't know. It hurts like hell. But, I don't think it's broken or anything." She said as she put slight pressure down on it. She winced some more. Molly closed her eyes and let out a deep breath. She was hoping this was all a bad dream and she'd wake with just the hangover and the chance to start the day over.

"Come on. Let me help you to the door. You need to get this elevated or something." Zack said. Molly shook her head.

"No, I'm good. I think it'll be fine. I just need to get myself cleaned up, again." She said. Molly stood and slowly let her foot make full contact with the ground. She took a slow step forward and realized each attempt made it hurt less. "See, It's good. Thank you for helping me up, though. I'll be fine." She lurched forward with small steps as she reached for the railing.

"Your shoes, Molly," Zack said.

He stepped in front of Molly and crouched down. Zack tied her shoes. Molly didn't know whether to smile, cry from pain, or recoil back to Nashville out of complete and utter humiliation. She looked down at the top of his head. He still had that black curly mane that made her swoon in school. Molly wondered if he had any idea she spent four years watching his every move and fawning over any pebble of attention he incidentally threw her way. Those were few and far between, but she clearly recalled each one. When Zack finished, he looked up and flashed that smile at her. In high school, that smile was usually followed by watching the back of his head as he made his way down the hall to class. This time, Zack extended his hand and refused to take 'no' for an answer. She gave in and let him help her hobble up the lodge steps and inside the door.

"Wow, this place hasn't changed a bit. I always loved that stone fireplace," Zack said as he helped her to couch.

"You've been inside before? I don't remember you coming over when I lived here," Molly said.

"Yeah, it was after I got hurt and left college. I did some work outside with my dad back in those days. Your dad would always insist we come inside and eat lunch in the dining room. And, when I was a kid, I came with my parents to see a few of the shows. Oh, and my aunt got married here when I was a kid, too." Zack said. He craned his neck upwards. "I always loved that moose up there. Glad to see it's still in good condition. It was the one thing that always stood out about this place. Your dad, he was a real good guy. I was sorry to hear about him passing away."

"Thanks, Zack. I feel awful that I couldn't make it back for the funeral, but I was in the middle of some stuff in Nashville." Molly said.

"Stuff, huh? Stuff that you aren't in the middle of right now, then?"

"You could say that. I guess. I'm in the middle of a divorce. I couldn't just up and leave Nashville without court permission to bring my daughter, a lot of issues had to be tackled before I could leave. Long story." Molly rubbed her ankle.

"Sounds like it. So, you're gonna sell this place, huh?" Zack said.

"That's the plan."

"Well, that's a shame. A few corporations have bought too many of these resorts in northern New England. They are strangling the real ones for business, the authentic ones. Which is ironic, you know?" Zack said.

"What do you mean?" Molly asked.

"People come from all over the country to get a real New England experience, a real Maine summer and fall feel, and they end up staying at the larger resorts and not the real ones. They sign up for zip lining, outlet shopping tours, and sit in front of fake stone fireplaces and pose in front of fake Moose heads. They want a flat screen tv, not a view of the ponds or wildlife. You know?" He glanced around. "The cabins here made of white pine with views and the birds in the morning, that's what's real. This old lodge building, the shows at night, and the homemade food, that's real, too." Zack said. "But, it's your place, your decision. Just a shame if it gets gutted and turned into one of those resorts, the kinds in the fancy brochures complete with spa services."

"I didn't really think about what kind of buyer might come along. You gotta realize, a few weeks ago, I never planned to be here taking over any of this. My dad never talked to me about what to do with the place once he passed. When he'd say he wasn't leaving anything to me, I kinda just believed him. We had what you might call a strained relationship after I left here. Honestly Zack, I just want to be able to start over with my daughter somewhere, and selling this place is the best way to do that." Molly said. She felt a twinge of resentment slip from her mouth as she felt the need to justify her decision to a man Molly hadn't seen since she was in high school.

"I guess we all just have different ideas about what starting over means." He said. "Well, I gotta get back to work. Here, give me your phone."

"Why?" Molly asked.

"I'm gonna put my number in it so you can text me if you need anything while I'm working out there. You need to stay off that foot for a bit. Okay?" He said.

Molly pulled her phone from her back pocket and handed it up to him. He tossed it back to her as he walked to the door. "Remember, stay off that foot." He said. She stared at the back of his head. When the door closed behind him, she scooted up the couch more and tossed her head back. The to-do list was growing by the minute and felt she had taken steps backwards, at least a tumble backwards. The paperwork from Mr. Castille was on the end table, just within reach. Molly pulled the stack to her lap and started to read. She was so busy signing every spot with a signature sticker, she hadn't read much of it. Her father's debts weren't as bad as she imagined. The overhead cost of the resort was lower than she remembered as kid, also. For being inebriated most of the day and night the last decade or so, he managed to stay on top of the business end of the business. But, the repairs he put off, the maintenance, and the overall lack of love for any space except the lounge certainly showed. Molly realized that neglect would surely override any savings he accumulated in other areas of the resort business.

The idea of some large corporation coming in and making it a cookie-cutter resort didn't sit well with her either. Then again, if she got a big enough check, she thought, what did it matter? It wasn't like she had any delusions of keeping the resort and running it herself. She sure didn't want to battle Kenny in court to keep Emerson a world away. Even if she wanted to keep it, what did she know about running it anyway? Sure, she ordered supplies and food from vendors as a kid, handled the 'talent' for shows, and made sure each cabin was ready, but doing that stuff as a kid was a far cry from running the place as an adult. She laid down the stack of papers on the floor next to the couch and let her head fall all the way back. The ankle pain was still radiating up her leg. Molly closed her eyes and rationalized that a nap was all she needed to regain full use of her leg and her mind. What started out as a day to take the wheel from Mr. Castille and stand tall as she worked towards making her own way had taken quite an opposite turn. She laid on a couch, hungover, absorbing the pain of a swollen ankle, still tasting dirt in her mouth, and feeling judged by the boy she couldn't have in high school all before lunch. Great Pines and Moose Pond Lodge was starting to feel like a curse rather than a gateway to a new life.

Chapter 4

Nature doesn't hurry, yet everything is accomplished –Lao Tzu

Just as Molly drifted off and let thoughts of defeat enter her mind, her phone buzzed. She perked up. Her heart quickened when she momentarily let the possibility of it being a text from Zack rush through her veins. It was Maxine. She and Emerson were invited to dinner. Molly shook her head and once again let guilt wash over her. She had completely forgotten about the conversation with Maxine in the grocery store the other day. She scooted up and let her foot hit the floor. The twinge of pain was much less severe than earlier. As she texted back to confirm dinner, she noticed the time.

"Dammit. The whole day is almost gone. Em will be home soon, and I'm still a mess. Get it together, Mol." She said.

Molly made her way to the bathroom and saw the dirt still smudged on her face and clothes from falling. She cleaned herself up and gave herself a mirror pep-talk. This was supposed to the day Molly started working towards a new life and all she had accomplished was making an utter embarrassment of her hungover-self. She gathered up supplies she had waiting by the door and decided it was better late than never. Molly made her second attempt at stepping outside like a grown woman and not a clumsy toddler. As she made her way down the stairs, she glanced around hoping to see Zack and prove to him she had herself somewhat together. She then realized what a sad state of affairs her life must be if walking down the steps of the lodge without falling on her face was now her barometer for having it together. The sun was bright and quick to remind her of the consequences of being bourbon-soaked the night before. She squinted as she headed toward the trail. There was enough time to clean up one cabin before Em was dropped off.

The trail was still a warm spot in her heart. The trees towered overhead and swayed in slow motion, even on the calmest days. Willows and pines intermingled and their branches formed the secret fort of her childhood, enclosing her below, where she felt a world away from everything and everyone. Molly smiled as a squirrel raced across. She heard chipmunks and knew spring was here to stay. The light danced through the branches and welcomed her in further. Molly remembered thinking the trees were talking to each other and her when the needles would swoosh. Whispering pines, her mom would call it. When the winds would pick up before a summer storm, that whisper would quickly evolve into shouts. She pretended those trees, those whispering pines, were friends who would hold her secrets close. Their hushed acceptance of everything she was and wanted to be was the purest parts of her childhood.

Molly stopped at the small wooden bridge that arched over a tiny creek. The water was sparse because the snowpack hadn't made its way down the mountain yet. She watched the stream wind the same path it did twenty years ago. It hadn't bothered to carve out anything more for itself. It reminded her of nearly everyone she left behind, unchanged. She gathered up the bucket of supplies and continued to the end. Once Molly reemerged from the wooden cocoon, the light once again made her squint. The clearing appeared with a circular path that measured a quarter mile. A dozen cabins were scattered on the outside and inside of that circle. The cabins looked smaller than she remembered. The oldest ones were painted green and white, like the fence leading to the resort. Others looked like miniature log cabins. There were shutters with small flowers cut into the wood. The green on the shutters was faded and peeling, but still brought back memories of her mother. The cabins with the porches and rocking chairs were set the farthest back away from the others, to give the high-end visitors and newlyweds a sense of privacy, even though you could see every cabin from one another.

The smaller ones had flower boxes under the two windows that flanked the door. She could almost smell the wildflowers her mother planted in each box and in-between each cabin.

She fished for the key to the first cabin. The handle was rusty but turned with some force. The musty smell made her flinch as she flipped the switch for the lights. Molly laughed to herself as she spotted the bed in the middle with her mother's quilt. That was the very cabin where she lost her virginity at sixteen. Molly had forgotten about it until the light shined on that quilt. Molly smirked when she remembered how she had to scoop up that quilt and wash it before her father returned in the morning. It was the one and only week he left her alone at the resort while he went deep sea fishing with friends.

Molly placed the bucket in the clawfoot tub and got the water as hot as possible. She added bleach and began the process of wiping away years of dirt and grim from the ceiling to the floor. She scrubbed harder as she saw the true white of the molding and chair rails. The cabin started to come back to life and her strange affection for the smell of bleach helped to clear her mind. Molly took off the rubber gloves and re-tied her long blonde hair. She felt cleaner as she revived the cabin. The mistakes earlier in the day, the last few years, and the dirt from her fall all seemed to fade. As Molly emptied the bucket and filled it anew with hot water and bleach, energy pumped through her entire body. She worked even faster on the floors. A dusting of the night stands, and good cleaning of the rest of the bathroom and fireplace would restore the cabin to its former glory. There was a breeze from the open door, which helped dry the wood floors even faster. The grain of the cabin floors always caught her eye. She knew it had probably been more than a decade since they were refinished, but the rustic and worn nature of their present state pleased her. As Molly stood in the middle of the cabin with her hands on her hips, she exhaled and blew a chunk of hair out of her line of sight. She nodded to herself.

"Well, that's about as good as it's gonna get. Not too bad for one afternoon."

She gathered up the cleaning supplies and rolled up the bedding. She figured with an earlier start, no hangovers, and no falls, she could have all the cabins cleaned in less than a week. Then, any repairs could start. Without warning or expectation, her thoughts floated to her parents. The quilt on the floor, the act of preparing a cabin for rent, and the breezy, damp April Maine air, all enveloped her senses, and she nearly forgot her parents were both gone.

Molly wandered to the path and over the bridge just in time to see the lights of the bus flicker through the small pines along the road. Her heart raced anticipating tales of Emerson's first day. Her eyes widened when she saw the shrubs and front lawn area. It looked as fresh and clean as the cabin. Molly hadn't seen a spring cleanup of the grounds take shape like that since she was a kid. She stopped in her tracks and gasped at the beauty of the front view. A few men were still on the side of the building laying mulch, and Molly heard drills coming from the gazebo. Her parents used to have morning coffee alone in that gazebo. One afternoon had transformed so much, at least aesthetically.

"What do ya think?" Zack shouted from the porch. Molly whipped around to see him standing on the first step resting up against the pole.

"I don't know what to say. Everything looks so good, so different than when I pulled in the other day. I can't thank you enough, Zack."

"No need to thank me. Just doing the job I was hired to do. Hey, how's that ankle feel? I see you didn't listen to staying off it for a while?"

"Oh, it's good now. I was just sprucing up one of the cabins after—" Molly said. "Hey, pumpkin! How was the first day?" She called out when she saw Emerson running up the drive. Molly instantly saw herself years earlier. "Sorry, Zack. What was I saying?"

"Oh, nothing. By the look on her face, it was a good day. I'll talk to you later. Gotta get back to work," Zack said.

Molly glanced back at him just as he disappeared on the other side of the porch. Emerson crashed into Molly to hug her. Molly peered down at her head and kissed her as Em hugged her tight.

"So, how was it?" Molly said as she peeled Emerson from her around her waist.

Her heart started to beat again when she saw the smile on her face. As the two of them made their way to the door and Emerson talked a mile a minute about her new friends and teacher, Molly glanced around hoping to see another glimpse of Zack. But, he was gone. Molly Settled for letting the relief of a successful first day take the stage for the rest of the day.

"Mom, I gotta call Dad and tell him everything, okay?" Emerson said as she tossed her backpack towards the dining room tables.

"Of course, honey. You can use the office phone if you want to call his office or use my cell. Whichever." Molly said as she opened the backpack to find the usual stack of forms needing her immediate attention. She wondered if she'd be so open to Emerson calling her dad right away if she had had a bad day. Molly knew a miserable school experience might push Kenny the Philander to want Emerson back in Nashville sooner rather than later.

"Hello, Mrs. Bordeaux? You in here?" a voice shouted from the lobby.

"Yes, yes I am. I'm coming." She said without looking up from the papers. Molly walked into the lobby to find the head electrician standing in the doorway. "Oh god, don't tell me something else needs to be rewired?" She muttered. "Oh, and its Watts, not Bordeaux. The Bordeauxs were my parents."

"Oh, sorry. Mrs. Watts. We just want to show you what we've done." The electrician said.

He was short and portly. His stomach hung over his belt to the point Molly didn't realize he was wearing one until he walked away. His team of electricians had worked for her father anytime he added on to the resort. Mr. Castille insisted Molly stick with them for any work that needed to be done to sell. Watching them work in various parts of the lodge proved to Molly that this group knew the lodge as well as she did. She followed him to the porch. Once outside, he nodded to his guys at the foot of the gazebo and around the willow trees. The group simultaneously flipped switches. The gazebo, willow trees, and porch lit up at once. Even though it was still light out, Molly could tell there were thousands of lights illuminating the main lodge and grounds.

"The gazebo? It has electricity now, Mr. Anderson?"

"It always did. It was wired when your dad built it, but after your mom died, he said don't bother installing switches and finishing the job. There was no need. Luckily, this morning, I remembered," Mr. Anderson said. He tugged at the sides of his belt.

"It looks beautiful. I can't wait to see it tonight. The porch, the trees, all of it." Molly's eyes widened as she stared at the lights. "How's everything else looking? The cabins and stuff?"

"Pretty good, mostly. I want to update wiring in some cabins, and a few will definitely need new water heaters. Tomorrow, we will go through the kitchen and appliances, to be sure everything looks good and up to code. Okay?" He said.

"Sounds good to me. Hey, you and your guys, the landscape crew, and the contractors redoing the porches, all you guys are getting a big dinner tomorrow night. You guys will be my first guests. Does that work?" Molly said.

Mr. Anderson shouted out the plan to the crew scattered around the front lawn, and all agreed. Molly giggled.

"That include me and my guys?" Zack asked from behind her.

"Oh, hi. Of course, it does. All of you. It's my way of saying of thanks, that and paying you." Molly laughed.

"Better make a ton. These guys like to eat, trust me," he said as he gathered a leftover weed whacker from the porch. "See ya tomorrow."

"We will leave them on, Mrs. Watts. Just flip the main switch by the door, the one labeled outdoor, to turn it all off when you want them off."

Molly was enamored by the lights strung everywhere. The way they crisscrossed from the porch to the trees and weaved their way to the gazebo her parents loved. Molly let her eyes bounce across the maze and her heart quickened in anticipation of nightfall. The sound of the tailgate closing snapped her out of her trance. Zack was opening his door to slide inside his truck. He flashed her a smile and a nod. She waved as he and the other trucks started to back out of the lodge driveway. Every corner she gazed at revealed so much progress. Molly took out her phone to take a few pictures. She texted her pictures to Samantha, her best friend in Nashville.

As she texted more pictures, Samantha texted back that the lodge was much nicer than she always described. Molly realized she was right. She always painted a grim and dreary picture of the lodge Even though her father had let it slide and hadn't taken steps to improve the place, it was never the hellhole Molly seemed to paint it to be. Maybe the memories of her father's descent into alcoholism after her mother died made the resort look dreadful, dull, and miserable in her eyes? The loneliness she felt those years of a motherless childhood were still there, too. She couldn't forget how the town, how everyone, rallied to her father and wrapped themselves around him to comfort and support him, while seemingly forgetting about her grief. He was larger than life, and so was his despair. It overshadowed everything else, even her when she needed him most.

She had clouded her own mind with the image of the resort as a hellhole for so long, she forgot the good things, the way things were before her mother passed and her father disappeared into his bourbon-soaked world. Molly looked up from her phone and absorbed the views from the porch. The sun pierced through the trees and cast slivers on the porch. The rocking chairs needed a fresh coat of paint, but were still strong, sturdy, and inviting. She sat in one and gently let it creak forward and back. The smell of the fresh cut grass and shrubs, the smell of new mulch, and the lingering bleach on her hands all transported her to every spring she had ever known in Maine. Molly smiled. She vowed that she'd never disparage this place again. It was time to see what the resort could be now and in the future, not just what it became all those years ago. Although, that would be easier said than done.

Waking the next morning to get Emerson off to school was a much easier task than the day before. The lack of a hangover made Molly feel as if she had already accomplished something. The improvements to the outside of the lodge and inside her mind caused energy to burst from her fingertips from the moment the alarm went off. She made scrambled eggs for Emerson while Em got ready for school. While she waited for her, Molly stacked a pile of pots, pans, plates, cups, and silverware on the counter. She wanted to give everything a good cleaning before hosting dinner for a dozen workers. She loaded the restaurant-style dishwasher and closed the lever. It quickly heated up, and the swooshing began. Her mother's voice echoed in her head. "Don't stand so close when you open it. That steam'll burn your face off." She filtered through the pantry in the back and front cupboards to generate ideas for dinner. A big spaghetti dinner would be the quickest, easiest, and the most sure-to-please option. She made sure everything she needed was still good and dragged out more pots and plates. Emerson came in the kitchen and suddenly looked so grown up. Molly sighed and smiled at her.

"Mom, why are you on the counter?" she asked.

"I'm washing these for dinner tonight. I invited all the workers to stay and eat, as a thank you, you know?" Molly said. "You look great. Are you excited for day 2?"

"Yep, today we're going into the woods to get soil samples for science, and there's gonna be a field trip to the beach in like two weeks. The beach! Mom, I can't wait to jump in." Emerson said.

"Oh, honey. I'm sure they won't be letting you kids jump in, and trust me, this time of year, that water is cold." Molly said. She swung the lever and pulled up the metal door of the dishwasher, unleashing a ball of steam.

"But you swam here growing up, right?"

"Yeah, in Moose Pond. The ocean, well, that's a different story." Molly said with a laugh.

"When can I swim in Moose Pond?" Emerson asked.

"By the time school ends, it'll be warm enough to jump in, okay?"

"But, when school is over, we're moving back, right? You're selling, and we're heading back home by then, you said." Emerson said.

"You're right, that's what I said. Listen, you'll get to jump in. I promise." Molly said. For a moment, the image of Emerson spending the summer jumping off the pier and squealing as her chubby ten-year-old body hit the water seemed a sure thing. Molly briefly forgot their time at the lodge was a starting gate to a new life and not the destination. "Hey, we might not live near where we used to. I mean, you will see your dad, of course, and be close to him anytime you want. But, I don't know for sure where exactly we'll end up. I just want you to know that and not think we are heading back to our old neighborhood. Okay? You okay with that?" Molly said. She slid the metal door down as she removed hot, freshly cleaned pots from the spare rack.

"Yeah, I know. I guess. I want to be near Daddy, and you," Emerson said.

Emerson hung her head and took the plate of eggs into the dining room. She slid her glasses back up her nose as she nudged the door open. Molly's heart beat against her chest. She hated the idea that she planted any seeds of uncertainty in her daughter. She never planned to upend her childhood and leave her in limbo about anything. Molly knew the importance of stability and couldn't believe her choices had led to instability for her kid. Nope, not going to get the guilt bug, she told herself. Kenny the Philanderer's actions did this. He put them all on this rollercoaster. Molly then wondered how long she could pin it all on Kenny. Kenny's betrayal and her father's death may have propelled her back to Great Pines when she least expected it, but whatever she did next was completely her call. And, whatever consequences that decision may have for her daughter was on her shoulders also.

As Emerson boarded the bus with emergency contact papers and a permission slip for the beach trip in hand, Molly walked back to the lodge. A misty dew was rising from the manicured lawn. The air was cold, but the sun signaled a gorgeous day was forming. She readjusted her hair tie as she walked and turned when she heard a truck pull in. It was Zack. He drove alongside her and rolled down the window.

"Hey, you're here bright and early," Molly said.

"Yep, I wanna get a head start on the grass around the cabins today, and mulch each one. You have a preference?"

"A preference?" Molly asked.

"For the mulch. A color. I can have the guys bring out black or red. Black is trendy right now at most commercial places, just so ya know."

"I didn't know anything about mulch could be considered 'trendy,'" She said with a laugh.

"Oh yeah, there's a lot of trends in these parts you've missed over the years, lady." He said. He revved the engine to make her jump as he rolled up the window. Molly laughed again.

As she made her way up the steps and Zack got out of the truck, she looked back at him.

"Red, please. I set my own trends, mister." Molly said. He smirked at her as she walked into the lodge. As soon as Molly pulled the door closed behind her, she leaned up against it and looked up at the ceiling. Her heart was racing again. Every time Zack unexpectedly showed up, her beats picked up. Her cheeks reddened. She shook her head and wondered how an old high school crush could still cause her to get a hot flash and feel dizzy.

Molly gathered more cleaning supplies to begin the other cabins as a flurry of texts arrived from Mr. Castille. He wanted constant updates on how the crews and contractors were doing and if she needed any more help. He was also concerned with any cost overrun. While Molly initially saw his obsession with the cost as a bit intrusive considering the lodge and any potential sale and profit was technically her business and her business alone, she started to accept that he was concerned with her best interest. She had cut her dad out of decisions and hadn't turned to him for advice or guidance for years. The idea that any older man needed to guide her life or financial undertakings seemed foreign. Kenny didn't even make financial decisions with her very much, especially toward the end of their marriage. He preferred to let her take the reins and only stuck his nose in when it would directly impact him or involved a big purchase. As she answered his texts and talked about market trends and comp prices if she sells before the season starts, Molly drew in deep breaths and tried to remember he was only looking out for her.

Molly climbed into her father's old truck to drive to the cabins. With so much bedding to wash, the idea of carrying it all down the trail and over the bridge was as overwhelming as Mr. Castille's flood of text messages. The smell of cigars unexpectedly made her cough. He never smoked in the lodge and only occasionally in the lounge. She squinted as she tried to remember the last time she smelled his cigars, or any cigar. She rolled down the window and let the fresh air fill the cabin as she drove toward the trail. The bumps in the dirt road sent her cleaning supplies racing to the floor of the passenger side. She yelped as she hit another bump just before the bridge. The ruts leftover from the snow melt were deeper than she anticipated. She had forgotten what a toll mud season took on dirt roads in Maine. Her head nearly bounced off the ceiling as the truck steadily climbed onto the narrow bridge. Molly stared straight ahead and tried to stay steady just as she noticed Zack's truck coming up behind her. She exhaled a sigh of relief as she got to the clearing. The sun was kissing the roof of each cabin and reflecting off the dirty glass of the side windows. Molly climbed out and went to the passenger side to reorganize her supplies and buckets. She heard a truck door close behind her.

"Hey, you gonna get these cabins gleaming today?" Zack said.

"Yep," Molly said as she laid two buckets and cleaning supplies at her feet. "Are you planning to come to dinner tonight? Along with the other guys, I mean."

"I don't know. I gotta ask around town and find out about your cooking ability before I commit." He winked.

Zack walked behind his truck and lowered the tailgate to retrieve a trimmer. Before Molly could think of a snappy comeback, she heard two riding mowers enter the clearing and knew his crew had arrived to help. She smiled back at him and attempted to wink back as she reached down for the buckets.

"You okay? Got something in your eye?" Zack yelled as he closed his tailgate.

"Um, yeah. I was trying wink back. I guess I kinda failed." Molly said, once again amazed at her ability to humiliate herself in front of him.

"Oh, thought maybe a black fly got ya." Zack winked again and turned to meet his guys.

"Jeez, Mol. Can you go one day without looking like an idiot?" She muttered to herself as she watched him walk away. She comforted herself with the thought that she wasn't tasting dirt like yesterday when she left him.

Molly adjusted her ponytail, pulled the gloves up to her elbows and let the hot water, bleach, white vinegar, and rags do the work they were meant to do. She washed away the dust, grime, smudges of hands and fingers that long left Maine, and washed away any traces of her father's neglect. With each swipe of a section of wall, a gray trail of water ran to the floor. She swiped over and over again until those trails of hot, soapy water ran clear. She let the puddles form on the floor and tried to avoid tracking more dirt throughout the tiny tourist havens. Start at the top and work your way down, she heard her mother say. Molly wasn't sure how young she was when she first helped her mother clean each season and in-between each guest. The seasonal clean-up after being closed all winter was the most intensive. The turn-around cleaning was much easier. She simply had to help clean the bathroom, do a light dusting, and help pile the bedding in the carts to take back to the main lodge. Once she added fresh bedding, Molly's mom would unfurl a quilt and let Molly spray it with fabric spray her mother made from scratch. She boiled down rose petals and lavender, along with other herbs and strained the water. She'd add that water to more water to dilute the residual color left by the herbs. The light scent would linger over the cabin and give it the first impression that Molly's mother wanted—an impression that is was home, that it was loved. She would also use lemon in the bathrooms. Molly's mom insisted nothing smelled cleaner than lemon. Molly had the fleeting thought of gathering some of the herbs around the lodge and making her own fabric spray. But it was only fleeting. Molly already felt up to her elbows in tasks. She added more bleach to the water. While lemon might smell like clean, she preferred the burning sting of bleach as proof of clean.

As she piled more quilts and sheets in the truck, Molly realized some of them had to be more than thirty years old. Her mother started to quilt after suffering the birth of a stillborn when Molly was in preschool. The baby was a boy and had a heart defect that wasn't detected until it was too late. The stress of birth was too much for his tiny, ill-formed heart to bear. While Molly didn't remember much of that time, she remembered her mother's pregnant belly. She had vivid memories of climbing onto her mother's lap and feeling the protrusion move. Molly didn't remember her mother going into labor or even being in the hospital. But, she remembered her mother sitting by the lodge window during snowfalls, crying and watching the sunset. She also remembered needles and scraps of material at her feet and in her lap as she cried. While she loved her mother's quilts, to this day when Molly saw knitting needles in a craft store, she pictured her mother crying with snow falling in the background. As she gathered up another quilt and held it close as she carried it to the truck, Molly realized she never asked her mother much about the loss. Her mother would've been around 25 or so when she lost a child. Molly felt growing pangs of guilt bubble up again. For too long, she had avoided Moose Pond Lodge to avoid her father and his demons. By doing so, she had also avoided memories of her mother, a woman whose memory should have been celebrated more.

One by one, she cleaned, prepped, and freshened each cabin. Molly left the doors to each one open to give the Maine spring breeze a chance to do some dusting for her. Zack and his crew's work provided the extra fresh scent of cut grass. The buzzes and roars of the lawn care equipment helped Molly keep pace with the cleaning. The growling of her stomach let her know lunchtime was creeping up fast. As she turned the key to one of the high-end cabins, a honeymoon cabin, the buzzes turned to a low hum that settled into silence. Molly figured if the guys could break for lunch, so could she. She got a sandwich out of the truck and went back into the honeymoon cabin. She sat on the edge of the bed. The sun blasted through the window and lit up the floor around her feet. She slipped off her shoes and drew her legs up. Molly glanced around and smiled as she chewed her turkey and swiss. The dust flickered in the sun, reminding her of the work she had to do. She noticed the half-burned candles on the night stand and the mantle. Her father built several of the mantles himself with white pine from the woods. A fall storm knocked down several trees across the trails, and he worked for days breaking apart the trunks with a chainsaw. He worked even harder that winter to carve mantle pieces to add to those cabins. Piece by piece, he laid the stones to create fireplaces and chimneys in four of the cabins in hopes of drawing in the destination wedding crowd. It worked. The pamphlets featuring the fireplaces, cozy quilted beds, and candle and champagne-flanked night stands all generated a sense of privacy and elegance that made marrying in the woods of northern Maine an exotic option. She stood up and ran her hands along the top. The dust piled and formed around her fingers. Neglect. She wasn't sure that level of dust could be from one season. Molly swallowed the last bite of her sandwich and riffled through a bucket for the dusting spray and a fresh rag. The door peered open more and cast more sunlight on the already glaring sight of dust on the mantle. She swung around to see Zack with two bottles of water.

"Hey, I got an extra water if you need it? You've been working hard in these cabins. All I've seen all day is you darting in and out of these things, carrying all those blankets." He stepped in and towered over her as he handed her a bottle.

She unscrewed the cap and took a long drink. She didn't realize how much her throat was burning from the bleach until the water hit the back.

"God, thank you. I didn't even think to bring a drink. I was just gonna get some out of the sink in a minute. Yeah, it's coming along okay, I think. These old cabins clean up nice. My mom always worked really hard to keep these places looking good. Don't know how much my father did," Molly said.

"He did alright from what I could tell the last few years. I mean, not like a woman's touch, though."

"Well, that's kind of sexist, don't ya think?" She shot back.

"I didn't mean it that way, really. Just, I remember your mom and I think she cared a lot more about this little stuff than your dad did." He said as he pointed to the table with the candle.

"Yeah, you're right. I think she did care a lot about that stuff. She was a romantic at heart. I didn't realize how much I miss her until I'm alone in these cabins. It's been a long time." She sat back on the edge of the bed and drank some more.

"I remember when you guys lost her. Hey, why didn't you ever come back much to visit anyways?" Zack said. "Never mind. That's none of my business. Sorry for prying." Zack went over to the sink in the bathroom and ran the water for a second before coming back out.

"It's fine. I just didn't want to be around my dad much when he was, well, drinking a lot. He kinda went into a downward spiral once my mom died. It wasn't too bad when I was in high school and college. But, by the time I graduated, well, you know. The whole town knows. He was the town drunk, from what I understand."

"Well, he might've had a problem. But, from what I knew, people here loved him. He liked to have a good time and made sure everyone else in that lounge had a good time, too." Zack stood in front of her. "You know, Ms. Matterson was a big help to him, if you know what I mean. Once they got together, he kind of eased up a bit. That's why I was surprised to hear he passed away like he did."

"What? Matterson? From down the road? I have no idea what you're talking about." Molly said. She stood up and swigged the last of the water.

"You don't? I'm sorry. I thought everyone knew about that. It was kinda common knowledge around here. I guess you could say they were dating? They were together a few years, from what I remember. You might want to ask her to be sure." Zack said.

Molly felt nauseous. She never thought her father moved on after her mother in any way.

"Did he love her? I mean, was it serious?" Her voiced cracked as Zack made his way to the door.

"Honestly, I don't know, Molly. I just know she was his, well, girlfriend, if that's what they call each other at that age." Zack said. "She was at the funeral. Hell, she handled the viewing like she was family, from what I hear."

Molly sunk back into the edge of the bed as Zack went outside. Part of her was comforted knowing her father had some level of companionship outside of strained calls and even more strained visits with her, Kenny, and Emerson. The other part of her felt like the worst offspring on the planet. Not only had she missed her father's funeral, but she was completely unaware that he had someone. How could he never tell her? Then again, once things fell apart with Kenny the Philanderer, she never called her father about it. He died having no idea she had left her husband and was sleeping on a friend's couch. He died, and a companion or significant other Molly never knew about handled the viewing. Mr. Castille never mentioned her to Molly. She felt as insignificant as the dust on that beautiful mantle. She felt neglected and as if her presence at the lodge was suddenly a piece of foreign matter that had collected around the edges, not meant to be there, not wanted. Molly was dizzy. Had her father fallen in love and spent the last few years happy and she was just too consumed with her own life a thousand miles away to notice it in his voice? Had he healed, cleaned up, showed affection and appreciation for another and Molly never bothered to ask? Or, had he kept it to himself because he knew it wouldn't change anything? Molly didn't know if knowing would have changed anything or not. She sat on the bed and tried to convince herself that she would've visited more, or at least once, or that she would've invited Ms. Matterson to visit with him. A tear welled up and escaped the inside of her left eye as Molly realized she probably wouldn't have done anything differently. She wouldn't have tried harder. The truth that he wouldn't have done anything differently ached even more. She shook those truths from her mind and stood up again. Regardless of what she would've done or what he would've done, she had work to do now. She grabbed a bucket and took it to the bathroom. Molly filled it with hot water and bleach. She reached up high above the toilet and started to clean that wall, then another, and another. She watched the dirt dribbled down and pool on the floor just as she had in the other cabins. It was all coming clean, finally. If she got those cabins clean enough, maybe the would've beens and could've beens would wash away clean, too.

Chapter 5

Rain is Grace –John Updike

As Molly started to prepare the largest dinner she attempted to cook in a long time, she thought about her parents and the massive meals they created in that kitchen. The sleek stainless steel and hard metal countertops gave the kitchen a sterile, cold impression. But to Molly, it was always filled with warmth, music, and a cleansing steam from the dishwasher. That steam felt like a hug, a hug from her past. As the steam permeated her freshly cleansed pores, the smell of simmering sauce wove its way to her nose. The boiling noodles, melting butter, and chopped parsley was inviting to her and the guys. She heard a few of the electrician apprentices commenting on the smells as they wandered through the dining room. Emerson even shouted how hungry it was making her as she did her homework at one the long tables.

"Hey Em, when you get a chance can you grab table clothes from under the window cabinet and throw them on maybe three or four of the tables?" Molly yelled as she slid a tray of freshly buttered bread into the oven. "Then, grab a few stacks of plates, please." Molly heard the cabinet open. She remembered doing those very same chores night after night when she was Emerson's age. Molly hoped the tablecloths weren't musty. She didn't have time to check them once she got dinner going. In-between trays of garlic bread, Molly dashed over to the full-length mirror in the cooks' closet. She tried to brush through her hair with her fingers and rummaged through her pocket for lip gloss. As she ran it across her lips, she got a whiff of bleach which had sunk into her fingertips after two days of virtually swimming in it.

After she finished cooking, Molly unwrapped an apron and tossed it onto the metal stool next to the dishwasher. She paused long enough to inhale the sauce, butter, and garlic before heading out to the lobby to call for everyone. Her arms were like jelly from the wall scrubbing and lifting heavy pots of boiling water. She thought about her mother and wondered how she did it every summer, every day, year after year. Molly pushed open the double doors of the kitchen, glanced at the tables, and headed for the main lodge doors. She thrust both heavy wood doors open and rang the dinner bell still attached to the side of the porch.

"Guys, it's ready!" She shouted to the dozen men scattered all around the lodge and porch. Eyes darted all around as the landscaping and electrical crew all glanced at their bosses. The bosses, Zack and Mr. Anderson gave the nod and everyone unstrapped tool belts, loaded up trimmers, and carried supplies back to their trucks. Molly watched as the crews disassembled everything and started towards the lodge steps. Before she turned to lead the way and serve the meal, she glanced across the yard at Zack. He was pulling off a grass-stained shirt and tossing it in his truck. He glanced back up at her just he reached in for a clean one. Molly knew he saw her watching him. She saw a tattoo from afar and wondered if and how she could get a closer look.

Molly and Emerson carried dishes of pasta and sauce into the dining room and anchored both tables with a heaping platter of garlic bread. Each of the workers washed up in the kitchen sinks and took a seat at the tables. Zack was the last to sit. He sat next to Emerson, right across from Molly. She walked around and poured iced tea into each glass as the men laughed and started to pass the dishes back and forth. As Molly poured the last of the glasses, Mr. Anderson stood up and clanked his with a butter knife.

"Hey guys, before we dig in, I just wanna say a few things to Molly here. Molly, your parents ran a pretty awesome place, and you know we all thought the world of them. Your mom's been gone awhile, but this meal would make her proud. I'm sure of it." He said. "And your dad, well, he and I were friends for many, many years. He'd be proud of ya, too, kid. I think fixing up this place for the summer is gonna do a lot of good for it, for this town, too. I know you have a ton of happy memories here. I think we all do. And I just wanna say thanks for this meal and the chance to make Moose Pond Lodge the great resort it once was. Cheers." He said.

All the men echoed his cheers and clanked glasses together. Molly smiled and wiped away a tear. She had spent so much of her time since entering that driveway thinking about how fixing the lodge would affect her and Emerson. It wasn't until that moment she realized a lot was riding on these renovations for each of the workers, too.

"Thank you so much, Mr. Anderson. That means the world to me. I'm so glad you're all here and can be part of this. My parents loved this place. I loved my childhood here. Being back here and seeing this place come back to life has brought back so many memories for me. Please, enjoy dinner, and maybe stick around for a few drinks in the lounge. You know my dad would want that. Please, eat." She said. Molly swallowed a lump in her throat at the thought of her father and the lounge. The men clapped as she made her way to her seat. She scooted closer to the table as Zack handed her the plate of bread.

"This is real nice, what you've done here. You didn't have to do all this." Zack said as he piled on pasta. Emerson giggled as the noodles slid off the side. "Guess I got a little too much, huh?" He said. "So, were you serious about having us stick around and have a drink in the lounge?"

"Yeah, I was serious. You guys deserve it. Hell, do you even realize how much you've accomplished already? The place looks great." Molly said.

"Well, it's not just us. You've busted your ass out there cleaning up all those cabins and this place, too. A nicely landscaped front and decent trails to hike might be one thing, but a clean bathroom and fresh quilts will be what keeps them coming back for more. You know?" Zack said.

"Yeah, I guess. I don't know how my mom kept up with all of it each year. I mean, I helped a lot when I was older. But when I was little, she must've been doing it all alone."

As they all finished dinner, each worker carried plates and glasses into the kitchen.

"You guys don't need to help clean up. I'll get these real quick then meet you in the lounge for drinks, okay?" Molly said as she tried to dart past a few of them.

"No, we got it, Molly. The more of us who help, the faster we can get those drinks poured," Mr. Anderson said.

Seeing more than a dozen men scurry to put away leftover food and load the dishwasher, Molly relished in the help and speed with which they got the kitchen gleaming once again. The laughs, conversations, and the scrapping of the last bits of sauce into containers made her smile bigger than she had since leaving Nashville. She got lost in the sea of men until Zack bumped into her. The sauce sloshed in the container as he quickly tried to step back. There was a slight splatter, and Molly saw the bright red dot on her nose.

"Oops, I'm sorry. Let me get that." Zack said as put down the container and reached for a rag from the counter. He wiped the dot off her nose and grinned at her.

She laughed. "Too many cooks in the kitchen." Molly glanced around and saw nearly everything done. "Looks good to me, guys. Who wants a drink?" Molly looked Zack square in the eyes. He smiled down at her and raised his eyebrows.

Emerson retreated to the lobby with school books as Molly and the dinner guests made their way to the lounge. She swung open the doors and waltzed behind the bar. Her eyes averted the spot where her father had died weeks earlier. She lined up glasses and reached for bottles with the same ease and confidence she had as a kid.

"There's no new beer on tap yet. I had the old stuff hauled away. But, there are some craft beers in the fridge, and the hard stuff is open and ready, guys." Molly said. Her mouth watered as she poured bourbon, vodka, and some scotch. Molly vowed to keep it in check this time. She'd enjoy a few drinks and go to bed without getting emotional and without waking with a massive hangover. She added splashes of ginger ale, cranberry juice, and dug cherries out of the jar she found in the back of the fridge. Zack pulled up a stool right across from her.

"You need any help back there?" he asked. The other guys pulled up stools and talked about old times in the lounge.

Molly shook her head, "Nope."

"You know, your dad and I had some great times in here, especially once he got the music hooked up." Mr. Anderson said. Molly smiled.

"Yeah, he certainly spent a lot of time here."

"You know, kid, it wasn't all bad. He wasn't, I mean. He kept it in check a good bit of the time. At least, from the nights I spent here a few years back." Mr. Anderson said. Molly gave him a sympathetic head tilt and slight smile.

"Yeah, I know, Mr. Anderson. I know," Molly said as she slid a drink to his awaiting hand. The last thing she wanted was to talk about her father's drinking in the room where he died from drinking.

"Let's all toast to Mason Bordeaux. To Mason." He said as he raised his glass. The group toasted in unison. Molly reluctantly raised her glass and let the bourbon slide down her throat. She closed her eyes as it warmed her.

"Hey, music? Where's the music?" Zack asked. Molly opened her eyes and reached under the counter to find the switches. She turned on the classic rock cd her father had in the player. She poured round two.

"Now, how about a toast to Molly and helping her get this place ready for summer?" Zack said. The cheers drowned out the clanks of glasses. Molly blushed. She wasn't sure if it was from the bourbon or the attention from the entire crew. She sipped some more. Memories of waking up hungover a few days ago led her to put the glass down. Zack was still watching her as she put some of the bottles on the shelf behind her.

After the second round, several of the guys needed to head home for the night. They each, one by one, thanked and hugged Molly for dinner. As Molly watched the men filter out of the lounge, she began to tear up thinking how they all knew her father. She wondered how many of them, if any, spent nights drinking with her dad. She wondered if any other them thought to tell him to ease up on the booze, or if they wondered where she was when he was put in the ground. She let words, questions, make their way to the tip of her tongue, but let them linger instead of escaping her mouth. She tasted those questions and fleeting thoughts. Molly swallowed hard as she made her way around the bar and held the door open. The smiles on their faces and redness in their cheeks told her their warmth and appreciation was genuine, as genuine as any exchange in that lounge. Molly let the mixed memories swirl above her. She could see her father laughing with these men, his laugh bellowing across the room. Molly could also see him alone, quiet, pouring glass after glass as he cleaned up the lounge. She knew there were nights that the sounds of crying coming from the lounge weren't a figment of her imagination. But tonight, laughs and hugs filled the room and crowded out those memories.

As the door closed behind Mr. Anderson, Molly looked back to see Zack behind the bar. He was taking glasses off the bar and running them under hot water.

"Hey, you don't have to stick around to do all that. I'm sure you've got plans, someone to meet up with or something. I got that." She said. Molly immediately regretted insinuating he had someone, mostly out of fear that he did.

"Nah, I don't have plans. I just want to help. You went to enough trouble tonight. Plus, once I get a good buzz, I like to clean." He said without looking up. Molly laughed.

"Can't say I've heard that one before. Hey, seriously though, thanks for all your help tonight cleaning up the kitchen, too. And of course, all the work you've done outside this place. It's made such a huge difference in a short amount of time." She said. Molly gathered up a few more glasses. She slid them over to the edge just as Zack reached out to stop them. He flashed her a quick smile. She grabbed a wet rag from the edge of the bar and started to wipe up the rings.

"There's no need to thank us all really. We're just doing our job. Plus, I remember how this place always was and want to see it like that again. You could really have a good season if we get it all done," Zack said.

"Yeah, I don't know about all that. I have no idea how my dad kept this place in business all these years as it is. It's not like people are flocking to the mountains in the summer to hang out, fish, hike, and all that. I think more people look for a way out of Great Pines instead of a way in." Molly said. She put down the rag and reached over to a table for her glass. She reached under the bar from the front and pulled out a bottle. Molly poured herself some. She slid the bottle back under the bar.

"Well, that's not entirely true. I looked for a way back in after I got injured, you know. Just because you couldn't wait to leave and never come back doesn't mean everyone feels that way. I tell you what, I couldn't be happier to have this place to come back to. And, you gotta understand, a lot of families love having a place like this to take kids to, to spend quiet time. No phones, no computers, no noise like out there. It's heaven in their eyes."

"Yeah, I guess. But not in mine. Once I drove away, that was it for me."

Zack dried his hands and poured himself another. "You mind?" He asked nodding to the bottle.

"No, of course not. Have what you want."

"So, you drove away all those years ago, and now you drove back with a kid in tow. What happened in-between?" Zack said as he sipped his vodka and tonic.

Molly nodded. "You know. Life I guess. Jobs, a kid, a condo, a cat, several affairs, and now a pending divorce." She shrugged her shoulders.

"Ah, I see. That's tough. So, a fresh start back here is more than taking care of your father's wishes, huh?"

"Yeah, I just hope selling pays for a fresh start for Emerson and me," Molly said.

"Wait, what? Selling? I thought you'd change your mind about that once it started to look good again? You still want to sell it?" Zack said. He put his glass down on the bar and walked around to a stool. Molly's eyes widened. She hadn't intentionally kept that plan from Zack or any of the workers. But, she also didn't see the need to discuss with them, either.

"Um, nothing's set in stone or anything. I'm just keeping my options open. I'm going through a difficult divorce and really need to start over somewhere with Emerson. On the other hand, her father has been an incredible dad, and I don't want to keep her this far away from him forever, especially after the way we left. Emerson needs him despite how he screwed up our marriage. She's acting fine about it all right now, but I know Emerson needs him to show her that she still comes first. As much as I hate him, I have to give him that chance to make it up to her," Molly sipped.

"Listen, Zack, I really don't know what I'll do or what's even right to do, but getting this place in order and stuff is the first step either way." She sipped some more and sat on a stool. "Anyways, what's it matter to you either way? I sell, or I stay and run this place? Seriously, what's it to you?" She said. Molly wanted to draw the words back from the air before they hit his ears. She knew the bourbon was starting to make her tone snarkier than she intended.

Zack stood up and drew his glass to his lips. He looked at her out of the corner of his eye as he sipped again. As he put the glass down, he said "Hey, it's no skin off my back whatever you do. I just thought you were putting all this effort in because you cared about the place. I just kinda assumed you were back for good. But, whatever."

"Whatever? I do care. This is where I grew up. Why do you even care if I am back for good or not? You never even noticed me in school much less noticed I left and never came back." She felt her cheeks grow red. Her temples started to throb. She took another swig and let the warmth flow down to her stomach. She hoped another swig would drown any words that threatened to reach her tongue. The last thing she wanted was to unleash more and create more regret in the morning.

"So, I didn't notice you in school. That doesn't mean I don't notice you now." He said. "But, you go ahead and sell and run somewhere else again. I'm sure that'll fix everything this time."

"Who the hell do you think you are? Run somewhere else? You have no idea what I've been through or what the hell needs fixing in my life." Molly said. She stood up and realized she was inches from his face. She was dizzy from the bourbon and the morsels of anger bubbling up and swirling around her mind. "And what the hell do you mean, you notice me now?"

"What do you think that means? Come on. You're a beautiful woman so of course I, well, you know," he said.

"No, I don't know. You see a klutz in her mid-thirties, falling down stairs, covered in dirt, and smelling like bleach from cleaning all day, oh and don't forget I have been known to stand there with sauce on my face, too."

"Well, I happen to think there's something, I don't know, kinda cute about all that. What's the word? Endearing?" Zack said. He flashed her that smile again, the smile that she caught glimpses of in high school and prayed to God he'd send her way someday. Now, he was directly in front her sending that smile her way as she rattled off all the reasons he shouldn't give her another look, much less a first. Molly could feel gravity pulling her closer to that smile, or perhaps it was drink-induced instability. She stepped back and lowered herself back on the stool before she unintentionally collided with his lips.

"So, you notice all I screw up, I guess. But what about you? You have someone at home? A girlfriend? Fiancée? Someone out there more 'endearing' I guess, huh?" Molly looked down, once again afraid of his answer now that she directly asked him.

"Well, yeah, there was. There is actually, someone very endearing. She's my kid, Hannah. She's four years old." Zack said. "She's my someone, that's for sure."

"What? I had no idea. Why didn't you mention her? Where is she? Are you, you know, with her mom?"

"That's complicated. I was, but it didn't work out. We split last year. Melissa, that's Hannah's mom, she took her and moved back down to Portland last summer. I get Hannah on weekends, mostly. And, I can drive down anytime to see her, take her for dinner, stuff like that. Wanna see a picture?" Zack said. He pulled his phone from his back pocket before Molly could answer. He sat on the stool next to her and swiped his screen a few times. "Here, here's a good one. This is a few months ago at Christmas. She got a puppy from Melissa's parents. Loves that little guy."

"Oh my, she's gorgeous, Zack. Look at those curls, those bouncy brown curls." Molly squinted at the phone.

"Yeah, I've had to learn how to braid to keep those under control. She gets those from her mom." Zack said.

Molly smiled as she swiped through more pictures. He had to have a thousand of her. There were pictures of the two of them together, then a few with a woman, too. Molly stopped. "So, is that Melissa? She's beautiful, too."

Zack leaned over and looked at his phone. "Yeah, that's her."

"How long were you two together? I mean, if you don't mind me asking." She slowly swiped to see more pictures without Melissa.

Zack took another sip. He told Molly that they met in college, the first year. She was there for him when he got injured and wasn't sure what to do with his life. When he came back to Great Pines, broken and lost, she stayed in college, but they stayed in contact. Once she graduated with a marketing degree, she got a position in Portland. They met up for dinner and drinks a few times. One thing led to another, and they dated for a few years. Once Hannah came along, he asked her to marry him. She said yes. Then, she said no. They continued to date until Melissa broke it off completely last year.

"We still get along though. We're just parents to the same kid now. We won't be a family like I thought, but that's what's meant to be, I guess. I've moved on. She certainly moved on—already living with another guy down there. But as long as he's good to Hannah, well, that's all that matters to me," Zack said.

"Yeah, but that kind of makes it harder, too--when they're good to the kid. I know it would almost be easier for me to move on if Kenny the Philanderer was a crap dad, but he's not. He's not at all." Molly sunk her shoulders and reached for her glass. "I think I've had more than I wanted to tonight." She exhaled deeply and took another sip.

"You and me both," Zack said. He closed the pictures on his screen and put his phone back in his pocket.

"You alright to drive or no? You can crash in one of the guest rooms tonight if you need to."

"Yeah, I think that would be a good idea. If you don't mind?"

"Of course, I don't mind. I have fresh blankets in all the guest rooms here in the main building. No problem," Molly said. "So, if you aren't driving, I guess you can another drink?"

"Why the hell not." Zack said. He got up and walked back behind the bar to retrieve the bottle. Molly slurped the last of her drink and slid her glass over to him. He poured and gave her a wink. Her heart quickened. Zack came back around and swung his stool to face her. He took a drink.

"So, Kenny the Philanderer. What was his deal? Why'd he run around on you?" Molly sat straight up.

"I don't want to talk about it—about him. I don't want to think about him, either." Molly sipped. The warmth was starting to burn. She was drinking too fast and not savoring the taste. She could often pinpoint the moment she crossed the line between enjoying the warmth and comfort of a drink and sipping to suppress what might come out of her mouth or enter her mind. She was at that moment.

"Hey, you okay? You seem a little, a little like you had one too many." Zack said. He put his hand over the rim of her glass. "You had a good night. Dinner, everything. It was real good. Don't get bogged down thinking of not so good nights. Well, I guess that's kinda my fault, too. Asking about it."

"Nah, it's okay. I'm okay. Or, I will be at least. You okay?" Molly said. She reached up to the top of his hand. "I'm good, really." She mumbled half to him half to herself.

Zack moved his hand from her glass and touched her cheek. He brushed her hair behind her ear as she looked down at her drink. He slid his hand under her chin and turned her to face him. She let her eyes meet his and hoped he wouldn't notice she had started to tear up. He pulled her chin closer to him and leaned over to meet her lips. He let his fall onto hers with ease and a gentleness she hadn't felt in years. He ran his hand along her cheek and put his other hand on the other side of her face. He started to kiss her harder. She relaxed her shoulders and began to melt into him as she leaned forward. He ran his hand down her cheek and to her shoulders. Then, he slid his hand to her waist to pull her closer. Molly reached up to wrap her arms around his neck. He suddenly stopped and pulled away. He looked to the left and wiped his mouth.

"Dammit, I'm sorry. I shouldn't have done that," he said without looking her in the eyes.

"No, no, really. It's fine. Trust me. It's more than fine." Molly said. She stood up and reached up for him. He pulled back again.

"No, you've had too much. I've had too much. This isn't the right time or place. Which guest room should I take?" Zack said. He glanced around.

"Um, the second down from the bathroom is fine. Jeez, you don't need to rush off. Really, I'm fine." She reached for the stool to steady herself.

"No, I gotta go lay down. I'll get out of here early enough tomorrow so Emerson or the guys won't see me, okay? No need to start any rumors over nothing." Zack said.

He nodded his head towards her and pushed his hands deep into his pockets. Before Molly could say another word, he turned and walked out the lounge door. She sunk further into the stool and looked at her drink. He was right. She had had too much. She had too much of everything lately. Despite being armed with that knowledge, she swigged the rest. Molly realized she didn't say goodnight to Emerson. She shook her head.

"When will you get it together, Mol?" She mumbled to herself. She stood up, placed the glass in the sink, and ran the rag over the bar top once more. Molly tossed the rag on the edge of the sink and put the bottle back underneath. She walked over to the door and light switch. Before she flicked it off, Molly's eyes found the spot on the floor. She forced herself to stare at it. "Nope, not going to become that, ever." Molly turned off the light and walked out the door.

The next morning rushed in like a tidal wave. Once again, she felt the pounding of her temples and a piercing headache roll from the front to the back as the sun peeked through the curtain. Molly squinted and reached for her phone. She was relieved to see it wasn't as late as she expected. As she laid back and slowly attempted to open her eyes and let the day sink in, her phone vibrated. Molly grabbed it anticipating a text from Zack, as the memory of kissing him and having him pull away pushed its way to the forefront of her crowded conscious. Once again, she squinted as she swiped her phone. She mouthed the words as she read *Hey Mols. Looking forward to dinner tonight. You guys will be here at 6 right?? Can't wait to catch up.* She groaned. As much as she wanted to reconnect with Maxine, she wasn't ready to think about being social. Molly peeled herself up from the bed and tossed aside the quilt. As Molly texted back and confirmed dinner, she was thankful it wasn't a phone call. The last thing she wanted to deal with was a chipper voice and feeling forced to reciprocate such chipper-ness. Before stumbling to the bathroom, Molly peered out the window to be sure Zack was gone. When she saw an empty driveway, a small pang of disappointment fluttered through her gut. Even though she wanted him to be gone, part of her also wanted to find him in the kitchen cooking her breakfast. Let that fantasy go, Mol—she thought to herself. Let that go.

Molly opened Emerson's door and let the light from the hall fill in the darkness.

"Come on, Kid. You've got school." Molly said as she tried her best not to sound hungover. Emerson turned and flipped down the covers. Molly smiled. She was so grateful Emerson wasn't one of those kids who was difficult to get going in the morning. "Hey, Em. I'm sorry I didn't make back in here to say goodnight last night. I just got busy chatting with the guys and cleaning up. Before I knew it, you were out like a light."

"It's okay. I talked to Dad right before I went to bed. He called the main office phone." Emerson said as she rose and rummaged through a pile of clothes still in a suitcase.

"Oh, what'd he want? Why didn't you come get me?" Molly said. She crossed her arms and leaned against the door frame.

"Nothing, just to see how the week was going. Dad did say he sent a package with more of my clothes and stuff."

"Okay, that's good. Did he ask where I was?" She immediately regretted the question.

"Yeah, I told him you had a dinner for the workers, and you were cleaning up from that," Emerson said.

"Oh. Now get ready for school. I'm gonna go make some eggs, okay?" Molly said. Emerson nodded and searched for more clothes.

Molly wandered through the lodge and started breakfast in the sparkling kitchen. She replayed some of the lounge conversation in her head. The feeling of kissing Zack filled her chest. But, the way he pulled away, his insistence on leaving, all left her with regret rather than elation. She watched the eggs cook and wondered how she should react when she saw him later. She decided to play it cool and not act like a love-sick school girl, even though that's how she felt. As Emerson ate, Molly got a quick shower, hoping it would ease her headache and allow some clarity to seep into her soul. Maybe Maxine could guide her next move or explain why Zack pulled away? Just like in high school, Maxine could be her sounding board over dinner. Molly rinsed her hair and thought, no, she couldn't bring it all up in front of Josh and Emerson. Molly threw on some clothes and ran a brush through her long, wet hair. She ran makeup across her face and lips as she watched the clock. Despite the headache and nausea, she looked somewhat put-together. She drew in a deep breath and played a few practice greetings in her head, as she knew Zack would be pulling in as she put Emerson on the bus.

"Hey, hope you had a good time last night. Sorry I drank too much. Sorry I asked too much. Sorry I seemed so desperate when we kissed. Sorry I have had this crazy crush on you since I was a freshman in high school and now that I'm a hungover middle-aged woman, I should really know how to act somewhat normal when I see you," she said in the mirror. "Ugh. Just get out there and stop being so stupid, especially in front of him."

Just as had been the case each morning since the men started to work at the lodge, Molly could hear Zack's truck pull in as she walked back toward the lodge. The sound made her heart skip a beat. She felt dizzy again. That was partly due to dehydration. She kept her stride as the truck slowed behind her. He beeped the horn. She jumped.

"Hey, didn't mean to scare you." He yelled from the window as he pulled alongside her.

"Yes, you did." She said without looking his way. She continued her walk with her arms folded and her eyes on the ground. "So, I didn't even hear you leave this morning." Molly hoped this would open the window to furthering the discussion.

"Yeah, I didn't think you would. I bet you passed out real quick, huh?" He said.

"Yeah, I guess I probably did," Molly said. She stopped walking and turned to face his truck. He put on the brake. "Listen, Zack, I'm sorry I had a little too much. I probably came on a little, what's the word? Desperate? Pathetic? Nosy?" Molly said.

"Stop right there. You weren't any of those things. Hell, I probably asked too much myself. Listen, two old friends, too much bourbon, it's all good. Okay?" He said.

She nodded. "Okay. Well, accept my apology anyways, please?"

"Apology accepted. So, how you feeling anyway?" He said. He pressed on the gas a little as she resumed walking to the porch.

"Not as bad as the other day, but not that great either. You must think I've got issues. Two hangovers in a week, huh?" Molly said. She looked down.

"Nah. You're going through a lot. You deserve a bender or two, or three." Zack said. He gave her a wink. She uncrossed her arms and laughed.

"Yeah, I guess," Molly said. She realized the 'benders' were starting to add up, especially when she added up the ones in Nashville the last year or so. As he turned off the truck and got out, he asked her what she planned to tackle today.

"Well, since it's pretty chilly and looks like it's gonna rain, I think I'll work on cleaning the main lodge building. Organize the office some, make a few calls about vendors to have stuff ready for the end of May, and maybe go through my dad's stuff. You?" Molly said.

"The rain will put a damper on trimming up shrubs, but I got some guys coming to help clear some branches from that old trail, the hiking one." He said. She stepped onto the stairs and looked down at him.

"The hiking trail to the lake?" Molly asked.

"Yeah, just clearing bigger branches blocking it."

"Oh, okay. Well, if you want a dry place to hide for lunch, you guys can come on in." She said.

He smiled up at her. He reached in his truck for a poncho. "Will do," he said as he unfurled it.

Molly nodded and walked inside. She swung shut the heavy oak door, leaned against the inside and let the scent of the lodge fill her lungs. It still had a musty smell when a good rain was about to come. Her eyes scanned the stone fireplace to the moose antlers close to the top. The cobwebs swayed back and forth—another sign of an incoming storm. Molly wondered if the janitorial closet still had the large broom with an extension. She smiled as she remembered balancing on her father's shoulders and reaching as high as possible to knock down the cobwebs. The feeling of swaying the broom extension back and forth with one hand and holding onto his head with the other warmed her. She relaxed her smile as she realized how unfair it was that Emerson won't get to share the same experiences with Mason. Molly wondered just what memories Em had of her grandfather at all. Two Christmases' ago, he flew to Nashville for three days. In a drunken stupor, he fell into the Christmas tree, breaking two ornaments—one made by Emerson at school and the only one Molly had from her mother. It was a crystal lighthouse her mother bought on a trip along the coast when Molly was 8 or 9. They spent the entire day darting in and out of lighthouses, taking pictures and collecting souvenirs from each. The ornament was the only thing Molly had left from that day trip.

As she heard the other trucks pull in the driveway and the faint sounds of chainsaws, the drops started to ping off the porch roof. Molly found the dusting supplies and window cleaner. She started with the books shelves, the main lodge windows, and then moved on to the office. Before cleaning, Molly had to tackle the stacks of paper on and in the desk. There were bills, invoices, vendor order forms, guests' receipts, and the tickets she sent last year. She came across a card envelope. Her father's name was scrawled across the front with two hearts drawn on either side. Molly slid out the card. "Happy Anniversary, my love" was elaborately written across a beach scene complete with the silhouette of two lovers, hand in hand. Molly's eyes skipped the poem on the inside and went straight to the signature. It was from Alaine, or Ms. Matterson to Molly. There was a heart over the 'l' in her name. Molly felt sick. Curiosity replaced the queasiness. It was a one-year anniversary. They weren't married. Molly was in high school the last time she saw Ms. Matterson. Molly only knew her as the neighbor a few miles down the road. She had a few horses on her land and children older than Molly. She lived all alone from what Molly remembered. She was also quite voluptuous. Her curves raised a few eyebrows when she was in the grocery store in tight riding pants and knee-high boots. Her shirts were all low-cut, or so Molly's memory told her. She also remembered Ms. Matterson as having bright red lipstick and very distinctive eyelashes and brows. Molly wondered when Ms. Matterson would've set her sights on her father, and why. If her memories of Ms. Matterson were accurate, she had no doubt what the attraction was for her father. He was, after all, not just her father and not just the town drunk. He was a man, a lonely man at that. Molly closed the card and sighed. She twisted her bottom lip and wondered if she should visit Ms. Matterson. Molly swallowed a lump in her throat. She wasn't sure if she wanted to know anything Ms. Matterson could or would tell her about her father's last days and years. Then again, if there was enough of a relationship between the two of them to warrant an exchange of cheesy anniversary cards, where was she when Mason died?

Molly filed the papers in order of relevance, keeping vendor information and lists of guests. She put the card in a pile all its own. It sat alone on the edge of the desk, being the only item of personal business in her father's desk. He had a picture of Molly, Emerson, and Kenny the Philanderer from Thanksgiving a few years ago. Molly smiled as she realized how much Emerson had grown in just three years. She had also gotten bigger around, more so than the rest of her friends. While Molly had been considered chubby as a kid and in her early teens, Emerson was reaching a point where Molly debated bringing it up with Kenny. She knew Emerson's diet was partly to blame, as the last few years Molly relied on prepared and fast food as she rushed home from work and Kenny worked odd hours, or did other things during those odd hours. Molly also knew their living situation was another reason. Living in a condo complex not far from the main streets of Nashville meant no real space to play. While generally safe, it wasn't like growing up at Moose Lodge Pond with woods, trails, and a lake to explore. Emerson was usually confined to the condo or a near-by park with Molly on the weekends. Her cheeks looked cute in the picture, but Molly couldn't help but wonder if those same chunky cheeks would make her the victim of bullying in Maine. She dusted off the top of the desk as she re-filed paperwork and put the card back in the skinny top drawer. Maybe a few months at Moose Lodge Pond would help Emerson's weight, she thought. Maybe even longer would make it a non-issue? Molly sprayed air freshener as she left the office. She made a mental note to buy some candles for the side table.

Molly spent the rest of the day mopping floors and cleaning the windows as the rain dribbled down the other side. She felt herself breathe a little easier as she moved on the next one. The air in the main lodge building was getting lighter with each day she spent cleaning. It was getting fresher, newer. She was starting to not only see a semblance of the place she grew up, but also the potential for a sale by June. Molly decided a concerted effort by herself, Zack and his crew, and the electricians and plumber could yield an alluring property ready for the market on Memorial Day Weekend. She planned to host an opening weekend with typical lodge events to generate buzz about the new and improved Moose Lodge Pond, then hope a buyer would waltz through and make an offer as the season began. Molly hadn't given much thought to what to do if that dream scenario didn't play out. Then again, she hadn't given much thought to what she and Emerson would do if it did, either. She glanced at the calendar on the wall behind the main desk. April 24th. While she had plenty of time to take care of the resort, she wasn't sure she had time to take care of the next chapter after that. Kenny's texts filled with questions and demands for a concrete plan were growing by the day. She tried to reply with some certainty and confidence that she had a plan, had it all figured out. But, as she saw the date, she knew she had nothing figured out. Then again,

Molly thought, when did she ever have anything figured out for herself? As she ducked behind the front counter to sweep some remaining dirt into a dustpan, she heard the door open. Zack and three of his workers entered with water rolling off their ponchos.

"We're gonna have to finish up that trail once the rain stops. Maybe tomorrow. Hey, Molly, you remember Alex from school? Think he was in your class." Zack said as he pulled the poncho over his head and shook the water off onto the front door mat.

Molly looked up and scanned the man next to him. "Oh yeah. Hey there. How are you? We had a few classes together. Your mom and dad used to play in a band here, right?" Molly said.

Alex smiled ear to ear as he wiped his boots on the mat. "Yep, they did. They still play at resorts, ski lodges, some open mic nights in Portland and Bangor, too. Makes them happy. How have you been?" He said as he walked closer. His eyes were dark, and Molly suddenly remembered sitting next to him at an assembly. They shook hands and exchanged the standard, condensed life story that people have prepared for those kinds of unexpected run-ins.

Zack laid his poncho on the floor and wandered up to the desk. "We came in to eat lunch if that's still okay?" Zack said.

"Of course, it is. I was just going to get myself some, too. I have a ton of left-over pasta from last night if any of you guys are interested?"

They filtered into the kitchen as she covered the counter in containers from the feast. As Zack put a plate in the microwave, he waved his shirt to dry it out where water had trickled through a hole in the poncho. Molly briefly thought about telling him he could just take it off, but she didn't have the nerve. She also wasn't sure she had the willpower or self-control to not ogle him if he did. She caught a glimpse of a tattoo on his upper arm. It looked like stems.

"Hey, Zack. What do you know about Ms. Matterson down the road? The horse farm lady?" Molly asked as she prepared a plate.

"I don't know really. Not much else than anyone else knows. She was with your dad for a while, but you knew that. She was widowed, like years and years ago. Her kids come back sometimes from what I see, with grandkids and all, but they were all older than us. Why?"

"I just want to know how close she was with my dad and why he never mentioned her, I guess," Molly said. She followed Zack and Alex with her plate. They sat at one of the long tables.

"Just go ask her, if you want. I'm sure she'd answer any questions." Zack said. He blew one of his floppy black curls from his forehead before taking a bite.

"Yeah, maybe I'll do that," Molly said. He winked at her as he took another bite. His green eyes swallowed her up for a moment, and she forgot what she agreed to do.

"Plans? Molly?" Zack asked. His words echoed in her head. She blinked.

"Wha..what did you say?" Molly said.

"I asked if you had plans this weekend? You okay?"

"Yeah, sorry. I just zoned out. Yeah actually, tonight I'm going to have dinner with Maxine Frost and her family. You remember her?"

Zack nodded. His curls flopped more. "Yep, her and Josh. I see them at their store." Alex nodded, too. "Great people. I think I remember you two were pretty close in high school, right?"

"Yes, yes, we were. She was my best friend." Molly said. The guilt of not staying in touch with Maxine came roaring back.

The memories of her and Maxine standing in the corner of the cafeteria watching Zack eat his lunch also came roaring back. She was trying not to stare at him the same way while he sat across from her eating his lunch more than 15 years later.

As Emerson made it home from school and the work crews packed it in early due to the worsening weather, Molly focused on dinner with Maxine and Josh. While she was looking forward to being side by side with her best friend, she felt prematurely defensive about never being around all these years. "It'll be fun" she kept telling herself as she dried her hair and repeatedly told Emerson to change.

Molly and Emerson sprinted to the car and navigated the driveway that resembled a river after the afternoon deluge. Molly leaned up to peer out the window and enter the main road. As she looked in the rearview mirror, she could already see an improvement compared to when she first drove up two weeks ago. She slowed down as she passed Ms. Matterson's place. It hadn't changed much. Two horses were standing in the field. As they entered town, Molly leaned forward more as she tried to remember the side streets. The rain made it difficult to see the road signs just as time made any shortcuts difficult to remember. "Frost," she saw on a mail box. She exhaled deeply.

"We're here, kid," Molly said. The two of them ran up the porch steps to avoid getting drenched. Molly glanced at the railings. They were yellow and scalloped. The front porch awning matched. They had a porch swing with their name engraved on it. There were pots of various colors and sizes lining the steps just waiting for flowers to come to life.

"It looks like a gingerbread house. Don't ya think?" Emerson said as Molly rang the doorbell.

"My thoughts exactly," Molly said. The door swung open. Maxine grabbed her by the arm before she could finish her sentence. She squealed as she hugged Molly, just as she had done at the store.

"Come in, girls. Dinner's almost ready. Emerson, you can go down the hall where the kids are playing. Molly, come on in the kitchen and say 'hi' to Josh." Maxine said.

Emerson gave her mom a wide-eyed look as Maxine nudged her toward a hallway.

"Go on, Em. It's okay." Molly said as Maxine pulled her by the arm. Molly glanced around. Family portraits covered the walls. There were also signs above every doorway with painted words of encouragement, Bible verses, and inspirational quotes Molly had seen a hundred times before. She smiled. The house seemed a perfect fit for Maxine and Josh and their little family. The walls were yellow and shades of blue. The kitchen was ablaze with bright white cabinets with red accents. Molly felt her eyes burning at the brightness of it all. Josh was at the counter putting the finishing touches on a cheese tray. He looked up with a grand smile. Molly immediately noticed he was at least two hundred pounds heavier than in high school.

"Molly, my god, you look great. Come in." He said as he put the knife down to walk around and hug her. His massive arms enveloped Molly. His squeeze forced the air out of her lungs. She gasped and laughed at the same time.

"Jeez, Josh. It's great to see you. Thanks for having us." Molly said as he unleashed her.

"So, what do you think of the place?" Maxine said. She reached for Molly's arm again and dragged her to the other side of the kitchen where a breakfast nook overlooked a small backyard.

"I love it. It's so homey. It fits you guys perfectly." Molly said. It was undoubtedly much homier than she ever bothered to make the condo feel. It reflected a family, a real family. Molly struggled to remember what she had on her old walls. A few pictures of Emerson and a painting they bought at a street fair? They never had a family portrait taken. For the life of her, Molly couldn't think of a good reason why. Maxine dragged her to the nook, and they sat on high stools.

"So, I want to hear all about Nashville, what you've got going on at the resort, your daughter, everything," Maxine said. Molly held the edge of the table as the flurry of questions made her dizzy.

"There's not much to tell. I'm fixing up the resort as best I can. The divorce is still going on." Molly said. She filled them in on the details of the resort cleanup, Emerson in school, and the antics of Kenny the Philanderer. Josh listened as he got pots off the stove and arranged chicken on a platter. The three of them called the children to the table and started to eat. Molly listened as Maxine and Josh talked about taking over the grocery store, the local PTO drama, who has moved back to town, how the new sheriff is related to the mayor, and the rumors of an affair between the code enforcement officer and the town clerk—who happened to be Josh's aunt.

As they cleared the dishes, Josh and Maxine ventured into the story of how they got together when she started working in the deli of Josh's father's store. Molly laughed as they told how Maxine ignored Josh's advances for an entire year because she was afraid she'd get fired. Their first kiss was in the break room after he wrapped her hand. She sliced it open in the deli, and he was the only one to step up and help stop the bleeding. Josh stood and retrieved a bottle of wine from the rack in the kitchen island.

"You want a glass, Molly?" Josh asked as he reached for glasses.

"Okay, just a little. I'm still nursing a hangover from the dinner I threw the guys last night." Molly said.

"Speaking of that, what are you going to do with that lounge?" Maxine asked.

"The lounge? What do you mean? You mean the whole resort?" Molly said. Josh slid over a glass. She took a sip.

"No, not the resort. The lounge, you know, where your dad died. I mean, you aren't going to keep it like it is, are you?"

"What? It's been cleaned, Max. What do you mean? What am I supposed to do with it?" She tilted her head to be sure Emerson was back down the hall with Maxine's three children.

"Well, you can't keep it open, right? Isn't that a little, I don't know, morbid? I mean, he died from drinking too much in there. Why would you want to have it open, and well, why would you feel comfortable drinking in there at all?"

"What do you suggest I do with it? Tear that part off the lodge? Not serve any alcohol at the resort? It's not like I'm going stay there and get sloshed in that lounge every night like my dad did, you know?" Molly said. She took a long drink of her wine.

"Don't get upset. But honestly, Molly, it sounds like that's exactly what you've been doing." Maxine said.

"Really? What the hell does that mean? I'm not my dad. And, I'm selling that God-forsaken place anyways, once its ready. It's not like staying there is part of my plan, trust me." Molly said. Maxine sat straight up, and Josh took a long sip from his glass with his wide eyes peering from over the top. They exchanged glances. "What? What's the look for, guys? Just say it."

"Nothing, Molly. It's just, well, that stuff is hereditary, you know? I'm just a little worried." Maxine said. She reached across the table to take Molly's hand.

"Listen, don't be worried about me. Seriously, isn't there any stupid petty PTO drama or grocery store scandal worth talking about? I and my father's drunkenness can't be the biggest story in this dumb-ass town, can it?" Molly asked.

"Dumb-ass town? Jesus, Molly. I'm just worried about you, that's all." Maxine said. She drew back her hand and looked down at her glass.

"Worried about me? You guys don't even know me anymore. You don't know anything about me now."

"Well, that's not our fault. You're the one who never came around again, who left and never looked back."

"What the hell was there to look back at?" Molly said.

Maxine stood up and stepped behind her stool.

"Us, Molly. Us. You know, I was your best friend our whole childhood. We went through everything together, your mom dying, my parents' divorce, your crush on Zack for years, everything. And you just up and left. You didn't just leave that resort or your drunken dad. You left me, too. You never looked back at me, or any of us. You painted this whole town with one big brush. You ran off to Nashville and created this entire other life for yourself. You thought that life or whatever made you better than all of us." Maxine said. "Guess what Molly, you aren't. Our life here means something to me, to us." She glanced at Josh.

"Jesus, Maxine. I'm sor--" Molly said.

"No. Don't. You don't mean it. I saw the look on your face glancing around my house. You still think it. You think because I chose a different path than you, that I chose a wrong path, a life for you to look down on. Going in a different direction doesn't mean I went in the wrong direction, you know?" Maxine said. "And really, Molly. You ended up right back here anyway."

"I never thought I left you, Maxine. I didn't mean to ever hurt you. My leaving had nothing to with you." Molly said.

"I know. Nothing you did had anything to do with me or any of us here. And, you coming back doesn't either. You set out to drive to that resort, sell it, and drive right off again without giving me or anyone here a second thought. You know It's true. Me, this town, that lodge, none of it means anything to you."

"Well, that's kinda harsh don't you think?" Molly said. She stood up and took the last sip from her glass. "Is that why you invited me here for dinner? So, you could shit all over me for leaving? You're not going to make me feel like shit for leaving back then or again. You got that? Emerson! Emerson, come on. We're leaving."

"Yeah, just leave, Molly. That seems to be all you know how to do." Maxine said. She wiped away two tears that suddenly streamed down her face. Her voice cracked. She swallowed the last of her wine and looked up at the ceiling. "Go. You'll just keep going anyways. I don't need you to walk back into my life just so you can walk right back out again." Josh came up behind Maxine and put his hands on her shoulders. Emerson appeared in the doorway. Molly tilted her head at Maxine and shrugged her shoulders.

"I said I'm sorry. What more do you want?" Molly took her purse from the stool and guided Emerson from the nook and through the living room. Emerson glanced back behind her shoulders. "Thanks for dinner, Mr. and Mrs. Frost." She shouted as Molly opened the door.

"You're welcome, Emerson," Josh shouted back as the door closed.

"Jeez, Mom, that was rude," Emerson said.

"Enough, Em. Just get in the car." Molly said.

She jumped in the driver's seat and turned the key as she fought back the tears. Molly backed out of the driveway and glanced at the porch before driving away. It was a cute porch, the kind she had to admit she always wanted. As she headed through town and down the road to the resort, she replayed Maxine's words over and over in her head. Maxine was right. Molly never thought about her or anyone she left behind once she drove to meet Kenny in Nashville. She never even sent Maxine her new address. What kind of person does that, Molly thought. Maxine was also right that Molly looked down on Maxine and her life there. She knew she had no right to, but she did. Molly regarded staying in Great Pines as a defect, an option for those without the guts or brains to do anything else. She didn't even see it as a choice because, in Molly's mind, no one would choose to stay if they could leave. As she drove past the streets and stores she knew all her life, Maxine was right about one more thing. No matter how far she went from Great Pines and Moose Pond Lodge, and no matter how she felt about those who did stay, she ended up right back there, back where she started. Molly realized blindly running from her past only brought her right back to where she started. Any lingering feeling that she was somehow 'better' than those she left behind got wiped away like the rain on the windshield.

As the street lights faded in the rearview window, the rain picked up. Molly drove the dark, winding road out of town on autopilot with Maxine's words echoing in her mind. As the horse fence came into view, Molly jerked the steering wheel and whipped the car into Ms. Matterson's driveway.

"Where are we going, Mom?" Emerson said as she leaned up from the backseat.

"I'm stopping real quick at a friend of grandpa's. Stay in the car," Molly said.

She saw Emerson roll her eyes from the back seat. Molly put the car in park and exhaled all she had in her lungs. There was a light on inside, but the rest of the property was dark. Molly darted out and dodged the massive drops as a few pelted her on the forehead. She couldn't tell if it was rain or residual tears streaming toward her chin. Molly found relief under the small metal awning. She was inches from the front door. Molly pounded. As the sound of dogs barking filled the main hall of the house, Molly realized she used more force than necessary. She was already prepared to apologize for startling an elderly lady on a stormy night. She squinted as the small light above her head suddenly illuminated. Eyes peered at her through a side window. Ms. Matterson seemed much shorter than Molly remembered. Molly waved awkwardly.

"Ms. Matterson? It's me. Molly Watts. I mean Molly Bordeaux." She said. The door slowly opened.

"Molly? Are you okay? Come in, dear." Ms. Matterson said as she slowly opened the door to reveal herself. She tied her robe closed and moved her long, gray hair behind her ear.

"No, no, I can't. My daughter's in the car. Can I just talk to you a second?" Molly said. Ms. Matterson opened the door completely as a gate held back a pack of yipping Yorkies. She nodded. Molly was distracted by her bright red lipstick and heavy mascara. "I just, I found a card inside my dad's desk. I guess you two were together? I had no idea." Molly said. The questions that crashed through her mind hours earlier were out of reach as she shook her head.

"Yes, yes, we were together, for a while anyway." Ms. Matterson said. She fiddled with the tie to her robe.

"Why didn't I know? Why didn't he say anything about you? Did you guys, you know, love each other, Ms. Matterson?"

"Please dear, call me Alaine. I don't know why he didn't tell you. Maybe it's because you didn't talk to each other much. Maybe it's because you never asked. I don't know." She pulled her robe tighter and retied the bow again.

"We talked. We talked whenever I could catch him sober, at least. If you guys were serious, where were you when he died? Why weren't you there? Why did he lay there for two days before he was found?" Molly said. She felt her heart beat harder against her chest.

"Where was I? Where were you? I was there for him for three years. I helped him to bed more than I care to remember. I tried to get him to stop or slow down at least. I tried to distract him from the booze. I tried to fill whatever void he was trying to fill with that stuff. I tried, dammit." She said as she put her hand on the doorframe. "I broke up with him a few months ago because I just couldn't be there anymore. I couldn't fix him. I couldn't save him. And, you want to show up here weeks after his funeral and ask where was I?"

Molly knew the rain was meshing with tears. She felt them bubble over. She felt a few drip from the tip of her nose as she stared at an overly made-up elderly woman. "Your father broke my heart. I gave him all I had to give, and I ended up alone, standing at his graveside with a handful of others who gave a damn and tried like hell to save him from himself. You want to show up here and ask where was I. That's where I was." Ms. Matterson shook her head and closed the door with a thud.

Molly stared at the wood grain on that door until the porch light went out. She blinked away rain and tears. Her gut churned, and her heart fluttered. Molly looked away from the door and back to the car. The headlights were shining right on her. She felt stripped away and naked in the dark, cold rain. She could see the outline of Emerson in the backseat. Molly wondered if her daughter saw her as Maxine and Ms. Matterson had seen her that night. She walked toward the lights of the car and stood in the rain for a moment. Molly let it wash over her.

She slid back into the car and put it in reverse. Molly made her way back to the road. She stared at the yellow line as she tried to fight tears. Emerson didn't make a sound until they reached the lodge. The rain started to subside.

"I'm gonna change for bed and call Dad if that's okay?" Emerson said as she pushed the back door open with her feet. Molly followed her up the steps to the main door. She fished for keys in her purse. "Okay, kid. Just don't tell him…" She paused.

"What? That you fought with your friends?" Emerson asked.

"Yeah, well, nevermind. Tell him whatever. Just don't stay up too late. I'm gonna go to bed early myself." Molly said.

She opened the heavy wooden door and flipped on the light. As Emerson disappeared into the lodge office to use the phone, Molly went straight to her parent's old bedroom to change clothes. Her wet clothes hit the wide pine floors with a thud. She didn't even bother to hang them up in the bathroom. Molly pulled on dry sweats and socks. She wandered back down the hall and heard Emerson laughing as she told Kenny the Philanderer about something that happened at school. The sounds echoed as she went to check the locks on the main door. Without thought, she went to the door of the lounge. Molly told herself she'd just check the lock on the outside door and then she'd go to bed. A good night sleep was the cure for a night of being confronted with her hypocrisy and inconsiderate treatment of people who once loved her. She flipped on the light and shuffled her wool-covered feet across the lounge floor, across the spot where her father faded away. The door was locked. As she turned to leave the lounge, she caught a glimpse of herself in the bar mirror. For a brief second, she saw her mother. Molly paused and tried to absorb the resemblance. She was almost the same age her mother was when she died.

Molly walked over to the bar and stared further at her reflection. She walked to the other side and took a glass from the shelf. Molly reached underneath and pulled out the bottle. It was only a quarter full. One drink will help me sleep, she told herself. It'll help ease the sting of the words thrown at her tonight and the sting of the words she had thrown at Maxine and Ms. Matterson. Molly poured a drink and fished ice from the freezer. She swirled the cube around the glass and let the smell wind its way up her nose. As she drew the glass to her lips, the resemblance to her mother was gone. One drink, she told herself again. Molly slid a stool over and sat down. She relaxed her elbows on the bar and swirled the cube. She watched it hit the sides and bounce back into the middle. It never stopped. It just floated from one side to the next and reflected the deep, golden brown around it. She sipped and let that familiar warmth roll down to her gut. It radiated, and her insides relaxed. She no longer felt her gut clench or her heart flutter. Her head didn't pound with the echoes of Maxine and Ms. Matterson. She felt light again, airy. She was lifted up from the reality of being back in Great Pines, in Moose Pond Lodge. Molly poured more in the glass. She told herself she'd call Maxine in the morning. She'd fix it. She'd fix it all somehow. Or, she'd finish fixing the resort and just run off again. As the bourbon engulfed another ice cube, Molly let that warmth replace all her feelings and responsibilities. She let it replace the guilt from her fight with Maxine, and the feelings of defeat on Ms. Matterson's porch. She allowed it to replace her feelings of guilt for not being there with her father. She let it replace her feelings of failure over her divorce. Molly let that brown elixir replace everything inside her once again, just as her father had done night after night.

"Maxine isn't right. I'm not like him. Never have been. Never will be." She muttered as she drew the glass to her lips once more. That warmth grew hot on her cheeks like fire. Had she just set everything on fire, everything she thought she was going to fix while in Great Pines? Everything she thought she could fix about herself? She sat on that stool and drew up her feet as if she was on an island and fire was swirling below. Even in the haze of bourbon and the warmth bubbling up, there was no comfort alone in the lounge. There was nothing but isolation, an isolation of her own making.

Chapter 6

A lake is the landscape's most beautiful and expressive feature.
It is Earth's eye; looking into which the beholder measures the
depth of his own nature—Henry David Thoreau

Once again, the buzz of her cell phone and a streak of light came barreling into her brain and jolted Molly back to reality. And yet again, she realized she never tucked Emerson into bed before she fell asleep. Molly shook her head, slowly so as not to entice yet another headache. The fact that her daughter spent another night falling asleep in her old room while Molly passed the night hours in the lounge settled in her gut. She sat up and let her head sink down. Molly's wet clothes were still in a heap in the middle of the floor. She turned off her phone and forced herself to stand. Queasiness radiated from her stomach to her entire body. While she wanted to crawl back into bed, draw up the covers to block the light, and let the hangover run its course, she couldn't. Life was waiting. Her daughter was waiting. The resort was waiting, and the calendar was a daily reminder that there wasn't much time left.

Molly slid her feet into slippers. She stepped over her damp clothes and wandered down the hall to her old bedroom.

"Hey, kid. Come on. Time to get up." She said. It hurt her entire body to force a fake chipper tone. Molly was tired of not only feeling that way morning after morning since returning to Maine, but she was tired of pretending she didn't. Emerson stirred. Molly drew her hand up to her head. "Come on, Em. Get up. I'm going to the kitchen." Molly said as she scooted back into the hall. Once she got into the kitchen and started coffee, Molly remembered the words exchanged with Ms. Matterson and

Maxine. She shook her head. As the coffee dripped, each word floated back into her head, and a headache emerged. The weight of what they said to her, what she said to them, was crushing. She wanted to open her brain and let the words fall out onto the floor to be swept up and forgotten. She wanted to feel light, like she had in the lounge, like it all didn't matter. But it did matter. Despite the momentary mix of amnesia and feelings of justification she felt in the lounge, the truth was at her feet, in her bones, and in her heart. It would always come roaring back regardless of how many nights she sat in the lounge. "Is this how Dad felt every day?" she mumbled to herself as she poured a cup. She blew then sipped. Whatever Molly could drink away would always return. She knew it, and she knew her father had to know it, too. The steam from the coffee collected on the tip of her nose as she stared across the kitchen. Why did he keep going back night after night, she thought herself? Why did she? She sipped again and vowed to call Maxine once Emerson left for school. She also vowed to make it all up to Emerson. She wasn't just a crappy friend; she had no doubt she was being a crappy mother.

As she walked up the lane after Emerson got on the bus, Molly slowed down and waited to hear Zack's truck come up behind her. She reached the steps and still heard nothing. Her heart sank a little. Molly paused and tried to remember if maybe in a drunken stupor she had offended or accosted Zack, too. She shook her head and pulled out her phone. There were no calls or texts between her and Zack. However, she saw three missed calls from Kenny the Philanderer last night. She exhaled and looked up at the sky. Zack's truck broke her from the trance of the clouds.

"Hey, you. How are ya this morning?" Zack yelled as he got out of the truck.

Molly turned toward him. "I'm okay. I've been better, but I've been worse."

"You had dinner in town last night, right? Your friend Maxine?" He said as he pulled down the tailgate. With the skies clearing, the sun pierced through and lifted the morning mist. It made the landscape behind Zack look fuzzy.

"Yeah, that didn't go so well. Which reminds me, I have some phone calls to make and fences to mend." She said.

"I'm going back to the hiking trail today, clear brush, mend the fence along the way, too." He said. Molly told him she might join him. It was going to be too beautiful a day to clean inside. She also wanted to avoid the lounge and figured the fresh air might help the all too familiar headache that plagued her.

"I'll come find you when I clean up from breakfast and make a few phone calls." She said. He slammed the truck bed shut and flashed her a smile. That smile still made her heart flutter like it did when she was fifteen.

Once she closed the door, her eyes followed the stone fireplace up to the antlers. It was nice to see the dust removed and the true majesty of the fireplace and antlers revealed. She glanced around the rest of the main lobby. It was looking clearer, fresher. Molly drew in a deep breath. The musty smell seemed to have dissipated. She smiled at the vast difference from when she followed Mr. Castille through the front door and now. That smile faded when her phone vibrated and she it was Kenny the Philanderer. She swiped to accept the call.

"Hey. Sorry I missed your call last night. I was—"

"It doesn't matter what you were doing, Mol. Listen, I want Emerson to fly down for a long weekend. I miss my kid. The judge said I have every right to fly her down anytime I want really." Kenny said.

"Okay, okay. Slow down. I told you I'm not trying to keep her from you. It's just that we're trying to get adjusted here, that's all." Molly said.

"Adjusted for what? You're coming back down this way once you sell that place anyways, right? You should've just let her

stay here in her old school and with her friends to begin with."
Kenny said.

"Listen, I'm not going to argue with you. Trust me; selling
is still the plan. I have no desire to stick around here any longer
than necessary. Just text me the flight info when you get it,
okay?" Molly said.

Her head pounded more. She scanned the lobby, the
couches, the bookshelves, and the pine floors. The lodge's beauty
might be shining through once again, but the old scars were still
visible. After last night and her run-ins with Maxine and Ms.
Matterson, it seemed she was only creating new wounds in Great
Pines anyways. She hung up and rolled her eyes. She hated to
think Kenny was right. She always hated it when he was right
about anything, especially when it involved Emerson. She was
both haunted and thankful for the simple fact that regardless of
how shitty of a husband he was, he was a good father. The fact
that he was a great father despite his cheating and lying made
Molly feel more inadequate as a mother. She knew she was
getting it wrong on so many levels, especially at night when she
repeatedly overlooked the basic 'mom duty' of saying goodnight
to her only kid. Before the feelings of failure and discontent grew
too great, Molly dialed Maxine's number. Relief filled her bones
when it went straight to voicemail. She decided short and simple
was best.

"Hey, Maxine. I'm so sorry about last night. You have every
right to hate me for how I left all those years ago, and last night. I
have no excuse for never looking back, never staying in touch with
you, for basically walking away from you, not just this resort.
You're right. I looked down on you for staying, on everyone else
who stayed. I don't blame you at all for losing it on me last night.
I'm gonna make it up to you. I promise. Well, I just wanted to say
I'm sorry. Call me back." Molly said.

She hung up and partially hoped that fifteen second effort
would be enough to smooth over Maxine's hurt feelings. She had
that slight sting and winced just like a band-aid had been ripped

off. Molly pushed herself from the door and slid her phone inside her back pocket. It was time to get to the business of really fixing things, hungover or not. The list of repairs and cleaning may have been decreasing, but there was still a lot more to check off. She took a few pain relievers and let them slide down her throat. There was a slight feeling of comfort when she told herself this would be the last hangover for a while. The lounge was not going to suck her in tonight, regardless of what took place while the sun was shining.

Even with a queasy stomach and the remnants of a bourbon headache, she went through the motions and stepped out into the sunlight. At the bottom of the steps, she stopped and looked up at the sun. The chilly, rainy days had floated off the coast and spring seemed to have found its way to Maine. It was the warmest day yet. Even though it had been almost 15 years since she spent springtime in Maine, she loved that earthy smell that indicated the mud and muck left behind by the snow was nearly all replaced by grass, ferns, and wild fiddleheads. This time of year in Nashville, she needed her air conditioning to get through the day and sweat would permeate her office clothes before she reached the car. This in-between the sleep of winter and rebirth of spring in New England was something she truly missed, even if she didn't care to admit to anyone.

Molly wandered down the trail to find Zack tossing a branch to the side with one hand while holding the chainsaw with the other. He flashed that smile she was getting a little too used to. He had sweat soaking through his back and under his arms. He walked toward her.

"What do ya think so far?" Zack said. She caught another glimpse of his tattoo peeking from under his sleeve as he raised his arm toward the trees.

"Looks good. I spent half my childhood running up and down this trail. Is the beach in good shape?" Molly said. She had been back for weeks and hadn't seen the pond yet. Zack nodded.

"Yeah, it's looking fine. A good combing is all that's needed. The canoes look good, the dock, too." Zack said. He pointed to another branch sticking out onto the path in front of them. Molly bent over and grabbed the end. She dragged it behind as she walked alongside Zack.

"You know, you're pretty lucky this place was your playground. Yeah, I'm sure as an adult, the responsibility is a bit much. But, for a kid, this is heaven. Don't you think?"

"You're right about that. It was. Listen, I know I seem like this all is such a burden and I can't wait to unload it. But you're right. As a kid, it was great to grow up here. Everything was great until my mother died. And, I am grateful I get to show it all to Emerson. She'd never been here before."

The trees were just as grand, and the tops swayed as the clouds passed overhead. Molly's headache and queasiness started to fade even more. She could almost see her mother running up the trail, in her bikini, with a towel thrown over her shoulder, chasing Molly. They raced to the pond every time they went down that path. She nudged Zack's with her elbow.

"Hey, put down that chainsaw."

"Huh? Why?" Zack said.

Molly repeated the command. He slowly lowered the chain saw next to his foot. Just before it hit the ground, Molly yelled, "Race ya!" She darted past him and felt the dirt of the trail kick up from her feet as she increased her stride. Her hair blew back from the wind as she realized she forgot to tie it up before leaving the cabin. She saw the break in the trail and water in the distance. Molly was running faster than she had in years. While she took up running with a group of co-workers in Nashville, she was the slow one in the pack. Molly did it for the company and the time away from Kenny. She had no destination, no set speed, and certainly no will to end the run sooner than necessary. But, as she let her legs pick up the pace and unleash power she hadn't felt since she was a kid, she felt free and strong. Molly pumped her arms and could sense Zack was catching up. She could hear his feet hit the trail in sync with hers. The view of the water grew larger as the trees grew sparser. Her eyes widened. Moose Pond was much bluer than she remembered. She couldn't believe she didn't miss it more. She slowed down as she reached the end of the trail. Molly glanced back behind her before her feet left the dirt and hit the sand. Zack had slowed to a walk.

"You win. My knees won't let me go that fast," Zack said.

She stopped and put her hands on her hips. Her breath rippled through her body at a rate she also hadn't felt in years. Her heart was pounding as was her temples. She felt beads of sweat form on her forehead and nose. Molly drew in one long, deep breath and looked back at the pond as Zack came up behind her. He put his hand on her lower back. Her eyes scanned one end of the pond to the other. The trees were sturdy and full. The sun bounced off the middle, and she saw a few bugs buzz the tops. Molly noticed a few bubbles here and there. She heard the birds as one skimmed the water in front of her. The sand and rocks were clean, seemingly untouched by anyone or anything. There were pine needle piles left behind from the occasional wave. She remembered gathering them as a child and making small huts for ants and other bugs.

"It's gorgeous. More gorgeous than I remember," Molly said as her breath grew steady and slowed. She wiped the sweat from her forehead. "I can't wait to see people back here again, in the canoes, fishing, families just taking a break and taking it all in."

"Yeah, that'll be nice. More families need to do that now, unplug and all." Zack said.

Molly remembered the mini-vacations she, Kenny, and Emerson took a few times in Tennessee. The woods, the Smokey Mountains, Rock City in Chattanooga, and just time away from the city on a Saturday afternoon. She knew she was guilty of still being connected. Kenny certainly was. His phone was always within reach, partly because he couldn't leave work behind and partly because of whoever he happened to be leaving behind at the moment. She relied on staying connected to avoid any feelings of rejection if she dared try to connect with him. It wasn't until she was standing in the silence and peace of Moose Pond that Molly realized she and Kenny both didn't bother to spend any of that time connected to Emerson during those trips. Had they ever taught her to disconnect? Molly realized even in the tranquil woods of Great Pines, she hadn't made any attempt to hand those lessons down.

"I'm gonna bring Emerson back here after school. Maybe we'll test out a canoe. I don't think she's ever been in one." Molly said. She folded her arms and nodded. She looked up at Zack. A bead of sweat lingered on a curl hanging in the middle of his forehead. She suddenly remembered his knee injury. "Oh, I'm sorry. How's your knee? I forgot all about it when I dared you to keep up." She let a smile creep across her face. Molly placed her hair behind her ears.

"It's good. I run still, just not that fast. How about you? When'd you get so fast? Did you do track, and I don't remember?"

"Nah, I just ran a little here and there for fun. That's the fastest I've ever even tried to run. I guess I had energy to get out. Or, maybe running from Nashville, life there, just now caught up with me." Molly said.

"Well, whatever you were running from, I'm pretty sure you left it in your dust now." He said. He moved his hand from her back and put his hands in his pocket.

"I hope so," Molly said. "I guess it's time to get back to work, huh?" Zack nodded.

She scanned the pond one more time. She could almost hear her father laugh as she remembered the time she fell out of the canoe when they went fishing. The glistening of the sun blinded her as she flailed and blinked water away. Her father's massive shadow crossed over the sun as he reached down and plucked her from the water. She laughed thinking of how swiftly he tossed her back into the canoe. "My dad loved it out here," Molly said. It was the first time in a long time she reflected on a memory of him sober. There were years of sobriety. As she and Zack started back up the trail, Molly made a silent vow to let more of those memories float to her mind's surface. Zack placed his hand on her lower back again. She looked up at him and smiled. The fluttering in her stomach and sweat under her arms when Molly would see him in the mornings was replaced by a feeling of contentment and what she could only describe as friendship. After her fight with Maxine, she wondered if Zack was indeed the only friend she had in town. As they turned to walk back up the trail, his hand slipped into hers. He squeezed it, and she squeezed his back.

Together, they spent the afternoon clearing the trail, raking over the sand and needles, and straightening the signs leading to the different paths. Molly had forgotten how intricate some of the trails were. She used to run from one to the other without a second thought. She stopped to listen to the wind sway the pines and smell the air. As she walked each path that connected to the main trail and the pond, Molly relaxed and refreshed. Her headache faded, and her mind's hurricane of thoughts slowed. There was a distinct and deliberate task in front of her. The practice of focusing on that one task, each moment, each branch and turn in the trail, all combined to fill her with peace. It was a peace she let overtake her body and mind. The sheer act of labor in the outdoors, the buzz of Zack's chainsaw, the intermittent song of the birds, all lulled the chaos that had cluttered her mind for so long. For the first time in a long time, the earth below her feet felt like home. She wanted to beautify it, honor it, and bask in it. She wanted those earthy trails to absorb through her pores and once again be a part of who she was. She stopped to glance around at the ground and the sky above her. Molly inhaled the fresh, piney, earthy air and realized she was falling in love with the woods again. She was falling in love with Moose Pond Lodge again.

As Molly and Zack gathered up the rakes, bags of leaves and sticks, and his chainsaw, she let her childhood memories bubble up to the surface. Molly realized she had buried them for all the years she spent in Nashville. Unearthing the trail was unearthing so much more. The smells combined with the passing clouds from one side of the pine-laden trail to the other made her hunger for more. She had let the memories of her father in the lounge, night after night, drown out the reality of her childhood. It was easy to stay away with those memories in the forefront. But, before her mother died, before the drinks and allure of the lounge sunk its teeth into her father, the resort was a country kid's heaven. Although, she had to admit it was a lonely heaven. It was still heaven compared to the childhood experienced by others she knew, even in Great Pines. Maxine's parents divorced and made her childhood a ruthless and resentful game of tug-of-war. Molly remembered love between her parents. She had distinct memories of laughing, dancing, flirting between the two of them. As Molly reached down for the handle of the last rake, she let the vision of her mother being twirled around the make-shift dance floor in the dining room fill her tired mind. Zack was up ahead of her.

"Hey, Zack? What kind of new stuff do you think we could add to the resort? Like, what do people want to do now? You know, outdoors? I know I run in Nashville, hike, and all, but I have no idea what's fun up here now." She shouted to him.

Zack stopped and turned around. He shrugged his shoulders.

"Nothing too different than before I guess. Zip lining is pretty big, but that's a huge liability, too. Hiking, fishing, scavenger hunts in the woods, classes, maybe? You know, like outdoor yoga, bonfires, that kind of stuff. What about talent contests and stuff? I remember your dad having that here." Zack was walking backward holding the chainsaw and dragging a few rakes and a shovel by the handles. He slowed down enough for Molly to catch up.

"Yeah, talent shows. I think I saw a karaoke machine in the supply room inside, too. Games and stuff, too. I'm just trying to think of new things to add, you know, to set this place apart," Molly said.

"How about an outdoor stage? For bands, maybe? You could revive the herb garden, all that. Paint the canoes, of course."

"Outdoor stage, huh? That's a cool idea. Could you build that or should I ask Bob Castille to recommend a carpenter?"

"I could build it. It'll take a few days after I finish clearing these trails and the planting right around the main lodge. I can add it to the gazebo."

"Well, I've got starter plants for the window boxes for the cabins. Emerson and I will do the flowers right around the lodge in about two weeks, once any danger of a freeze is gone," Molly said as she caught up with him. "Outdoor stage. Hmm. The more I picture it, the more I like it." A smile crept across his face. As they made their way from the main trail, over the bridge, and back to the truck, Molly saw Mr. Castille's car parked in the main drive. "Speak of the devil. I gotta go find him and figure the funding for some of this stuff."

Molly leaned the rakes up against the side of the dusty yellow truck. She brushed her hands off on her jeans and skipped up the steps. That short sprint to the pond gave her new energy. She opened the large wooden door. Mr. Castille was standing at the counter flipping through the old guestbook.

"Hey, kid. How's it going out here? Everything's looking great, inside and out." He said.

Molly sunk into the couch next to the fireplace.

"Thank you. It's been exhausting. Thank God I've got Zack and the others here to help. You should take a walk down to the cabins and take a peek. So, what have you got for me today?"

"Well kid, I've been talking this place up and toying around with the numbers. I think once we get some good pictures and get it on the market, you'll have quite a few offers to choose from," Mr. Castille said. "Do you know exactly when you think you wanna do that? Put it on the market?"

"I thought we'd have a grand opening Memorial Day weekend and then sell? You know, once it's all up and running, we have bookings and all. I was just talking to Zack about what to add, like an outdoor stage, new activities, and such." Molly said. She sat up and leaned her elbows on her knees.

"Of course, you can add whatever you want. I just thought you'd want offers lined up before that, so you and Emerson can get back down south or wherever sooner rather than later. But hey, it's up to you. Whatever you want to do is fine. I think you need to strike and field offers before the season starts, which is in a few weeks. Not too many people are looking to a buy a summer resort once the summer has actually started," Mr. Castille said.

"I guess you're right. I haven't really thought too much past getting the place ready, honestly."

"Listen, Molly. It's no skin off my back when you sell or whatever. But, if you want the maximum possible for this place, well, I'd get my head in the game now. Adding more than necessary, planning a big opening weekend, and all that is just putting more on your shoulders than you need. Certain things need done--the electrical, cleaning up the landscaping, updating the cabins, plumbing, all that. But all this other stuff isn't necessary to sell."

"What happens if I, I don't know, if I don't sell right away? Do I get the trust at least? For the summer?" Molly said.

"Well, yeah, of course, it's yours. Are you thinking of staying?" Mr. Castille said.

"I don't know, Bob. I just want Emerson to experience a little of this place, the parts of it I loved. I guess. You know, the people, the guests, the Friday nights and bands on stage, all that. I don't know. Maybe I'm just feeling sentimental or something."

"This place. It's your home. Hell, I'd love to see you stay forever. That's what your parents wanted for you anyway."

Molly stood up and put her hands in her pockets. "Staying here forever? I'm not sure that'll ever happen. A summer? Maybe. Forever? No."

"You never know, kid. You never know." He said. He zipped up his bag and reached to hug her with one arm. Molly leaned into him.

"Thanks for everything, Bob. I don't know what I'd do without you."

"I'm serious about deciding very soon. I can post pictures and get the real estate agent right on advertising this place ASAP. Just say the word." He released her and stared her up and down. Mr. Castille then looked around the main lobby, ceiling to floor. "It's all looking so good. Your dad would be proud."

Molly nodded and looked around, too. She knew her dad would be proud of how the place looked. She had no idea, however, if he'd be proud of her.

As Mr. Castille walked out, Molly heard the bus stop at the end of the lane. She reached for the door and followed him to his car. He tossed his briefcase on the passenger side and watched with Molly as Emerson meandered up the lane.

"Why does she look so down? I thought she was having a great time in school here?" Mr. Castille asked.

"Yeah, she was. The novelty has worn off. She misses her dad and her friends in Nashville. And, well, you know kids. I think she's getting some crap from a few, but I'm not sure." Molly said.

"Really? That sucks. She's such a sweet kid. I'm sure all this upheaval is bad enough without kids making it worse. But, we've all been there, huh?"

Molly nodded. Emerson grew close enough to flash a fake smile Mr. Castille's way.

"Hey, kid. How're you liking Great Pines Middle School?" Mr. Castille asked.

"It's good. I love my teacher. She's awesome." Emerson said. She released her overstuffed backpack from her shoulders. "And, the resort is cool. Mom? Can I go call Dad before dinner?"

"Of course, you can. I'll bring your bag in." Molly said. She reached down and kissed the top of Emerson's head as the girl darted past and jumped up the steps. Emerson opened the great door and disappeared inside as Molly picked up the backpack.

"As much as I hate to say it, I'm glad she calls him every day. He might've been an ass to me, but he's a good dad, and that contact makes her day," Molly said.

"Having a good dad is important for a girl. A dad who will drop everything and be a rock when a kid needs it." Mr. Castille said with a wink. He reached for the car door.

"Yeah, well you know I wouldn't know what that was like." Molly quipped.

Mr. Castille closed the car door and shoved his hands in his pockets. "Now, Damnit, Molly. Your dad thought the world of you. Don't you go around painting him like some awful guy who neglected you. I'm getting sick and tired of hearing you bash him. It's not right, and it's not fair. You got that, kid?"

"Excuse me? Don't you go around painting him out to be some kind of saint. He wasn't there for me, and you know it. He was in that damned lounge night after night. I cleaned it up after school each day. I counted and filed deposits on cabins. I signed vendor slips and food orders. I did all that while keeping up with my grades, filling out my own permission slips, and making us dinner every night. Me, Bob. I was two years older than

Emerson." Molly said. She wiped sweat from her forehead with the back of her hand. She felt her cheeks getting red again.

"Molly, he had a disease. You know that. He loved you more than anything. I checked on him all the time while you were away. I know where his heart was. You were all that mattered after your mother died. Listen kid, I know he didn't seem to show it all that well. I know you felt alone, but you were his whole world. Once you left, he just fell further down that rabbit hole. Then, he was just as alone as you felt you were. Holidays, birthdays, the anniversary of your mom's death, all of it hit him harder and harder each year. I was here with him for all of it.." Bob lowered his head and looked at the ground.

"What about the night he died and the days afterward? Where were you then? Huh? You, the guys who worked here with him, Ms. Matterson? You say he had a disease. Why didn't any of you guys help him deal with it? God damn it, Bob, he laid there for what? Two days? Where were you then?"

"You're seriously asking me that? You can sit there and blame us all you want. Alaine Matterson called me this morning and told me about last night. But blaming us won't make you feel any better in the end. You're the one who wasn't here for him. You're the one who ran off and never looked back. Going and making a life for yourself was great and all, but you never turned back. You say you left because he wasn't there for you, but you never gave him another chance to be. That's all he wanted, especially after Emerson came along. You know he was dry during some of those times. I was there when he called you over and over again." He folded his arms across his large chest. "A ticket to Nashville here and there and a few pictures of Em, that was it from you. You never called and rarely answered when he did. He tried so damn hard, Molly. You never gave him a chance to make it up to you. It's like you wanted to keep punishing him and then got more pissed when he fell deeper. I swear, Molly, it was as if part of you needed him to be that drunk that didn't give you the attention you deserved just so you could justify not coming around." Mr. Castille said. He leaned closer to her face, turning as red as Molly was. "You burned a lot of bridges when you left, Molly. Now you're gonna walk back into town and have the nerve to ask where all the smoke's coming from?" He shook his head and pulled the door open again. Mr. Castille started the car and stared forward as he backed out.

Once again, Molly found herself standing alone absorbing the sting of words that cut. Her only friend in town, her father's last love, and the only father figure she had left, all three asked her the one question she couldn't justify with an honest answer, the one question that would haunt her the rest of her life—where was she? She looked back at the lodge steps knowing Emerson was on the phone with her father, laughing and getting much-needed attention and comfort. Even after getting caught with a nurse on her knees in front of him, Kenny the Philanderer was being a more attentive parent than Molly had been the last few weeks. Where was she when Emerson needed her? Fixing trails with Zack, repainting canoes, and building an outdoor stage was all going to fix the outside, what the rest of the world and Great Pines could see. But, none of it would fix what she was reminded of time and time again since she returned. She wasn't there when her father needed her, just as he wasn't there when she needed him most. Molly knew as she stood looking up at the lodge steps that she could very well be on the path to repeating the same pattern with her daughter. More frightening to Molly was the realization that she was also repeating the same pattern as her father—drinking away the nights in the lounge expecting bourbon to provide an answer, a relief. However, it was going to take more than avoiding the lounge to prevent that fate. It was going to take putting out a lot of fires, fires she seemed to stoke since she returned.

Chapter 7

I go to nature to be soothed and healed, and to have my senses put in order---John Burroughs

Molly stood against the wall and listened as Emerson filled Kenny's ears with every detail of her day. She smiled hearing that Emerson finally had a girl and two boys to sit with at lunch. Despite the blur of work she strived to complete each day and the blur of bourbon more nights than not, Molly did manage to worry about how Emerson was fitting in. The same problems that plagued her in Tennessee were only amplified in Maine. Her weight had been an issue for the last several years. From the first grade on, Molly believed Emerson would slim down as she grew taller or as she played more soccer and softball. Only, a 'slimming down' period hadn't arrived. It had been a growing source of contention between Molly and Kenny as he wanted her to eat better and participate in more sports. However, Kenny never wanted to be the one to cook better meals or take her to countless practices. Knowing he wouldn't put in the effort to help her show Emerson a better way and knowing part of the reason was it would interfere with his philandering made Molly's blood boil the last few years. She blamed herself, too. It was easy to bring home fried foods, especially in downtown Nashville. It was easy to grab bags of dinner on the way to grab Emerson from school, much easier than chopping and cooking well past any normal dinner time. It was easy to sleep late on weekends instead of taking her to the park or hiking. It was easy to lounge around on the couch with a glass of wine rather than find healthy ways to get Emerson out and about. If she was happy in her room reading or on Molly's phone face-timing friends, Molly used that time to wallow and wonder where Kenny was, and with whom. It was all easier than the alternatives. Emerson was now paying the price. Molly knew Emerson was already self-conscious about being bigger than the other kids in Nashville and that was more obvious in Great Pines. It was a different way of life up here. Molly hoped

Emerson would embrace it and the results would begin to show. However, Molly knew she had to set that plan in motion.

Molly peered around the corner to see Emerson sitting on the desk with the cell phone in her hand as Kenny was now on speaker.

"Hey, Mom. Say 'hi' to Dad." Emerson said.

"Hey, Kenny. How're things going?" Molly asked. She wondered if her concern sounded as fake to Kenny as it did to her.

"I'm good, Mol. Emerson was telling me about her new friends. And, we've been talking about her coming down in two weeks. I'm off work, and she can miss a day or two of school. There's a festival downtown, too."

Molly drew in a deep breath. As much as it pained her, in her gut, she knew this was best for Emerson.

"Yeah, Kenny, I think that would be doable. She misses you for sure," Molly said. Emerson flashed a big smile. Molly flashed one back.

"Told ya," Emerson said into the phone.

"Well Ken, we can work out the details later tonight if you've checked out flights. But for now, I want to show Emerson the lake. Tell your dad bye, sweetie." Molly said. She raised her eyebrows at Emerson.

"She hasn't seen the lake yet? Isn't that like the main thing there to see?" Kenny asked.

"It's been raining a lot, and I've been busy fixing up the place. Just haven't had the chance yet." Molly said. She walked closer to the phone.

"Yeah, Mol, I hear you haven't had the chance to tell her goodnight much lately either. Must be pretty busy at night, too, I guess?" Kenny said. Molly reached for the phone. Emerson shot her mom a scowl. Molly pressed the speaker button and drew the phone to her ear.

"Mind your own damn business, Kenny." Molly said as she turned to face the door. She rolled her eyes and tried to whisper. "I'm not. It's not your business anyways. Is it?" Molly left the office and stood in the hall with the phone. She could feel Emerson following her out. "Maybe I need a little something to take the edge off what you've done? Maybe that's the only way I get the image of you and that whore on her knees in my house out of my head? Huh?" Molly paused. "Yeah, like you're a model parent yourself. Screw you." She pressed end on the phone. Molly looked up at the ceiling. She promised not to be that parent, ever. Yet, she was that parent at that moment. She turned around to see tears in Emerson's eyes as she stood in the doorway.

"Can I still go back to stay?" Emerson asked. Molly knew she was trying to will the tears away as her voiced cracked. Molly went to her, bent down, and drew her daughter close.

"Of course, you can. I'm so sorry I did that in front of you. You can definitely see your dad in a few weeks. He loves you to pieces and misses you so much. I shouldn't have said those things and lost my temper. I really don't want to be that mom." She said. Molly could feel her start to cry. She pulled her back and wiped her eyes. "Emerson, listen. Things have been crazy and not fair to you at all lately. I know. And, I know I've messed up. I haven't helped you enough. I haven't been saying goodnight or asking you much. That's gonna change. I'm gonna change."

Emerson's eyes darted around. Molly placed Emerson's hair behind her ears. She looked at her daughter's round face and squeezed both her hands tight. "I mean it, Em. Things are changing right now. I know we've put you through a lot, your dad and me. This move has changed your whole life, your school, your friends, and I haven't helped at all. I'm here, Em. I'm going to make it all up to you, I swear." Molly said. She stood and pulled in Emerson for a hug. Molly patted the top of her brown hair. "You trust me, Em?" Emerson nodded yes. Molly held her tighter. She didn't want to let her go. She wanted to squeeze her hard enough to shrink her down, reverse the years, and start raising her all over again. "Get your bathing suit on, kid. We're going to the lake." Molly said. Emerson looked up at her. She had Molly's big brown eyes and her father's smile. Molly knew she'd have to find a way to work with him to make everything right for Emerson.

As they walked the trail, Molly pointed out the paths and told Emerson which led to the cabins, fire pits, other hiking trails, and which looped back to the lodge. She told her about growing up running the trails, climbing the trees, and sitting alone in the woods once her mother died. Emerson took her hand and asked Molly to tell her more about her grandmother. Molly squeezed her hand and spent the rest of the walk describing every detail of her mother. Molly found herself searching the back closets of her mind to find more in-depth details. She hadn't realized how much she forgot until she was asked to remember.

As they came to the piney opening that led to the sandy beach, the water came into view. Emerson slid her hand out of Molly's and started to run toward Moose Pond. Molly watched her chubby legs pick up speed and let the echo of her giggles fill her ears. She was hopeful a cleansing in the lake could be the new start she needed, for herself and Emerson. Molly trotted off and stayed close behind. She wanted to drink in the sight of her daughter running toward the lake she grew up running towards. Molly wanted Emerson to soak it in, the sight of the pines flanking the lake all around and the sun bouncing off the water. She wanted to see Emerson squint and hear her squeal when a fish brushes by her leg. Molly wanted Emerson to fall in love with the lake, the lodge, the way of life at the resort, or at the very least, to appreciate it. Molly slowed her jog when she thought of allowing to Emerson to fall in love with it all only to take it away. Was it fair to dangle the lure of the resort in front of Emerson at all? The thought of forcing another transition on her daughter made her slow down even more. Molly stopped short of the sand and watched as Emerson made it to the water. Emerson turned around. She was huffing and trying to catch her breath.

"Mom, this is so cool. It's beautiful. Can I go in?" She shouted. The water was teasing her ankles and Molly could already see the pine needles float passed her daughter's toes. Molly put her hands on her hips and drew in the pine air.

"Yep, of course, you can. Just be careful." She said. Emerson slowly inched in up to her thighs. Molly could see the goosebumps form. Even though it was May, the water still gave visitors an icy introduction.

"It's freezing, Mom!" Emerson said. Her smile and shrieks filled Molly's heart. Despite her failings the last few weeks, and failures the last few years with Emerson, Molly saw a happy and vibrant girl enjoying life. Molly peeled off her shoes and reached down to roll up her jeans. She kept her eyes on Emerson as she rushed to join her in the pond. Emerson splashed Molly's face as she inched closer to her. Molly flinched and splashed her back. Molly laughed as the water coated her hair and dripped from her eyelashes. Emerson swirled around in a circle as she ran her hands along the water. Molly was out of breath from laughing. She made her way back to the sand and plopped down. She felt it stick to her legs as the goosebumps rose. Emerson trudged out and sat next to her. The sun kissed the freckles on Emerson's shoulders, and Molly stared at her daughter.

"What?" Emerson said. She was trying to catch her breath again.

"Nothing. You're just a beautiful girl, Em. I don't think I tell you that enough. You like it here?"

"Yeah. It's fun to run around out here and stuff. I love having a pond like this, too. It had to be cool growing up here, swimming anytime you wanted and stuff." Emerson said.

"It was. It really was." Molly said. She looked away from Emerson to watch the sun dance on the water. Black flies started to skim the pond.

"Why didn't we come vacation here, like when Grandpa was alive?" Emerson said.

Molly shrugged. "I didn't want to come back, I guess. It's, well, kinda complicated adult stuff, I guess. But, I do love it here."

"I do, too. But, how long are we staying before we head back to Tennessee? The whole summer or what? I want to see the shows and stuff, the people staying at the cabins." Emerson said. Molly looked forward and squinted.

"I'm not sure. I don't really know when it'll sell for sure or even when I'll list it for sale. I gotta work that out with Mr. Castille. I promise I'll keep you in the loop, whatever I decide. Do you think you'd like a whole summer here?" Molly said. She squinted looking at the sun.

"Yeah, I think so. I mean, if I can still visit Dad. I don't want to go the whole summer away from him or anything. But, yeah, I think it'd be cool to live here, too."

Molly nodded. She picked up a handful of pine needles and ran them between her fingers. Molly let them drop on her wet jeans and to the ground in between her legs. She picked up a few more to block an ant headed toward her knee.

"Whatever happens, I gotta decide quick, though. I think by the time Memorial Day comes, it'll be ready for guests and then I'll decide. I gotta talk to your dad tonight about sending you down to see him, okay? Maybe I'll have it all figured out once you get back here." Molly looked straight ahead as she weighed her options out loud, half to herself, half to Emerson. She reached over and took Emerson's hand. "I meant what I said earlier about things, me, changing. Okay?" Emerson nodded as Molly squeezed her hand and smiled down at her. She saw the goosebumps rise on her daughter's legs and felt the burning of her own. "Come on, let's head back and get dry." As they rose and started back the trail to the lodge, Molly tried to picture her life a year from now or even months from now. While the divorce was a certainty, the details of the next chapter weren't. It was all up to her, the path she would choose for herself and Emerson. The diverging paths on the way back to the lodge only brought that reality home more. She wished it was as simple as darting off the main trail, exploring the paths through the woods, and darting back anytime she felt like it. Only, life wasn't unfolding in that manner, and Molly knew it never would.

She remembered driving from Maine to Nashville with Kenny ahead of her. There was nothing but excitement, anticipation, and hopefulness. There was no trepidation or second-guessing. There was no need to question whether following Kenny for a thousand miles made sense or what the future may hold. She trusted him, trusted his lead. Now, there was no one in the lead, no one to follow. And now, there wasn't even a father to ask for advice, not that she asked him when she took off for Nashville. It was all up to her, and her alone, and so much was riding on not getting it wrong. Molly vowed to call Mr. Castille later and get some hard numbers if she sold or if she kept the resort for one summer. While never an option she seriously considered when she pulled into that driveway weeks ago, it suddenly seemed like a possibility. One summer could help her regroup, mentally and financially, and it could give Emerson a season of memories to carry with her for a lifetime. It could be like handing her daughter a piece of her soul, a string of the fabric that made her who she was. As they approached the opening to the main drive and side view of the lodge, Molly caught a glimpse of Zack's truck. A smile crept across her face as she realized a few added days, or months, in his presence might give her a few memories also.

After dinner was cleared and night fell, Molly joined Emerson on the couch next to the fireplace to go over her homework. It was the first time since Emerson started at the new school that Molly had devoted a night to help her. As they finished, Molly decided she put off calling Kenny the Philanderer long enough. It was time to dial, jot down flight numbers, and prepare herself for the inevitable trip to the airport to see Emerson off. Her stomach clenched at the thought of watching

Emerson walk off with a flight attendant, but she knew Emerson could handle it and it was best for her. The sound of Kenny's voice as he relayed the details was oddly comforting. Despite not trusting him regarding anything else between them, she knew when it came to Emerson, he was on top of details and would never steer them wrong. Molly listened and felt a slight pang admitting to herself that on his worst day, she still admired his natural parenting skill.

Molly wandered into Emerson's room after her daughter changed. She slid into bed next to her and caressed her hair. Molly kissed the top of her head as she had done nightly for years. She let the warmth of her daughter's breath and the scent of her hair be all the elixir she needed that night. She had promised herself and Emerson it would be. As she rose to leave, she reiterated her promise to change, to get this right. Molly closed the door, the door to the room she once occupied for years, and stood in the dark, wooden hall. As her eyes scanned the knots in the wood walls and ceiling, she resisted the gravitational pull of fate. The words 'one drink' entered her mind. She inhaled and exhaled that idea out. Molly shook her head. Before another word or rationalization could materialize, she turned her body toward her parent's bedroom door. She shuffled her feet and let the idea of waking up without a hangover be her motivation for going through that door and staying there. Tomorrow wouldn't start with a headache or a feeling of confusion. It wouldn't start with frantically checking her phone to be sure Emerson didn't miss the bus or to be sure Molly hadn't called Kenny or anyone else late into the night. It wouldn't start feeling queasy, regretful, or stuck in a cycle that scared her. It would start with welcomed sunshine, a clear mind, and plan. It would start the way she needed the rest of her days at the lodge to start—out from under the curse of being her father's daughter.

Before she changed from her pajamas and started Emerson's breakfast, Molly told Mr. Castille she wanted to host a grand opening, advertise cabins and activities, and spend the summer ensuring the place was the best it could be before a sale.

Once the season got underway, it could go on the market with a closing date near the end of the season. She wanted that one last summer for herself and Emerson. Molly wanted to hand over the resort in a way that would make her parents proud. She wanted to sell and start fresh somewhere after soaking in a successful season. Molly didn't want to drive away remembering what she drove up to in April. A new energy filled her soul, and her mind raced with ideas, just as it had when she ran to the pond with Zack chasing behind. Motion, it was all set in motion. As Zack's truck pulled in the drive, Molly rattled off her ideas and the plan to stay the summer. As he turned off the truck and the engine settled, Molly waited for a reaction.

"Is that right?" Zack said as he slid out of the driver's side. Molly stepped back from the door and leaned against the front end of the truck.

"What do you think? I gotta work the phones and go through the old guest list and stuff. There're a few deposits that poured in from guests. Oh, and a couple called about a wedding. A wedding...can you believe it? I think by Memorial Day I can have it all ready. The wedding might take some extra time, but it's a small party, a family wedding beginning of July." She said. Molly was out of breath as Zack reached into the bed of the truck.

"Well, girly. Will you need a landscaper all summer then?" He said with a wink. Molly's smile widened.

"Yeah, I guess I will need someone out here on a regular basis to keep up with the grass at hedges at least. You know any good ones in town?" Molly said as she turned to hop up the steps. "Seriously though, can your team take on another client all summer? Please say 'yes.'"

"I'll see what I can work out. Come find me after lunch, okay?" he said. Molly tried to throw him a wink as she stumbled up the step. She shrugged her shoulders as she caught herself and felt the blood rush to her cheeks. He laughed. Molly laughed back as she went inside.

The next week and a half was a flurry of preparations to have Emerson fly alone and confirmations for guests. The office phone was constantly warm to the touch as it was never far from Molly's cheek. Once she hung up with one client seeking to confirm a cabin reservation, she was on the phone with another. Molly felt her heart flutter when a guest would remember her as Mason's daughter. Some would ask where she's been. Others would offer their condolences and tell a story or two about her father. It was cathartic to hear strangers tell her something she didn't know about her father or a story of how he went the extra mile to make a week in the woods memorable. One past client told her how their cabin plumbing sprung a leak and started to flood in the middle of the night. Mason promptly turned off the water and moved the family's belongings to the main lodge. He then made up Molly's old room to house the two children and gave the couple his bed. Mason slept on the couch after making sure they were tucked in and dry for the night. He then gave them back their deposit and gave a deep discount on another week's stay the following summer. Molly felt her eyes start to water as she pictured her father sleeping on the couch. She imagined him carrying bags and trekking down the trail in the dark to make sure the family had all they needed. It was four years ago. He must've been sober to have done it all. Molly listened and found herself squinting. She was trying to remember the last time she saw him sober at night. Her eyes darted around the office, scanning the thank you notes on the board and pictures lining a shelf next to the door. The voice on the other end had happy, sober memories of her father. Had he gone through periods of being dry and never told her like Mr. Castille said? Had he spent nights, maybe even months clean and didn't bother to call and talk, ask her how she and Emerson were, or apologize? She stayed away because he was an alcoholic. Molly drove off and never looked back because his drink consumed him and his lounge was where his heart and mind was. But, hearing these stories over the phone, stories that were tender, funny, and inspiring, made her wonder if she really did paint him that way to justify staying away. Did she need him to be that person, a drunk who didn't love her enough to quit, so she could stay away and not feel guilty? As Molly hung up with a guest from Rhode Island coming for the 4th of July, she pictured her father on the lounge floor, bloated, and alone for days. Regardless of how sober he was while helping a family find a dry place to sleep or how sober he may have been in spurts, he died drunk. He died soaked in the one thing he loved more than anything—his liquor. Molly wiped a tear away with her finger and wiped her nose with the back of her hand. She dialed the next number on the list of returning guests. She had a successful season to plan and, hopefully, more memories to hear from strangers. Molly hoped those stories from others could replace some of the memories that still haunted her.

Chapter 8

There is pleasure in the pathless woods. There is rapture on the lonely shore—George Gordon Byron

Molly pulled up the handle on Emerson's bag and made sure it was at the right height. A poised flight attendant rattled off the flight number, seat number, and verified who was picking up Emerson in Nashville. Molly listened to the bright-eyed attendant's words as they pierced through the whitest teeth she had ever seen. She couldn't help but notice how young the attendant seemed. Molly jokingly asked who was escorting her on the trip. The attendant's smile shined even brighter as she let out a giggle so childlike that Molly truly wondered how old the woman actually was. The encounter meant to reassure nervous parents was only serving to make Molly worry more. She watched Emerson's reaction to the young escort and marveled how at ease Emerson was with this stranger. Molly raised her eyebrows and told herself that Emerson's comfort and safety was what mattered most.

As Emerson's plane raced towards the clouds, Molly headed back to the lodge. She triple-checked with Kenny the Philanderer that he had the right flight information. Then, she ran through her mental checklist for the lodge. A few more trips into town and a few more calls to vendors might be all that is needed before the keys are ready for guests. Zack had finished the stage and fixed the gazebo. The canoes were shiny and emblazoned with new names. Each was named for a county in Maine. The outdoor games were cleaned and organized in the sheds. The main lodge was cobweb-free and smelled like fresh lilacs. The food vendors were all set and menus planned. She had finishing touches to handle, such as planting flowers in the boxes of each cabin's porch. Molly also had stacks of clean quilts to drape over each bed and bathrooms to touch-up. Mantles needed one more swipe with a dust cloth, and the rocking chairs needed one more wipe down to remove the haze of yellow pollen. It was looking, smelling, and feeling like the opening of the resort she loved as a kid. It was her childhood coming to life before her eyes, and by her own hands. Moose Lodge Pond was on the brink of being open for business. She had used a hefty chunk of her inheritance to bring it back to life. Molly knew she'd get a return on her investment financially. She wasn't sure what it would bring mentally. The cleanliness and newness of what Molly spent weeks creating gave her some peace, some moments of feeling healed. But, she wondered if the day to day work of running the lodge for a summer would serve to open old wounds, wounds she couldn't imagine would ever heal.

When Molly pulled in from the long drive, Zack's truck was still in front of the steps. His workday ended hours ago. Molly walked through the main lodge doors to hear music from the kitchen side. She walked behind the stone fireplace. The distinct scent of lobster boiling smacked her in the face. She smiled and let her shoulders fall.

"Hey, is that you, Mol?" Zack's voice called from the kitchen.

"Yep, what's all this? What are you up to?" She called back as she lowered her purse and followed the music.

"You've worked so hard since coming back, and I know you have a busy two days lined up, so I wanted to cook dinner, give you a night to just relax and enjoy what've you've done here," he said. "That's all."

"That's all?" She said with a laugh. "It smells and looks incredible. You didn't have to do this." She was happy he did.

"Plus, I didn't want you to come home to an empty place. I know it's hard watching your kid go off like that, even for a weekend."

Molly pursed her lips and tilted her head. He knew better than anyone how hard it was to watch them go. She was thankful Emerson was older. She couldn't imagine how hard it was to hand over a 4-year-old and go weeks without seeing her. Once Zack told her about Hannah, he only mentioned her more and more. He adored her as every father should adore a daughter. Molly told him often how lucky Hannah was to have him and how lucky Melissa was to have him as a co-parent. Molly gathered plates and set the table as Zack pulled the lobster from the water. He had melted butter steaming in a bowl and corn already waiting on a platter. As she placed the plates on the table in the dining room, she heard him uncork some wine. Molly paused for a second. She hadn't drunk anything for over a week. She inhaled and closed her eyes for a second. Molly swallowed the lump in her throat. Emerson was gone for four days. There was no one to wake up for school. There was no co-parent potentially calling to chastise her for not saying goodnight to the kid. Plus, she didn't have a 'problem' like her father. She merely had a few bad nights, or weeks, after a stressful life-altering situation. Molly let the fact that she drank too much in Nashville wash over her. It wasn't a constant thing. It wasn't night after night, like her father. It was only when Kenny would 'work' late or when she'd find notes, texts, or receipts that she didn't want him to explain. She chose to drink a few, crawl into bed, and try to forget. She chose to drink and ignore what was happening until it was right in front of her face. Tonight though, she could choose to drink with Zack and celebrate. There was no harm in that. Molly told herself she deserved it.

The wine flowed as the lobster claws cracked. The grand lodge that was dusty, empty, and sullen on the night Molly returned was suddenly a different place more than a month later. As the wine gurgled into the glasses, laughter echoed, and Molly felt at home. It felt natural to sit across from Zack, talk about high school, and make more plans for the summer, her first summer in Maine in 15 years.

"So, you haven't taken her to the beach at all yet? Or to hike up a few of the Presidentials?" Zack said as butter dripped from his chin.

"Well, I guess I've been just a tad busy. But, I will. Once we get things really kicking here, I'll take her. Wanna come with us?" Molly asked. As the words escaped her lips, she slurped claw meat into her mouth. What if he said 'no'? She had gotten so used to him being around; she didn't picture too much of her daily life without him within earshot.

"Yeah, sure. I'd love to. Maybe on a weekend I have Hannah, we can take her to the shore for the day. She loves chasing the waves, at least she did last summer. Everything she loves and hates seems to switch on a dime each time I get her."

"That's girls for you. Trust me, that won't change." Molly said. She raised her glass to her lips and let a sip slide in. The gentle mix of tartness and sweetness made her mouth water. She closed her eyes and let it go down. Zack sipped his wine and poured a little more into both their glasses.

"So, a wedding is going down soon, huh? That'll be a big undertaking."

"I guess it will be. My parents made it look so easy when I was a kid. God, come to think of it, I haven't been to a wedding in forever. What about you?"

"A few last year, mostly guys from college. Not my own, that's for sure." Zack said. He took the last bite of lobster from his plate and dipped it in the murky, thickening butter.

"You and Hannah's mom planned to get married before, you know, she left?"

"Yeah, I thought we did. Well, I did. She just wanted more, I guess. Someone more. But, hey, it worked out alright. As long as I get to see Hannah, it's all good." He said as he rose his glass again.

"I'm not looking forward to all this shared custody business. This is the first time I've sent Em to see him and it's really hard already, you know. They probably aren't even home yet and it feels like forever." Molly said. She sipped the last of her glass. Zack stood up and took her drink.

"I got another bottle in the kitchen. I'll grab it. Hey, it gets easier. It becomes, well, I guess normal after a while." He said as he slipped off through the double kitchen doors. Molly watched the doors swing back and forth, slowly crossing each and coming to a stop, barely touching in the middle. She saw his shadow through the slit in between. Normal, she thought. She wasn't sure she knew what normal was anymore. She was in the one place she never expected to be, having dinner with the one person she never expected to see again, and her daughter was a thousand miles away with Kenny the Philanderer. There was nothing normal about what her life had become. She suddenly realized nothing about what life had been like the last few years was quite normal either.

Zack reappeared with two full glasses wedged between his fingers and the bottle in the other hand.

"Enough about all this divorce, wedding, custody stuff for tonight. Tonight, we celebrate a clean and fixed resort just itching to reopen for the season." He said as he slid into the chair across from her. She used her fork to scrape the last of butter and scattered pieces of corn up from the plate. Molly smiled as he slid the glass in front of her. She sipped. She smiled. Both were effortless as she sat across from him.

The two of them cleared the table and took their wine into the lobby. Molly collapsed on the couch as Zack sunk into the oversized leather chair. She sipped some more and felt light-headed. The wine was taking hold. She needed to squint to read the text from Kenny about making it to the house. Molly placed her glass on the side table and held up a finger to Zack. She dialed and felt a rush of relief leave her body when Emerson's voice answered on the other end. She shot a smile toward Zack as he smiled back with a wink. He stood up and poured a little more into her glass. Molly mouthed 'thank you' to him as he slid back over to the chair. After listening to Em tell her about the plane ride and Kenny relay the flight information for picking up Emerson, Molly sent a few 'I love you's to Emerson and hung up. She glanced toward the large picture window that overlooked the pine-flanked driveway. Slivers of the last remnants of the sun pierced through the cluster of needles.

"The sun is setting later and later, huh?" She said as she drew the glass up to her lips. Zack nodded as he sipped more wine. She could tell by his flushed cheeks he was feeling the wine buzz, also. That realization made her giggle.

"What? What's so funny?" He said. He chuckled at her.

"Nothing, really. I just never expected to be sitting across from Zack Preston drinking wine and watching the sunset at my parent's lodge. I would've killed for this chance in high school. You know, I guess it's no secret I had a serious crush on you back then." She said. Molly's cheeks warmed.

"Yeah, I know. It was kinda obvious," Zack said. She laughed. "That's alright. I thought I was big shit back then, too." He said. "Man, I'll tell you though, getting hurt kicked that attitude right out of me." Zack shook his head.

"I'm sorry that happened to you. I remember you were gonna leave here, make it to the NFL, never look back. I had no idea really."

"It's alright. Everything happens for a reason, you know? Coming back here was the right thing. I know it. I wouldn't have Hannah if I didn't get hurt. I wouldn't have been here to help my dad out," Zack said. "Oh, I'm sorry."

"Oh, no, don't be. My situation was completely different." Molly took another sip. "This wine is certainly starting to take its toll on me."

"Yeah, me too. I guess we've put away a good bit and it's not even dark. I should make some coffee, head home."

"Nah, stay awhile. Hey, I gotta an idea. Wanna go down to the pond, maybe watch the sunset or something?" Molly said. She cringed, knowing she sounded desperate. She had never stayed alone at the resort, except as a teenager when her dad left one week, the week she lost her virginity. Zack's eyebrows raised. He drew in a deep breath.

"You sure? You don't want me heading out of here to give you some alone time? You've had a long day taking Emerson to the airport, trudging through dinner with yours truly, and all." He sent her another wink. His sly winks made her heart skip.

"Yeah, I'm sure. Let me turn out the kitchen lights and get my shoes." Molly said as she swirled the last of her wine. She walked around the fireplace and through the double doors to be sure the oven was off, and the dishwasher was done. There was no one to wake for school, she told herself again as she walked back to the lobby. Molly grabbed a quilt off the couch and threw it over her arm. She grabbed the bottle from the side table.

"Well then. I guess we'll be taking our glasses." Zack said as he opened the front door. "Listen, if I have any more tonight, I might need to crash in the spare room again, okay?" He said. Molly winked at him as she passed him and started down the steps. He took the bottle of wine from her hand so she could lean down and put on her shoes. She reached up and held his arm as she balanced on one foot. The wine was kicking in even more as she tried to slip on her shoes. His laugh echoed as they made their way to the trail. The sunlight danced on the trail as the wind rustled the needles. Molly looked up and smiled as she thought about how much taller the trees were.

"My God, I loved this trail as a kid." She said, half to Zack and half to herself.

"I can see why. It really is beautiful. And to think, you're selling this place and leaving again, huh?"

"I don't know yet what I'll do. I mean, I do plan to sell, eventually. I am excited to stay this summer and show Emerson how I grew up, though." She said. Molly looked forward and tried to focus on the trail rather than the passing clouds, light, and clusters of needles above her.

"Well, who knows. Maybe you'll want to stay forever after a great summer back home." Zack said as he put the glasses in his other hand with the bottle. He took her hand in his and pulled her a little closer as they walked. Molly loved the feel of the callouses on his hands. It gave him a ruggedness Kenny the Philanderer never had. She let him hold onto her as the trail opened to the beach. As they stopped, she let go and laid out the quilt. Zack took a seat and opened the bottle. Molly sat next to him as he handed her another glass. She watched the last slivers of sun reflect off the water, the water she knew all her life. Molly slipped off her shoes.

"Wanna go in?" She raised her eyebrows at Zack as if to dare him. He shook his 'no' and laughed. "Come on. It's not that cold. Come on." She stood up and reached her hand down to him.

"You're serious? We'll freeze. Nope." He said. Just as Zack went to take a sip, Molly slipped her shirt over her head. She reached down for his hand again.

"Come on. You're not going to leave me standing here in my bra begging you to join me, are you?" She felt light-headed and stumbled back a bit. She grabbed his hand to steady herself. He laughed. Once she regained her footing, she reached down and started to unzip her jeans. "Come on, Mr. Preston. I dare you. Are you scared?" Molly said. She started to shimmy her jeans down to her hip, being careful to keep her panties from sliding down, too. She winked at him, or least gave a half-wink as she once again started to stumble.

"Whoa there, lady. You sure you can even walk to that water without falling?" Zack said as a huge grin slid across his face. "I'll tell you what though, I think that water will sober you up."

Molly stepped back and slid her jeans down more. She peeled the jeans from her calves and kicked them off to the side. She glanced down enough to realize her bra and panties didn't match at all. Molly laughed at the expectation that they would match in any way.

"Come on, Zack. Come in with me." Molly put her hands on her hip and tried to suck in her belly and appear somewhat sexy standing there with the setting sun hitting her back. Zack squinted. Just as he started to nod 'no' again, he jumped up and bolted past her.

"Race ya!" He yelled as he sprinted full-speed toward the water. Molly squealed and followed. He tossed off his shirt and stopped short of the water to undo his pants. She stopped and watched him from behind for a second. His back muscles and thighs caught her off guard. She had seen him shirtless a few times working and changing by his truck, but she hadn't seen him like that from behind. She inhaled and felt goosebumps rise on her arms and legs. Water splashed on her chest as Zack ran in, turned and threw a handful at her. She cringed and laughed as she made her way in up to her hip. Zack dashed backward and floated as he looked up at the clouds. Molly waded in further a few feet from him. She drew up handfuls of water to her chest and shoulders.

"You tricked me." She said as she tossed some water on his stomach. He laughed.

"Damn, it's colder than I thought. But, you're right. It feels good. It feels perfect right now." He said. He floated closer to her. "Come on, lay on your back. Look up with me." Molly let herself fall backward and swayed her arms side to side. She let her legs rise to the top. The water danced around her hairline and ears. She giggled with him. They both stared at the sky. He reached out and let his hand brush her arm.

"Thank you for this, Zack."

"For what? I didn't want to come in, but I sure as hell wasn't gonna just sit there while you jumped in half-naked."

"For dinner, for the wine, for all of this. Thank you." She reached out and brushed his arm. He dropped his legs down and stood next to her. Zack reached down for her arm. She let her legs fall and stood in front of him. The icy water rolled off her chest and down her stomach. Zack slid his hands behind her and onto her lower back. He pulled her closer. She reached up to his shoulders as the setting sun bounced off them. Her goosebumps multiplied as she started to shake. Just as her teeth began to chatter, he reached under her chin and leaned down to kiss her. His lips were wet and felt warm against hers. She froze all over and welcomed the slight warmth of his tongue as he kissed her harder. Molly let her body lean into his. He drew her in so close that the water sloshed between their stomachs. He slid his hand down her hip and squeezed. She drew up her arms and wrapped them around his neck. Zack reached down with both arms and pulled her up off her feet. She wrapped her wet legs around his waist as he started to walk her out of the pond. As her flesh met air, the goosebumps grew worse.

Zack walked her toward the blanket, without letting his lips release hers. She held his face and released the grip her legs had on him. "Lay down" he whispered while still kissing her. Molly peeled the rest of her body from his and laid back on the blanket. She squinted from the remaining sunlight. He leaned down over her and shielded her view. Drops of water from his hair and chin fell on her as he slowly lowered his body on top of hers. The goosebumps started to melt away. Her teeth began to chatter again, but Molly knew it was overwhelming anticipation, not the cold. He reached down for her hips and pulled her into his as he kissed her even harder. She moaned as he ran his hand from her cheek, her chin, down her chest and hip. She reached her arms around his back and drew him even closer. She moaned and felt dizzy, both from the wine and the prospect of making love to Zack

Preston on the sandy beach of Moose Pond. She moaned again as he touched her in a way she hadn't been touched in what seemed an eternity. He had complete control of her, and she wanted him to. She surrendered to him in every way and let the sandy beach, the smell of the wine, and the drops of water running off their bodies fill her senses. The softness of the sand underneath the blanket as he made love to her made her feel one with him and the beach at the same time. Their slick, wet bodies meshed with the beach and each other. Sand clung to her hands as she grabbed his hips and held onto his shoulders. She didn't want it to end. She didn't want him to let go and peel himself from on top of her. She didn't want to move a muscle or think about anything. She just wanted more of him, more than she had ever wanted anyone in her life.

When they finished, he collapsed on her. She ran her sandy hands through his hair as he kissed her shoulder. His breathing lulled her. She felt her heart slow, and the dizziness subsided. Molly didn't want to forget anything about how Zack felt on top of her. She wanted to lay there on the sandy quilt and melt into him as the day ended. Molly looked up and noticed a star. The sun was nearly gone and the night was rolling in above them. He whispered to her as he kissed her earlobe. She giggled and couldn't stop smiling. He leaned up and looked her in the eye. She let his stare engulf her. He leaned down and kissed her forehead as one more drop lingered from his hair. It ran down her cheek and neck. As he started to peel himself from her, the goosebumps returned. He reached for his underwear and jeans. She reached for hers. Zack sat back on the quilt and placed his elbows on his knees. He stared at the water as she finished getting dressed.

"That was beautiful, Molly. You're beautiful." He said. She sat next to him and leaned her head on his shoulder.

"It was," she whispered and kissed his shoulder. "I guess you have to stay the night now, huh?" She smiled at him. He bit his bottom lip.

"I ain't going anywhere tonight. I don't think I'll be staying in the guest room either." He said followed by that wink she was beginning to love. He reached over for the glasses which had tipped over. Zack used a corner of the quilt to wipe away the sand. He poured what was left of the wine into them and handed one to Molly. She leaned back on her elbows. Her wet underwear started to soak through her shirt and jeans. He leaned back next to her and exhaled deeply. She watched his ab muscles ripple as he stretched back further. Molly wanted to climb on top of him and make love again. It seemed as if she had been with him on that blanket in front of the pond for hours, yet the explosion of passion between them only lasted seconds. Molly wanted to relive every second of it again and again. The high school girl in her wanted to run back the trail and call Maxine to tell her she was just with Zack Preston. The adult woman in her wanted to lay next to him, sip more wine, and let herself fall in love with him.

Molly let her mind float forward in time as she wondered if she could spend all summer making love to him. She sipped and thought how could this go anywhere if she sold the resort. Then, Molly glanced at his body, his wet hair, and his tattoo. She wondered how could it *not* go anywhere? She spent years fantasizing about him, longing to be with him. Suddenly, at the age of 35, she was with him, alone and basking in the afterglow of having sex with her high school crush. Molly's goal of making her time at Moose Pond Lodge a cut and dry transaction, so she could get on with life as a single mom away from Kenny the Philanderer was morphing into something else. Just like she always did, at least anymore, Molly had let her impulses and need for instant gratification override everything. She let things get complicated. The intensity bubbling up inside of her, the twinges of passion still rippling through her, and the buzz of too much wine, complicated things. But, it felt too good to resist those complications. It felt right. And, even if it wasn't, Molly knew one thing for sure. She sure as hell didn't want it to stop, at least not anytime soon. She knew once they wandered back to the lodge, they'd shower and make love again. She didn't dare think about a moment past that.

Chapter 9

I felt my lungs inflate with the onrush of scenery—air, mountains, trees, people. I thought, "This is what it is like to be happy."—Sylvia Plath The Bell Jar

The minutes of passion unleashed was like a damn breaking for Molly. It had been years since she gave herself so freely to another. With Kenny, even in the good days, or the days she believed weren't so terrible, she held back a little. But as those minutes at the beach of Moose Pond morphed into days at the lodge, she felt herself letting go and falling. There was a sensory overload as she took in Zack's scent, felt the sweat on the back of his neck when he kissed her, his breath, his skin. All of it set off an electrical current running through her, confusing her. She was dizzied after each time they made love. Molly was becoming addicted to that dizzy feeling, that buzz. She let it engulf her, swirl around in her gut, and ignite a fire of passion in her that she let lay dormant. Zack was simultaneously making her feel alive and off-kilter. Like the bourbon in the lounge, she wanted to keep drinking him in. She realized there might never be enough of him. Molly knew the more she let herself fall for him, the less likely she'd know when to say when.

By the time Molly drove to the airport to pick Emerson up from the long weekend in Nashville, Molly was a glowing, hot mess. She was breaking out in a sweat just thinking of crawling on top of him again. Her mind kept replaying the last few days over and over again. She tried to pull herself out of the fog he enveloped her in and listened to every word Emerson had to say during the drive. Emerson got to see many of her old friends, go out to eat with Kenny at her favorite BBQ place on Music Row, and sat on the curb listening to live bands well past her bedtime. Molly remembered her first few years in Nashville with Kenny, before Emerson was born, before she caught him messing around. Kenny would take her downtown, and they'd sit outside of clubs with a cover charge. They'd have drinks in travel mugs and take out from Jack's BBQ. The two of them would sit on the curb and listen. Then they'd move down the street to listen to another band until closing time. It was her favorite time there. She couldn't help but smile as Emerson brought it all back to life.

As they pulled up to the lodge just as the sun started to set, Mr. Castille's car came into view. Emerson perked up.

"What's he doing here? Are we still selling this place?" She said.

"Yeah, I guess I'll be putting it on the market once the season gets going," Molly said as she removed her sunglasses.

"Then back to Nashville, right? Oh, Dad wants me to fly down for the fourth, too. Said he'd talk to you about it."

Molly nodded and turned off the car. Mr. Castille stepped out of his car and walked over to her door.

"Hey, what's up?" Molly said as she slid out. Emerson ran over and hugged him. She had become close to him over the last few weeks. Molly knew he was probably filling the void left by Kenny the Philanderer. He was also filling the void of a grandfather who should be there, the one she could only see now in pictures and read about on postcards tacked up on the office bulletin board. Molly, Mr. Castille, and Emerson walked up the steps. Emerson dragged her weekend bag behind her.

"Pick that up, kid. It's got wheels for a reason." Molly said.

"Well, I've put some feelers out there about the resort the last few days. I called around to a few guys I know and other resorts up north. There's a resort company interested in buying, but they want to make a deal before the summer is over. Guess they want to get a jumpstart on snatching up the place and capitalize on the leaf peepers," he said as he held the door open for them.

"Wow. I didn't expect any offers or anything just yet. I thought we talked about putting it on the market mid-summer then selling as the season ended?" Molly said. She flipped on a light and threw her purse on the couch. She remembered Zack was coming by later. Mr. Castille set his briefcase on the table and opened it.

"Well, you gotta understand, this isn't the best market so you might need to jump on an offer quicker than expected."

"You said a resort company? What's that exactly?"

"There's a few larger corporations that've bought up smaller resorts the last few years. They combine them, spruce them up some, I guess. The small-time family-owned resorts like this place are just becoming far and few between." He placed the papers on the table. "Places like this, like Moose Pond Lodge, are just a dying breed." Mr. Castille glanced up at the antlers on the fireplace.

Molly picked up the stack of papers and scanned them.

"If I were you, kid, and I really wanted to make a few bucks and start over down south or wherever, I'd think about this offer. God only knows if another offer will come in later in the season, or at all." He closed his briefcase and slid it off the table. It dangled by his side. "Think about it. You've invested a big chunk of what your dad left you to fix it up. If you don't get a buyer by the end of the summer, you're pretty much stuck with this place until the next spring at the earliest. It won't sell in the winter. Nothing here sells in the winter. You know that," Mr. Castille said.

"I'll look it over. I just wanted the whole summer, you know? I wanted that for Emerson and, well, and for myself, too. But I know you're right. I can't afford just to disregard a great offer." She said as she flipped through the pages. Mr. Castille leaned down and kissed Emerson's head.

"Glad you made it back safe, Em." Mr. Castille walked over to the door. He turned back around. "You know, Mol. You do have another choice. You could stay." He didn't wait for her reaction. Mr. Castille closed the door behind him just as Molly sat on the couch with the stack. Emerson sat next to her. The word 'stay' lingered over her head. Emerson leaned her head on her mom's shoulder.

"Hey, you've had a long day, flying alone and all. You go ahead and get ready for bed. It's almost nine.." Molly patted her daughter's knee.

"But what about what he said? What happens if you sell early? We just go back home or what? What if you don't sell this place at all? We just live here?" Emerson said.

"Well, I guess yes. Those seem to be our options, kid." Molly said. She tossed the stack of papers on the table. "What do you think we should do? I want you to be happy, and I've already disrupted your life enough. Haven't I?"

"I do miss Dad. I wish we were all closer together, honestly. But I like it here, too."

"I promise you this, kiddo. No matter what I decide, you'll always get to see your dad. We'll both make sure of that. He loves you more than anything. I do, too. More than likely, I'll be selling this place. I want us here for the summer, but I have no desire to stay forever, okay?" As soon as she said the words, she heard Zack pull in. Suddenly, her desire to leave faded and staying forever didn't seem like such a far-fetched idea.

"Is that Zack's truck?" Emerson said as she jumped up and ran to the window. She flung open the door. Zack walked in with an armful of flowers. Molly stood up.

"What's this for?"

"Emerson. I wanted to welcome her home." He handed her the bunch of daisies and daylilies. Emerson smiled.

"Thank you, Zack. They're huge. I don't think anyone's gotten me a bunch like this before." Emerson said. Molly's heart thumped against her chest. She wasn't sure if it was because he was so close to her or because he made Emerson feel special.

"Go put them in water, Em. They'll be perfect right here in the lobby unless you want them in your room?"

"My room. Definitely my room." Emerson darted off to the kitchen. Once Molly heard the doors swing open, she rushed to Zack's arms and kissed him.

"Well, that's one way to win her over. You didn't have to do that."

"I know. I wanted to. She's a great kid. I wanted to make her homecoming a little special." He leaned down and kissed her. "Listen, I won't stay because she just got back and I'm not sure what you wanna tell her."

Molly nodded. "Yeah, I need to figure out what to say this is. What is this, anyway? I mean, what do you think I should tell her?" Molly instantly wished she could take back the question. She didn't want to push him away.

"Well, what do you think this is? I know I'm happy with what it is right now. But, I think a lot of it depends on what you end up doing. Right? I mean, what can it be if you move off after this summer?"

Molly knew it wasn't the right time to tell him a move could be sooner if she accepted an early offer.

"I'm not sure, Zack. I mean, there's no definite plan to move, and I don't have to move at all."

"Don't go anywhere then. Don't move. Stay and run this place. I know you love it again. Plus, honestly, I ain't going off anywhere. I've got Hannah. I'll be in Maine as long as she is." Zack said. He put his head down and let his hands slide onto her hips. She looked up at him.

"I know," Molly said. "Everything just seems so heavy right now. The lodge, guests coming in a matter of days, me and you, all of it. I guess. I'm still interviewing people for cleaning and serving positions." Molly said. She lifted her head and looked up at the ceiling. "I just feel like it's all happening so fast. I don't know how my parents did it each year. I haven't even booked bands or anything for weekends." Zack pulled her closer. He leaned down and kissed her shoulder.

"Hey, hey, hey. Slow down. It'll all get taken care of. Just relax. You know, I can do more than trim hedges, cut grass, and clean up trails. I can help with the other stuff, too."

"I have a feeling I'm going to take you up on that."

"Go say goodnight to the kid, get a good night's sleep, and I'll see you in the morning. Okay? I'll come by a little early and help with anything else. Think about what I said. We can do this together if you want?" He kissed her again. She wanted him to stay but knew she needed to focus on Emerson and the resort for the night. He let his hands slip to his side. Zack kissed her forehead and said goodnight. Molly put her hands in her pocket and watched him walk out the lodge door. Her heart fluttered, and she fought the urge to run after him. She wanted to grab him, throw herself into his arms, lure him back to her room for the night. Every time Molly caught a glimpse of him walking away, a twinge rippled through her heart and gut. She would curl her fingers up into her palms and close them tight. Her pulse would quicken and her breath increase. Molly knew she was falling fast and hard for Zack. As her feelings for him overwhelmed her, Molly couldn't picture herself willingly walking away from him and what they had. If she sold, that's exactly what she'd be doing. The word 'stay' lingered in the air. Moose Pond Lodge was becoming less of a curse and more of a destiny, one she could share with Zack.

The next few days were a flurry of hiring local high school kids for cleaning and kitchen staff, most of whom had worked there the summer before. She also re-interviewed the cooks who all worked for her father. Most of the interviews consisted of hearing stories about her father and all he had done for them over the years. When Molly wasn't interviewing and finalizing pay paperwork, she was buzzing from cabin to cabin to ensure all was in order. Planting herbs and flowers on and around the porches was the last touch before sweeping and declaring each cabin ready for guests. As she dug in the dirt of the planters, Memories of planting with her mother flooded her mind. Then, memories of running from cabin to cabin to water plants with Maxine so they could head into to town also came roaring back. As the sun beat down on her head and the dirt flaked on her eyelashes, Molly pulled off her gloves and decided to call Maxine. She swiped call without allowing herself to overthink it. Like ripping off a bandage, Molly wanted to jump past the pain, the slow pull of regret, and just get it over with. Once she heard Maxine answer, a wave of relief washed over her. Molly drew her dirty glove across her forehead and said 'hello' to the best friend she had ever known.

"Hey. I've wanted call you back. How's it going out there?" Maxine said.

"It's going. I'll say that. I meant to keep calling, too. I wasn't gonna let you avoid me forever." Molly said with a slight laugh. Hearing Maxine laugh in return lifted a weight from her shoulders.

"Hey, Mol. I'm sorry I was so hard on you that night. I shouldn't ha-"

"Nope, you don't have to apologize. You were right. Everything you said. You were right. I didn't like having it all thrown in my face at your house like that, but everything you said was true. I've owed you an apology for a long time, a really long time." There was a long silence on the other end. Molly blinked away more soil as she looked up at the sun. "Um, so guess what?" She said to break the quiet.

"What?" Maxine said.

"So, Zack Preston and I are a thing, kinda. I guess. I don't know what we are technically, but let's just say, things have happened, things I only dreamed of back in the day." Molly bit her bottom lip as she was transported back to the sandy quilt on the beach and her bedroom in the lodge. Maxine gasped.

"Oh my God. Do tell." She whispered to Molly.

A smile grew across Molly's face as she fell back into a comfort with the voice on the other end. She rattled off details, squealed like a teenager, and felt her cheeks turn red as she told Maxine everything. As they talked, Molly let her guard down. She let the years apart fall to the wayside. She let the feelings of trepidation and the guilt she carried fall from her shoulders. All she felt was openness and comfort hearing Maxine laugh and squeal on the other end. They ended the call with a vow to get together for dinner again soon, at least once the kids were done with school and the resort was operating smoothly.

As Molly made a move to repair her most cherished friendship, Emerson was inviting friends home after school and becoming more independent. Emerson was melting into life in northern Maine with ease. This gave Molly more time to take care of the minor details of the resort. It also gave her more time to exchange glances and steal moments away with Zack. As soon as Emerson asked about a sleepover, Molly thought it would give her and Zack a night alone. A night alone with him could be the calm before the storm. She found Zack spreading mulch in front of the lounge door. As she walked up behind him, she let the view infuse into her memory.

"Hey, so Em is going to stay at a friend's house tonight. A girl in town she's gotten close to at school. Do you have dinner plans?" He stood up and turned around. He had sweat dripping from his face and through his shirt. The heat of summer suddenly decided to barrel into the valley.

"Nope, none. You want to go out? Stay in?" Zack asked.

"I was thinking stay in, see what happens maybe after dinner." She said with a wink. He laughed. She knew her winks weren't seductive, but comical.

"Once I drop her off in town, I can bring back some Chinese. Will that work?"

"That would be perfect," Zack said as he crouched back down in the flower bed. "Just about done here, then I think you're all set for guests. Well, at least in the landscaping department. How ya feeling about people showing up this weekend?"

"A little nervous. I've got everything done I can remember, but who knows what I'm forgetting. I keep wandering around, mostly to the cabins that will be rented tomorrow just to be sure." She said.

"Well, tonight over dinner, we can brainstorm and see if you've forgotten anything, okay?" He said. She flashed him a smile.

"I hope there's more to the conversation tonight." She tried to wink again.

"Please, please don't try to wink," he said with a laugh.

Molly laughed back at him. She walked past the flower beds and to the door of the lounge. She knew she needed to take another walk-through and be sure it was ready for some adult time. But, Molly avoided walking in there all week. Thoughts of her father were never far from her mind as she took calls, processed credit card deposits for guests, and organized kitchen deliveries. However, picturing him the lounge, being where he died on the floor, was more of her father's memory than Molly wanted to let in. Molly also had to admit she didn't fully trust herself to be in the lounge alone, especially at night. It wasn't just the memory or vision of her father that taunted her in that lounge. It was the smell and sight of the bourbon. Once she opened some and let its scent invite itself into her mind and soul, she knew she would get sucked in for the night. There could never be just one glass alone at night. Too many weeks of hangover after hangover made that point a fact for Molly. She stood right in front of the door and saw her reflection. Molly drew in a deep breath and twisted her lip to the side. She saw her father in her reflection. She closed her eyes and let the good stories of the kitchen staff, vendors, and past guests wash over her. He wasn't just the man who died in that lounge. He was more. She was more. Molly reached up and opened the door. The place needed one more cleaning, and she couldn't put it off another minute.

Molly stepped in and inhaled and smell of the wood, the handmade bar. She took a rag from the side of the sink and wet it. Molly then sprayed the bar and wiped away the cleaner. While the bar was clean to anyone else's eyes, she wanted to do a once-over to be sure. She also needed to keep herself moving, busy until guest arrived in the morning. She smiled thinking in just a few hours she'd be alone with Zack. That would keep her mind and body occupied until morning.

As the preparations wound down and the last shovel, dishrag, and mop was put away, Molly raced to town with Emerson. She raced back with dinner and tried to settle her nerves as they ate.

"Relax, Mol. It's gonna all go great. Guests will be coming and love every second here. You've done great since you got back here." Zack said as he finished an egg roll. He scooped more rice onto his plate.

"I know, I know. I just feel like everything's riding on this. If I can keep this place full and keep people happy, then I'll relax a little." She said.

He reached over and took her hand. Molly's eyes darted all around. While she tried to focus on him and listen to his advice, she was still glancing all around trying to spot anything she had forgotten, anything that needed to be cleaned or dusted again. He squeezed. She looked at him and tilted her head.

"They'd be proud of you, you know?" Zack said. Molly relaxed her shoulders. She squeezed his hand back. Her eyes started to well up.

"I hope." Molly looked down and felt a lump in her throat. "I just, I just owe it to him." Her voiced cracked. "I do. I stayed away so long. I let him down. I let him die al—"

"No, don't do that. You can't change any of that, Molly. He wouldn't want you to carry that around. Just focus on what you've done here now, not what you could've done. Okay?" He said. She wiped away her tears. It only seemed to open the gates for more. Tears she couldn't predict, or control found their way to the surface and escaped the corners of her eyes. Molly let go of Zack's hands and hid her face with a napkin.

"Hey, don't cry. It's all good, Mol. Everything is going to be fine." Zack reached for her hands again. "You've done a good thing here. No Matter what, you've created a place he'd be proud of, both your parents would."

She nodded as she wiped away more tears. Molly blew her nose into the napkin.

"How is it possible to feel all of this at the same time? I do feel proud of what this place looks like now, mostly thanks to you and everyone else. And, I'm excited to see it filled with people again. But, I just wish I had come back sooner." She said as she put down the napkin. "Then, all this divorce stuff, not knowing what to do next, it's all just a lot to take in at once. I swear, some days, especially lately, I think I'm feeling every emotion possible all in one punch."

"That's the way it works, I guess. Life. It just piles it all on. But, you gotta just deal with each thing as it comes and move on. You know?" He said. "Just deal with right now. What are you feeling right now? I mean, besides regret, fear, and all that?" She laughed.

"Right now? I guess, well, I guess, mostly grateful. Grateful that I have you here to help me, and not just with the resort, everything."

He reached over and took her hand once more. Zack drew it up and kissed her hand gently. He smiled at her. She drew in a deep breath and let out much more than pent-up air. She let out fear about the opening and possible sale. She let go of her resentment and uncertainty over the divorce and where to go with Emerson. She let go of guilt about her dad. Molly was learning that would be an ongoing process. There was no one-then-done moment of healing and forgiving herself for not being there. However, each time she told herself it was okay or Zack told her, she felt some of it dissipate. She felt a little lighter, freer.

As they cleaned up from dinner and moved to the front porch with some wine, she asked Zack to spend the night. She was relieved to know that was his intention all along. She blushed when he mentioned what all he had planned once the sun went down. As they made their way down the hall to the bedroom with some wine, Molly briefly worried about what exactly would become of this relationship if she moved. She only let that worry infiltrate her mind for a second before pushing it aside and allowing her body to take over. She also let the idea of staying forever sneak into her busy mind. She let him scoop her up at the door and burst through with her as if the hall was on fire. He stumbled with her to the bed and tossed her down. She scurried up to the pillows while trying to remove as much of her clothing as possible in a few seconds. Before she could utter a word or finish undressing, Zack was on top of her. She let him sink into her in every way. Molly wanted the heaviness of his body over her to drown out the outside world. She wanted to see nothing, feel nothing else but Zack's chest on hers and his lips engulfing her lips and shoulders. Molly let passion crowd out all reasoning and every other emotion she had felt that day. The world only existed in that room, in that bed. Molly even forgot it once had been her parents' bedroom.

When the sun snuck in and danced on the floor, she was hit with the reality that today was the day. She glanced over at Zack asleep next to her. Molly bit her lip. Love was the only word she could conjure up to explain what she was feeling for him. The prospect of staying and running the resort with him seemed to make sense. It was the only vision for her future that did. Everything about him made sense to her. He was comfort, stability, reason, passion, and adventure all rolled into one. He was everything she never realized she was missing. She seared the image of his sleeping face into her mind.

Molly checked her phone and see the time. Guests were scheduled to arrive in a few short hours. Employees would be in the lobby and kitchen in two hours. She reached under the quilt and searched for Zack's arm. As she drew it close, she heard him moan as she watched each of his facial muscles awaken.

"Damn, it's morning already, huh?" He groaned as he scooted up. Zack reached over the side of the bed to find his jeans. "I gotta go get Hannah for the weekend." Molly reached up and touched his back.

"Why don't you bring her here later? Maybe for dinner? She could meet Emerson. Em loves younger kids to play school with her." Molly said as she slid her hand down, noticing his muscle tone. He stood and pulled up his jeans. He turned around and faced her, further distracting her with the sight of his flesh and his floppy black hair.

"Maybe. I dunno. I might. I really don't bring her around other women much. Don't take that wrong, though." He said. "I just haven't thought of introducing her to anyone." Molly's heart sank for a moment. She searched for her shirt as he pulled his over his head.

"I'm not saying you have to introduce me as her next mom or anything. I mean as friends, you know. She could meet

Emerson and play with someone new. Besides, you've certainly been around Emerson enough."

"Yeah, well, as a guy who works here and an old high school friend. That's it. It's not like you'd have me here right now if Emerson weren't at a sleepover in town. Right?" He said. Molly stood up and found the rest of her clothes. He was right. She nodded.

"Maybe we could change that." Change that forever, she thought. Molly tilted her head and realized she was picturing a future with Zack and a future at the resort, none of which she planned when she pulled in that driveway. She didn't know whether to laugh out loud at the idea of changing her entire plan or just throw her hands up and let herself fall even harder for Zack Preston. She couldn't decide what was more unexpected, falling for him or falling back in love with Moose Pond Lodge.

"Maybe we can." He shoved his phone in his pocket and walked around to the other side of the bed. He kissed her forehead. She closed her eyes. "I gotta go home, shower and stuff. Maybe I'll be back with her for dinner. I'll text you, okay? Oh, and good luck today." He headed for the door before she could think of a reason to make him stay longer. Molly sat on the edge of the bed. She waited until she heard the lodge door close and his truck start before she headed out to the hall. Molly wandered into the kitchen and started the coffee. Breakfast, she thought. She should've asked him to stay for breakfast. Molly comforted herself with the thought that she'd have plenty of chances to ask him to stay. Images of staying and falling deeper in love with Zack replaced any desire to leave Moose Pond Lodge that summer or, perhaps, ever.

As she made last-minute touches, the smells of lunch and dinner started to pour from the kitchen. Molly lifted herself on the stool behind the front desk just as a car pulled in. She saw a Rhode Island license plate. She knew it was her first family coming for a week. Three more groups were checking in that day. There was a young couple from southern Maine, a set of grandparents with their teenage grandson, and two couples coming together renting side by side cabins. The family from Rhode Island was a middle-aged couple with a toddler and an eight-year-old boy. The husband's parents had been regulars, and he wanted to show his son the hiking trails, how to canoe, and how to fish at the pond. When their car doors slammed shut, and the sounds of feet shuffled up the steps, Molly adjusted herself on the stool and picked up a pen for the guest book. She felt a like her twelve-year-old self again. Molly had that rush of anticipation to meet new people and the feeling of wanting to please these strangers in every way. Just as when she was a kid, she played her introduction over in her head as the door opened. The toddler scooted out of her mother's arms and ran straight for the fireplace. She teetered as she looked up at the antlers. The eight-year-old boy's eyes widened as he scanned the lobby area. He sank into the couch as the parents approached the desk. All of Molly's fears faded as she rattled off the information, fished for their key, traced the trail on the map, and had them sign their reservation. She fell into a routine and comfort zone, a position of authority, which she hadn't felt in so long. She was surprised by how happy it made her to help guest orient themselves. Molly rattled off the dinner times and the menu for the night, the hours of the lounge, the babysitting service number, everything she'd thought she'd forget. The information flooded her mind, and she unleashed it with ease.

The couple smiled at her, asked questions, and relief appeared on their faces.

"Thank you so much, Ms. Bordueax. It's everything Henry said it was. I love it already." The mom said as she wrestled the toddler from her leg.

"Mrs. Watts. Bordueax was my maiden name, my family's name. And, thank you. I hope you enjoy your stay. Please ring the desk if you need anything at all. Oh, take this card. My cell is on it so if I'm not at the desk, feel free to text me with any questions or concerns." Molly said. "Oh, I forgot. We noticed from our records that this week is your birthday, Mr. Perrault. Here's a complimentary bottle of champagne for your cabin. Just give me a second, and I'll escort you down the trail and show you where you are." The couple lit up. Molly learned early on that those personal touches are what made guests and families return year after year. That was the one lesson her father instilled her when she manned the front desk or ran extra towels down the trail, hand-delivered bug spray and yes, even delivered bottles of wine to cabins at night even though she was only ten years old.

Molly called to Emerson from the back hall.

"Hey kid, man the desk while I take the Perrault family to their cabin. Okay?"

Emerson scooted up on the stool and picked up the pen. She stuck it in her mouth and fiddled with the guest book. She then twirled the pen like a baton as she blew strands of hair away from the front of her face. Molly stopped and turned at the door before stepping out to help the family unload. She let the image of her daughter at the desk sink in. Molly saw herself twenty-five years earlier. She noticed one difference. Emerson was still overweight for her age. Even though she had slimmed slightly since moving to the lodge, she still had a long way to go before she could lose the pudginess that wasn't as cute on a ten-year-old as it was on a five-year-old. Molly smiled at her and made a mental note to take her to the lake and down the trails more before she sent Emerson back to Nashville in a month.

As the afternoon slowly descended into the evening, the parking lot started to fill up with cars from all over. Time flew by as Molly rushed from check-in mode to guest services duties, tourists guide, and weather expert giving out advice about best times to take out the canoes or hike the trails. She buzzed from one cabin to another, one car to another, and back and forth updating the kitchen on allergies and number of guests. Once dinner time arrived, the lodge doors were propped open, and the sounds of laughter and clanks of dishes twirled around the fireplace. Molly sashayed from table to table chatting, refilling drinks, and listening to stories of summers past. She lit up hearing about her father, burned dinners when he was between cooks, late nights at the lounge. She also lit up hearing from the couples who had never visited before. Hearing that the lodge and cabins were more impressive and beautiful than the pictures online indicated made her heart swell. She loved that others were falling in love with her childhood home.

By nightfall, guests had gravitated to the lounge and front porch. Music from the lounge poured across the porch and gazebo in the yard. Guests sat in rocking chairs as towels hung over the railings, drying as day one ended for everyone who checked in for the weekend. Molly took a chair close to the door as Emerson sat on a step. The lights were turned on. Molly closed her eyes. She could almost hear her father's laugh above the others coming from the lounge. Molly thought how he'd love to see the place so alive. He'd love getting to know these guests and see them enjoy his resort, the woods, and the fresh pine air. The head cook from the kitchen, Samson, wandered out and nudged Molly's shoulder. He handed her a glass of wine.

"Freshly opened from the lounge. Thought you could use a glass. It's been a long day, Molly." She smiled and took the glass. "Hey, Emerson. You want some cake?" He said as he raised his eyebrows. Emerson jumped up and followed the cook. Molly laughed. As much as she wanted to ensure Emerson slimmed down, she wasn't about to deny a 10-year-old a piece of cake after an exhausting day working the front desk. As she sipped her wine and rocked, Zack's truck turned up the driveway. A smile crept across her face. It took everything she had not to jump up and run to the driver's side. As he parked at the far end of the lot, she could see he wasn't alone. His daughter was in the passenger seat. Molly sat up when she heard the door close, then the other door. Zack walked across the lot holding the tiny hand of his 4-year-old daughter.

"Hey there. Is it too late to stop and visit my new friend?" He said as he made his way to the steps.

"It's never too late to visit. Who is this?" Molly said as she put her glass down. She walked to the edge of the steps as Hannah took each one with both feet. Her brown curly hair dangled in front of her face. Molly held out a hand. "I'm Molly. What's your name, sweetie?" Hannah smiled up at her and bit her lip. She grabbed her father's hand and pulled on it.

"Hannah," she whispered.

Zack nudged her with his leg. "Go on, shake her hand." He said as she leaned down to her ear. Hannah held out her tiny hand and reached for Molly's.

"You want juice, Hannah?" Molly said. Hannah nodded 'yes.' Molly attempted to wink at Zack as she led the girl into the lodge. Molly tried to picture Emerson being that young. It seemed a lifetime ago. As she walked Hannah past the fireplace, she watched the little girl's eyes scan the rocks and widen as they met the moose antlers.

"Big, huh?" Molly said. Hannah once again nodded as she bit her lip. Once settled with a cup of apple juice, they made their way back to the porch. Zack sat in a chair next to Molly and pulled Hannah up on his lap. They watched the few kids staying at the lodge play on the gazebo. They talked with the other adults who weren't in the lounge and the occasional straggler who came out to smoke in the parking lot.

"She's gorgeous," Molly said to Zack. He moved Hannah's hair from her face.

"Thank you. Hey, honey. You wanna go play in the yard with those kids?" He asked his daughter. She slithered off his lap and handed him her cup. She held the railing and took one step at a time, being sure both feet were grounded before taking the next. Zack laughed.

"She's overly careful on steps. She fell a few months ago, right outside the store. Ever since, she takes forever to go up and down, which is fine by me."

"She certainly loves you. She doesn't like letting go of you at all," Molly said.

"Well, I'll take that for as long as I can cause I know that'll change soon enough. She'll be embarrassed and run from her old man before I blink."

"Yep. You're right about that. It all happens fast." Molly said. "I watched Emerson handle the desk duties today, and I swear it was only yesterday that I was up there doing that. 25 years sure went by in a blink." They both rocked and watched Hannah pull blades of grass and teeter behind a few other kids running around the gazebo. The sun was hitting her brown hair. She seemed to sparkle as she ran.

"Thanks for inviting us. I'm always looking for new places to take her." Zack said. Emerson came out of the front door.

"Hey, I brought my kid to meet you, Em." He said. Emerson lit up.

"The brown-haired girl, that one, running around the gazebo. That's Hannah." Molly said as she pointed to Zack's daughter.

"Alright. I'll give her some cake, too. If that's okay?" Emerson said as she scanned the group of kids. "She kinda looks like you, Zack."

"Nah, she got her looks from her mom. A lot of good about that kid comes from her mom." He said.

Molly's eyes darted around, and she shifted in her seat. The compliment for his ex-girlfriend left her with an uneasiness she hadn't expected. While he hadn't said anything negative about her, he also hadn't been so quick to throw her praise. On the one hand, she found it refreshing to hear him be so open and positive about what she knew was a painful subject. She wondered if Kenny the Philanderer ever had the sense or inclination to say anything positive about her.

Emerson took Hannah under her wing and spent the rest of the night entertaining the girl, making her belly laugh in the grass and on the front porch steps. Just before the sunset and some of the families gathered their kids to head to their cabins, Zack reached over and took Molly's hand. He squeezed it. She squeezed his back.

"What a perfect day, huh? Just like I told you. See, you were worried about nothing. It all went off without a hitch, and I'd say, from what I saw, everyone seems to love it here." He said. Molly rocked a little in the chair and nodded in agreement.

"I must say, you were right, Mr. Preston. It feels good, honestly, to look around here and see these guests having fun, eating, laughing, drinking. My dad would be happy; I have to admit." She exhaled long and slow as she looked straight up at the porch ceiling. "I owe a lot of it to you, you know? You went above and beyond to make it possible. I'll tell ya, when I first pulled in here, I sure as hell didn't picture any of this happening. Have I said thank you, yet?"

"Yeah, you did. You thanked me plenty," he said with that wink. She laughed and squeezed his hand tighter. "Seriously, this feels good, you know. Me, you, the kids, sitting out here on a summer's night."

"It does. It really does. I didn't expect any of this either."

"I know I didn't. But, unexpected can be the best thing for you. I've certainly seen that in this life. The football scholarship, getting injured, falling in love, having it fall apart, having Hannah, all of it, unexpected."

"That whole 'meant to be' stuff, everything happens for a reason, blah, blah?" She said.

"Yeah, I guess. Look at this here right now. Me and you. You had this obnoxious, mad crush all those years ago; now we're here together. It happened when it was supposed to happen."

"What did? This? Us?"

"Yeah. Don't you think?"

"So, there is an 'us'? An official us, huh?"

He leaned over from his chair and kissed her.

"I think so. I want that. Don't you? I know a lot of it depends on what you decide to do. But, right now, right here, I want this. I would love a whole lot more of nights like this, nights like last night," he said.

She felt her cheeks turn red and hot.

"You can't stay tonight, can you?" Molly said.

"Nah, I gotta get Hannah home. We've got bath time, story time, all that good stuff. But, I'll bring her out tomorrow. If you want?"

"Of course, I want you to." The thought of him doing bath time and story time warmed her insides. It seemed a lifetime ago that she did bath time. She always did it alone. Kenny was always working late, always. Molly found herself letting the idea of her and Zack and the girls being a family swirl around her head. If she stayed, she thought, they could do it. She thought about what he said, things happen for a reason, at the right time. Maybe this was all happening at the right time, her divorce, inheriting the resort, hiring Zack, all of it. Perhaps they collided at the perfect moment and the family she was meant to have was meshed together right before her eyes.

Zack scooped up Hannah in his strong arms. He leaned over and kissed Molly on the forehead while balancing the girl. Hannah giggled, which made Molly giggle. Molly saw Emerson's eyes widen followed by a smile.

"I'll see you ladies tomorrow. In fact, I think I can put a screen, over there by the gazebo. A movie screen, like an outdoor theater? What do you think?" He said as he nodded his head toward the gazebo.

"That would be awesome. I think the families would love it. I can serve popcorn and stuff." Molly said.

"I can stream something from my laptop," Emerson said. Molly squeezed her shoulder.

"That would be perfect. We'll pick a movie tomorrow then."

Zack loaded Hannah into the truck and buckled the booster seat. He winked at Molly again as he made his way to the driver's seat. Just as he fired up the truck and shifted into reverse, Hannah blew her a kiss. Molly wanted to run and hug the tiny girl. She blew a kiss back and giggled again. Molly reached down and took Emerson's hand.

"What do you think, kid?" Molly said to Emerson. Emerson looked up at her. She squinted as the last slivers of sun pierced through the pines and into her eyes.

"You look happy, Mom."

"I am. I really am." Molly said as she waved goodbye to the truck. She tugged on Emerson's arm to pull her towards the door. The front desk phone was ringing. It was cabin 5, the family of four from Rhode Island, looking for extra towels and pillows. Molly let them know she'd be right down. The work of the lodge was never over if there were guests in any cabins. Unlike when she was a teenager, however, she was happy to oblige. She smiled, gathered what was needed from the linen closet, and started off down the darkening trail. Her entire childhood seemed to revolve around running up and down that trail with supplies for guests. This time, it gave her pleasure. It fulfilled the need to nurture others, which was something she knew her father always had despite his faults. She shined the flashlight on the way back, scanning the trees and pine needles along the path. It was home. She was home.

Molly lingered in-between being awake and asleep. A sense of contentment and satisfaction danced around her. She also thought of the paperwork in the office, the offer to sell. Molly decided she'd tear it up later. She wasn't going to sign an early offer. If things kept going the way they were, she wasn't going to sign any offer to sell ever.

Chapter 10

The best remedy for those who are afraid, lonely, or unhappy is to go outside, somewhere, where they can be quiet, alone with the heavens, nature, and God...I firmly believe that nature brings solace in all troubles.—Anne Frank

The first weeks' influx of guests came and left. There were 'thank you' notes signed and left on cabin mantles. There were signatures etched in the guest book and promises of reservations for next summer. The two couples who rented cabins put a deposit on the largest cabin for a week next July. Molly beamed with pride as she prepared for the next guests and hugged those who were leaving. There was immense joy in hearing that the little touches she included made time more than memorable. It made the northern Maine camping experience meaningful. As new guests signed in and cabins were prepared, Molly grew increasingly thankful she had Zack to share it all with. His attention to Emerson didn't go unnoticed also. Even though Emerson still talked to her father each night and texted him throughout the days, Molly felt Zack's presence made the transition of the divorce easier for Emerson and herself. While common sense and Maxine told her to slow down and not jump into anything quickly, her gut told her to jump, to dive, and swim towards Zack as fast as she could. He was there every day, for work, for dinner, for evening help. He became a constant and Molly loved every second of it. She smiled each night knowing she was falling in love with Zack, and she was confident he felt the same.

June wore on, and local acts lined up to perform on weekends clear through September. The stage lights shone, and the sound of heels, music, and microphone squeals filled the dining area after dark. The lounge was lit up each night with a bartender who told jokes, made exotic drinks, and insisted on learning everything about everyone who stayed at the resort. Molly would wander in after saying goodnight to Emerson. She would have a glass of wine, but no more. She considered it her duty as the owner to mingle with everyone. Molly sat in the back or the corner of the bar and listened, laughed, and fell in love with lounge again. She could enter without seeing her father on the floor. She let the new sights and smells slowly replace the old.

Her divorce papers arrived in the mail just as June waned and July waited to break through the calendar on her phone. The wedding being held at the resort was just around the corner. It was a relatively small party as far as weddings were concerned; yet, it was large for the resort. Guests of soon to be Mr. and Mrs. Parker would fill nearly every cabin soon. While Molly slid into the responsibilities of running Moose Lodge Pond, the thought of a wedding caused increasing anxiety. Part of it was the need to ensure it was perfect for the couple and guests. Part of it was the need to ensure some of them would return. However, a small part of it felt like her divorce made her utterly unqualified for the task. As she signed the papers, Molly thought back to her wedding. She never expected to sign divorce papers, to fail. Every detail emerging for the upcoming wedding reminded her that she indeed failed. They failed Emerson and each other. As much as she wanted out, needed out, and didn't regret driving away, she wished that one aspect of her adult life had been a success story. While Em was adapting and happy by most accounts, Molly wondered about the long-term effects on her daughter. Kids of divorce can't escape some damage, regardless of how amicable or how much the parents try to avoid causing any. The damage would seep in one way or another. Her failure would change who her daughter was meant to be. Each call confirming flowers, the date of the cake delivery, tent rentals, and the number of chairs needed reminded her of that impending damage. She couldn't reverse it. Molly felt like a hypocrite putting on the show of a wedding for strangers, in front of her daughter, when she knew nothing of how to make a marriage work. Hers was a show, and she was booed off stage at the end. She hoped this new couple's wedding wasn't a show that would lead to a marriage that was for show, also.

Mr. Castille arrived to look over the divorce papers to make sure Molly wasn't being raked over the coals, as he said on the phone. He plopped down his old briefcase on the front desk and called out to Molly just as she was walking from the office.

"You didn't sign them yet, did you? I want to read every word before you agree to give Kenny the Philanderer anything. You know, you're probably getting low-balled on child support?"

"Nah. If there's one thing I do know it's that Kenny will always take care of Emerson. He'll make sure she has everything she needs. You know, I did work in a law office in Nashville. I kinda think I've got this." Molly said as she pulled up the stool and laid the papers on his briefcase. She scooted up and nearly fell off the side of the stool. Mr. Castille smiled and nodded as he watched her try to regain her balance. Molly smiled back at him. He had been a witness to her klutzy nature nearly her entire childhood. Mr. Castille started to peruse the papers as he continuously pushed his glasses up his nose. Molly noticed he was sweating. She never realized how big he was until he took off his suit jacket and tossed it on the couch.

"Yeah, everyone thinks that until it comes time to pay up." He said. "Like here, you're giving him way more time with her than necessary."

"Well, he deserves it. And honestly, if we're going to stay here, I want her to see him still as much as we can afford."

"That kind of answers my next question. You've had a few weeks to think about that early offer. They aren't going to wait forever. Are you going to sign the offer and sell or not?" he said as he laid his glasses on the guest book. "Mol, for what it's worth, I think the smartest thing to do is to sign that offer and get what you can for this place rather than hem and haw. You'll be stuck here in the fall, offers all dried up, and pumping a shit-ton of your inheritance into maintaining a place you can't sell until next summer." He raised his eyebrows at her.

"I know, Bob. I know. But, I'm not going to take it. I think we're gonna stay. This place needs me, and I need it." She said. She let her head fall to the side. "Is it the smartest idea? No. But, I love it, again. I love it, and I think I can do it."

"Love it or love something else you got going on here? Listen, It's not my business. But, I don't want to see you decide this based on an old high school boyfriend and some summer fling." He said. "Don't get me wrong. I know Zack, his family, all good people. But, people talk, you know? The whole town knows what's going on. Like I said, it's none of my business. I just don't want to see you make a mistake business-wise based on this guy."

"It's not based on some guy. And, he wasn't my high school boyfriend." Molly said. She knew instantly she sounded more defensive than necessary. Bob was only looking out for her. "Listen, I know you think it's best. But this is my home. You said yourself this is what my parents wanted."

"True, girly, true. Keep the paperwork though. Don't do anything just yet. Promise me you'll still let it linger as an option, okay?"

"I will. I promise." She smiled at the closest connection she had to her father. At that moment, she heard her father's voice. She knew he would say the same thing to her. Keep your options open, girly, he'd say. Mr. Castille put the divorce papers in his briefcase.

"Gonna take these home and review them thoroughly, okay?"

Molly nodded and walked him to the door. Mr. Castille turned and looked back at her as he reached for the handle.

"He'd be pretty proud of you, you know? You, Emerson, staying here, fixing this up, throwing a wedding, all of it. You did good, kid." He glanced up at the antlers. "Even climbed up there and cleaned up those dusty old antlers." He winked at her as he pulled the door closed. Molly reached up and placed her hand on the door and closed her eyes. Tears started to well up. They were a mix of happy tears and those all-to-familiar tears of regret that plagued her since she pulled in the driveway in April. Molly turned and looked up at those antlers. They were the anchor of the resort during her childhood. They still were.

The next morning was one day closer to the wedding. Molly could almost hear a clock ticking at she confirmed details and talked daily with the wedding party to ease nerves and ensure perfection. Daily briefings on the weather forecast were texted back and forth. The couple, Allie and Jonah Parker, lived in Boston and were downright paranoid about rain ruining the occasion. Molly found herself obsessively checking her phone for any signs of upcoming storms in the extended forecast. Everything at the resort and with Zack seemed to be smooth sailing. She just needed this wedding to be the same. Weather-related texts soon morphed into the quelling of cold feet on the part of the bride. Molly had yet to meet Allie in person but had already reassured her of a successful wedding and marriage more than she could remember anyone doing for her years ago.

Zack pulled in the driveway a week before the wedding with a truck bed full of pots and flowers. He intended to spruce up the flower boxes, add potted roses to either side of the wedding cabin and gazebo steps, and ensure fresh bouquets were in each room before anyone arrived. Molly was amazed by the tiny details he swooped in and took care of long before they entered her mind.

"Everything's looking so beautiful. Almost makes me want to remarry someday," she said as he pulled pots from the back of the truck bed.

"Yeah, weddings bring out the romantic in me, too. Well, the romantic landscaper, I should say."

"You handle other weddings in town over the years?"

"Yeah, a few each summer, I guess. I did a winter wedding out here about five years ago. I made kissing balls of holly, poinsettias, all kinds of winter greenery. It was nice but cold as hell."

"I can imagine. The bride and groom, parents, and some friends will be here next Thursday. I can't wait to meet them in person. They seem sweet." Molly reached over and helped pull a pot of roses off the truck. Zack smiled up at her.

"It's gonna go off just fine, you know? They're gonna love it, all of it."

"I hope so."

Zack lifted a pot and put it on his metal cart.

"I'm gonna take these to the cabins. You want to have lunch later?"

"I'd love to. You know where to find me." She said as she stumbled back. Zack laughed.

"Don't break your leg, honey. Then I'll be left to do all this wedding stuff alone." She laughed back at him. He walked to the other side of the cart and kissed her. She slid her arm up his and to the back of his neck.

"You wanna stay tonight?" Molly said.

"You think Em will be okay with that?"

"Yeah, I do. She's getting kind of used to the idea of us, you and me. Plus, she adores Hannah. You could stay tonight, bring her over when you get her tomorrow, and make a weekend of it. If you want?"

Zack leaned back and looked her in the eyes.

"Yeah, I think I'd like that a lot. I'll see you later for lunch, okay?" He pulled the cart forward and started towards the trail. Molly watched him disappear through the pines. She let herself imagine, for a moment, setting up her own wedding at the lodge someday. She pictured herself walking toward him from that trail as he stood in the gazebo. Molly smiled. She knew it was silly and way too early to even think about marrying again, but something fluttered in her stomach every time Zack kissed her and walked away. Something awakened in Molly just by the sight of him. She exhaled and slid her hands into her jean pockets just as he completely disappeared. Months before, as she drove from Nashville to Great Pines with her Emerson sleeping the in the backseat, the image or thought of Zack hadn't crossed her mind in nearly two decades. Suddenly, she couldn't imagine going a full day without seeing him, kissing him, hearing him call her 'honey.' While Molly had assured Mr. Castille she wasn't keeping the resort because of Zack; she quietly admitted to herself he was a big part of her decision to stay.

After a day of preparing for weekend guests and preparing for the wedding to follow the next weekend, Zack and Molly both cleaned up at the deep kitchen sink as Emerson took dinner to the tables. There were four families and one couple staying the weekend. Two of the four were anxious to hit the pond and fish from the canoes. The other two were avid hikers who took advantage of the winding trails before dinner. The couple was older, childless, and looking for a relaxing spot to watch stars. They were from the city and missed the wide-open views of skies unobstructed by streetlights.

Zack planted a kiss on her cheek and took her hand as they pushed through the double doors to eat and socialize. Zack talked to each table about the town, history of the area, and best trails. Molly watched him from afar with admiration. The way he interacted with others, including the children, warmed her heart and led her to fall harder for him. She spread butter on a roll and let herself fantasize about the next summer and summer after that. She pictured Zack by her side at the front desk, showing guests cabins, and running the resort together. He swooped behind her and placed his hands on her shoulders. Zack leaned down and kissed the top of her head.

"Are you two married?" asked the wife of the hike-loving couple.

"Oh no, Mrs. Hindman. We're just—"

"She was madly in love with me in high school and has stalked me ever since," Zack said. Molly slapped the top of his hand.

"Not quite! We knew each other in high school. I just moved back a few months ago and we started dating. But, no, not married." She said. Zack kissed the top of her head again.

"She wishes though." He said as he squeezed her shoulders and made his way back to the kitchen. Molly giggled and relished in the sight of him walking away.

"Well, you two seem happy, certainly like you should be married," Mrs. Hindman said.

"Thank you. He's really a wonderful guy. I'm very lucky to have him around here, that's for sure."

As the night wound down and guests made their way to the cabins, Molly and Zack helped the bartender close the lounge. Emerson wandered to her room to watch a movie. As Molly placed wine glasses on the top shelf, Zack tickled her side. She laughed and steadied and glasses. The bartender laughed along with her.

"Watch it, Mol. Those are the good glasses," he quipped as he wiped the bar one last time.

"I think that's your hint to quit for the night," Zack said with a wink. "Right, Carl?"

"Yep, get out, you two." He said. Molly let Zack guide her from behind the bar and to the door to the lobby. As they made their way to the hall, Zack pulled her close and kissed her.

"You sure this is alright with Em?" He said.

Molly nodded as he kissed her. She reached for his belt loops and pulled him further down the darkened hall. She reached behind her and opened her door as Zack started to scoop her up from the ground. They made their way into the bedroom and Zack pushed the door closed with his foot as he inched closer to the bed. His phone buzzed in his pocket. He laid Molly down and whispered "sorry." Zack crawled on top of Molly and kissed her harder. His phone buzzed again. They both sighed together.

"Who the hell is calling this late." He said as he stood up and reached into his pocket. Molly pushed herself up on her elbows as the phone lit up the room. "It's Melissa." He swiped to answer and mouthed 'sorry' again. Molly watched his face drop and could see the color drain despite the few slivers of light in the room. She sat up at the edge of the bed. "What? I mean where?" He said as his eyes darted around. Molly stood up and went to the light switch. She could see Zack's hands start to shake. Molly reached for his free hand. "Yeah, yeah, I'll be right there as soon as possible. Jesus. Tell her I'm on my way, please." His shoulders dropped. "Don't worry. Just hold on. I'm on my way." Zack removed the phone from his ear and swiped end. His eyes filled with tears. Molly squeezed his hand.

"What? What happened?"

"It's Hannah. An accident. I gotta go. They're at Maine Med. It's bad, Mol. It's bad. I gotta go." His eyes were darting all around the room.

"Your shoes, right there," Molly said as she reached for his shoes. "What happened? Is she gonna be okay?"

"I don't know, Mol. Melissa said it's pretty bad. They wrecked. She's in ICU. Jesus, Molly. She's four. She's four." He shook more and started to cry.

"Hey, hey. It's gonna be okay. You want me to drive you?"

Zack drew in a deep breath and looked to the ceiling. He steadied himself. "No, I'll be fine. I gotta go. I'll call you when I know anything. Okay?" He leaned down and kissed her head just as he had done at dinner earlier. Before Molly could reach for his other hand, he darted from the room. She followed him down the hall and heard him grab his keys from behind the front desk. As she heard the door swing open, Molly yelled, "Be careful, please." The door closed before she could get out another word. By the time Molly made it over to lock the lodge door, she heard his tires peel out from the gravel and down the driveway. His lights faded and the lodge fell silent.

Molly sat on the couch and thought of Hannah. She pictured her brown, bouncy curls and her high-pitched giggle. The lively little creature had become a weekend fixture at the resort for Saturday night movies, canoe trips, and learning to swim at the pond. Emerson took her by the hand and led her everywhere when Zack had her at the resort. Molly struggled with the urge to wake Emerson and drive to Portland to be by his side. It was midnight. She thought how devastating it would be as a parent to wait outside of an ICU room while a child struggled to live. She pictured being in Melissa's shoes and having to call Kenny to tell him Em was gravely injured. Then, she pictured Kenny walking into a waiting room with a random woman by his side. Molly knew she couldn't follow him regardless of how badly she wanted to. She knew Zack and Melissa needed to be there together, for each other and Hannah. She pushed herself up from the couch and went to bed. Molly barely slept as she constantly checked her phone.

When the sun came up, she sat up and checked her phone, again. There was still no word. Molly decided to give Zack another half hour before texting for an update. She gathered clothes and showered. As the water ran down her back, Molly did something she hadn't done since she drove back to Maine. She prayed. She asked God to watch over that little girl and to watch over Zack. As she dried off, she rechecked her phone. A half hour had passed. Molly texted Zack. She stood in front of the mirror, dressing and combing through her blonde hair, while never taking her eyes off her phone. She heard Emerson stirring outside. The phone dinged.

Hey, sorry didn't text earlier. Still waiting to see her. She has broken legs, head injury, punctured lung. The text read. Molly's hand shook at the thought of little Hannah being so badly injured.

What happened? I'm so sorry. I can still drive down. Molly texted back.

Her phone rang as soon as she sent the text. It was Zack. "Hey, she was hit by a car. She was on the sidewalk with Melissa walking downtown. They were both hit. Melissa is okay though, bruised and stuff. A teen driver hit the gas instead of the brake. Hannah got the worst of the injuries. We've been sitting here all night waiting to get in to see her." He said. His voice sounded so far away. He talked slowly. She could tell he was tired.

"Oh Jesus, Zack. I'm so sorry. I'm sure they're doing everything they can. When can you see her?" Molly said.

"Oh hey, the doctor just walked in. I'll call back later." He pushed the words through the phone and hung up before she could respond. Her door opened, and Emerson walked in asking what was wrong. Molly let the phone fall on the bed as she fought back the tears. She told Emerson everything she knew, as she realized she knew very little. Molly promised to update Emerson when Zack called again.

For the entire day, she fought the urge to call him. She was desperate to hear his voice, to hear how Hannah was doing, and desperate to comfort him in any way she could. Leaving him alone was what she knew to be right and most helpful, even if it was killing her inside. Molly spent the day trying to pay attention to guests needs and handle the lodge duties, all the while her mind kept wandering back to Zack and Hannah, even Melissa. She hadn't met her but felt a motherly connection, even though she was Zack's ex-love. Molly checked her phone every few minutes. There were no new texts or calls. She decided to text again if he didn't update her by nightfall. Molly couldn't decide if this was a case of no news is good news, or if she should fear the worst for tiny Hannah.

She did the dishes and the lounge was getting busy, as it had every Saturday night since the lodge reopened. Molly slithered out to the front porch once she had a spare moment. There were still no calls or texts. She hesitated before dialing his number. Molly stared at the driveway. She wished his truck would pull up and they would have the weekend they planned. She dialed his number.

"Hey there." She said as he answered. "How is she?" She heard him breathe deeply.

"She's looking better, much better than this morning. We can only see her a few minutes at a time, but she might get moved in the morning. Sorry I didn't call sooner. We've just been a little overwhelmed here."

"God, no, don't be sorry. I wanted to wait to call, but I've been worried sick. I'm glad she's improving. How are you doing? I can still come down if you want?"

"I'm okay. My dad is here. Melissa's parents and sister are here. We're doing alright right now."

"Good. Good. I'm glad you've got family around right now."

"Yeah. Hey, I'm gonna go. It's almost time for the doctor to come back around. I'll call in the morning, okay?" He said. "Oh, thanks, hon."

"What? Thanks for what?" Molly said.

"Oh, nothing. Sorry, I was talking to Melissa. She just handed me coffee. I gotta go. I'll call later, okay?"

"Oh, okay. Please keep me updated, Zack."

"I will. Bye." He said. The call ended before she could say anything else.

"Thanks, hon?" She said to herself as she stood on the porch. "Hun?" Molly's mind swirled. She felt nauseous suddenly. She squinted and slid her phone into her pocket. The sounds of the lounge rippled past. Everything sounded far away, distant, and hollow. Molly shook her head. "Damnit, Mol. Don't be like that, not now. He's going through a traumatic experience. They both are. Let it go," she told herself in a low whisper.

She was ashamed of herself for letting the slightest wave of jealousy creep into her mind when Zack was dealing with every parent's worst fear. She shook her head again and made her way to the lounge door. When she opened the door, a wink from Carl, the bartender, and the greetings of the guests already feeling the buzz of locally crafted beers swept over her. Molly figured she could spend the rest of the night analyzing the tone, inflection, and intention. Or, she could take a sip of what Carl was pouring and release herself to the lounge. She chose to focus on the guests and put on an act for the night. Part of that act was to push the word "hun" from her memory. She didn't let the lounge suck her in. She wouldn't turn to bourbon to drown that word floating in her mind. She'd deal with that word later. One thing was for sure, she'd deal with it sober because Molly knew bourbon would only wipe away that word temporarily. It would still be there in the morning.

The next morning, the sunlight pierced through just as her phone buzzed. She scrambled to pick it up. "Zack?" she said before realizing it was her alarm. She let disappointment flood her mind and her heart. As she sat up, Molly realized she was selfish, again. Instead of focusing on Hannah getting better, she had spent the part of the night focused on half a word Zack muttered to his ex-girlfriend as she handed him coffee, coffee bought to get through the night as their daughter was ICU. Molly felt foolish, petty, and small.

Molly went through the motions of accommodating guests and making time to enjoy the pond with Emerson in the afternoon. She fought the urge to call Zack again. She decided texting would be safer, less intrusive. It would also eliminate the chance of hearing Melissa in the background, or hearing Zack talk to her.

Hey, is she doing okay? Better today? And how about you? She texted. Molly watched Emerson kick up water and flop around as she waited for a reply.

Yep. In her own room. Talking to us. Thank god. She's going to be okay, except for therapy for the legs. Bad concussion though. Dr. says walking will be tough for months. I'm good. All good there? Sorry I didn't call earlier.

No, don't be sorry. Glad she's doing better. You want us to come down? Or take care of anything at your house? Molly texted back. She wanted to dial his number.

No, the house is fine. My mom checked stuff. Don't come down. Too much to do there. And I'm good here. It was touch and go for two days. Never been so scared before.

I can't imagine. You sure you don't want company? When do you think you'll be back? I miss you. She texted. She regretted it as soon as she hit 'send.' Molly stared as she waited for a reply. Fifteen minutes passed before the phone dinged.

I don't know when I'll be back. I might send some of the guys out this week for the wedding stuff. Sorry. But don't want to leave before she's out. Don't need company though. Plenty of family here now. She read and her heart sank. She reread every word over again.

Don't be sorry. Glad family is there to help. Let me know if you change your mind. Molly texted back.

The phone didn't ding for the rest of the day. She focused on what he didn't text to her. He never said he missed her back. He never said she was family, too. He never said he loved her. Even through texts, Molly sensed a distance. The words said so little but she read so much into them. Each space was filled with what he couldn't say or didn't feel. Molly let the day slide into night and into the next morning without bothering him again. Now that she knew Hannah would be okay, she wanted to wait until he reached out to her, called or texted. She tried to push him from her mind, but each second dragged on. Each hour of no contact stretched and made him seem further away. She reread all their texts. She scrolled through social media checking if he posted updates. Molly even scrolled through Melissa's feeds to check for updates or pictures of Zack with her. There was nothing.

The wedding was days away. The only dings on Molly's phone were the bride as she constantly sought updates about weather, chair counts, wine cases, and the flowers. Zack said he had the flowers handled. Molly lied to the bride, telling her Zack was on top of it even though no one had come out yet. Molly decided to call Zack by Thursday morning to ensure the flowers were ready if she didn't hear from him sooner. As much as Molly wanted to give him space and could tell that's what he needed, she couldn't let any detail of this wedding fall to the wayside. She needed it to succeed so the resort would succeed. After the demise of her marriage, her stumbling as a mother for months, and letting down her father when he needed her most, this wedding could reset Molly's life, reset her path. It would clear the clutter, the brush, and broken branches. A wedding would envelop the resort and wipe away the failures, the memories she needed to be erased. At the same time, Molly felt her heart start to splinter with each passing hour of not hearing from Zack. Had she let him too close, in too soon? Did she do exactly what Bob Castille accused her of doing? She pushed those feelings aside and confirmed chair numbers, plate numbers, and put together a bucket of cleaning supplies to give the honeymoon cabin a once-over before the couple was set to arrive.

Molly wandered down the path to the cabin, bucket in hand, as clouds rolled in. She had just appeased the bride the rain would hold off the next few days, and all would be roses and sunshine. Her shoulders slumped. Nothing would ruin this day for the bride, groom, guests, or for her. She walked on the screened porch. The rocking chairs creaked as she brushed past and opened the door. The sun was shining through the back window even though clouds rolled across the trail. It illuminated the fireplace and the neatly stacked pile of wood next to it. The turquoise circular rug gave the space a brightening. There was a loveseat directly across from the fireplace with two of her mother's quilts draped over the side. Even though Molly had washed the quilts a week ago, she leaned down to smell them. All traces of her mother, the smells of her childhood, were gone, but Molly couldn't resist trying. She wished for one more hug, as she had done countless times since returning. She reached in the bucket for a rag to wipe off the mantle and nightstands. Swirls of yellow pollen danced above as Molly disturbed the stillness. She sneezed. As she reached in the bucket for cleaner, she heard the door creak open. Molly glanced from under her arm.

"Zack! Thank God you're back." Molly said. She dropped the spray and ran to him. He stood still and put his arms around her shoulders. Molly squeezed him then pulled back to look up at him. "Is she okay? Is she out of the hospital?"

"No, well not exactly. She's been moved to an out-patient facility for rehab. Her legs are pretty messed up, and it'll be awhile before she's running around again." Zack rubbed his chin and looked up. Molly could tell he was trying not to cry. "Listen, I just came back to let you know the wedding stuff is all set. I brought Dustin over and showed him where everything goes. The flowers, pots, and the arrangements on the gazebo. He'll take good care of it tomorrow and the weekend. Okay?"

"Yeah, yeah that'll be good. I knew it would get handled. I'm more worried about Hannah though. Are you going back down or staying here for the wedding. They arrive tomorrow afternoon,

3 o'clock, I think." Molly asked. She clutched his belt loops. "After all, we gotta pick back up where we left off." She tried to wink at him. As she smiled, Molly realized the last few days were the longest she had gone without seeing him since she got back to Maine. He looked down at her and stepped back. "What? Are you heading back right away? What is it?" Molly said. She held his beltloops tighter.

"I need to talk to you. Sit down, okay?" Zack motioned toward the honeymoon bed. He took her arm and guided her. She let the rag fall and followed. Molly sat on the edge and squinted. The sun was in her eyes. She noticed more dust dancing around in the air in front of her. "Listen, Mol. You know how great you are? This resort? This spring and summer. It's been amazing." Molly squinted more.

"Yeah. What we've got is pretty special. I don't know what I would've done without you." Molly said. "We make a great team. Don't you think?" She reached for his hand.

"Yeah, we do. I started falling for you the second I saw you trip down the steps of the lodge." He smirked. Molly let a slight laugh escape. "But, being there watching Hannah, well, Melissa and I—" Zack said as he looked down at the floor. Molly stood up before he could finish.

"What? Just spit it out, dammit."

"Molly, please sit down. Please." He reached for her hand. She let it fall limply into his. He pulled her close in front of him. She looked at the floor at his feet. He slid his hand under her chin and made her look up. "This is hard for me, okay? But, sitting there, just sitting helpless, we had nothing to do but talk, Molly. I mean, really talk." Molly heard him swallow. She glanced around everywhere but into his eyes. There were black and white framed pictures of the beaches of Maine, the lake with the setting sun, and the harbors on the shore. The water glistened in the pictures. Molly felt a tear escape. She swallowed as her eyes darted around.

"Melissa and I have a complicated relationship, and we had an even more complicated break-up. Molly, I fell in love with you this spring and summer. I really did. But..."

"Just say it, Zack. Just say it." Molly said. Her hands started to shake. She wished she still had the rag to wring or twist to occupy her hands.

"We think we owe it to Hannah to try again. We, well, we still have a lot of feelings for each other. If we can make it work, it's really what's best for Hannah, you know?"

"No, Zack. No, I don't know. Running back to Nashville and making it work with Kenny wouldn't do a damn bit of good for my kid except give her a miserable mother to grow up with. Just because you have a kid doesn't mean you're better off together." She said as she met his eyes. "You were just emotional cause of the accident. Think about it." Molly said. She reached to touch his arm. "That's all it was. That doesn't mean you should get back together."

"Molly, it's more than that. I'm sorry, Mol. I'm sorry. I know this is hard."

"You do? Really? Jesus, Zack. You said you loved me. You, you convinced me to keep this place. Dammit. You...you made me believe we could do this together. You made me want to be here, here with you."

"I know, I know. I do, Molly. I meant everything I said. I did. But—"

"There's no 'but' when you love someone. There just isn't. How can you be in love in with me, stay here, everything, then just want to try again with her? She left you. She took your kid and left. She gave up on you. Jesus." Molly folded her arms and turned toward the fireplace. "I knew it by your voice. Damn it. I knew it and just let it go. I thought I was being paranoid, just like I always thought with Kenny and his late night calls."

"Don't compare me to him. Don't. This isn't anything like that. You know this isn't like that. I'm not Kenny." He said. Molly turned around to look at his face. She tried to stop the tears and bit her lip. Her shoulders shook. He stepped towards her as she put her hands up. She wanted to block the view of him, the sound, his very presence. At the same time, she wanted him to lunge for her, scoop her up and make love to her right there in the honeymoon cabin. She kicked the cleaning bucket across the cabin. His shoulders slumped. "Molly, I did fall for you. I really did. I loved being here. I loved being here with you." He started to step forward.

"No, just go. Go, run to Portland. Start over with her. Do whatever. I got a lot to take care of today and this weekend. Then I'll just go back to Plan A. Sell this shit-hole and move on."

"Don't say that. Don't. I never meant to hurt to you."

"Yeah, no one ever does, do they?" Molly's arms unfolded and dropped to her side. "Just go."

"Molly, for what it's worth, I'm really sorry. I didn't plan any of this."

"Is that supposed to make it easier? I knew I shouldn't get involved with you, with anyone here. Shit, I had a plan. I came here to sell and move on. You convinced me to stay and for what?"

"Hey now, I never told you to stay. I didn't make you do anything. We both fell into this, this thing we had, pretty damn fast. I'm not trying to screw up everything here for you. I'm not. But, shit, Melissa and I agree, we, well, we gotta give this another shot. I can't help that. I think it's the right thing to do for me, her, and for Hannah."

"Yeah, well, that doesn't leave me with much now does it? I fell in love with you, with this stupid idea of us here, and it got me nowhere. It got me nothing."

"This place is doing great. You can take pride in what you did here. Don't just throw everything away because we didn't work out." He said.

"There's nothing here for me. I should've rolled up that driveway in April, sold right away, and moved on. Sticking around, falling for you, showing all this to Em, it's all just turned to shit again. All of it." She walked closer to the fireplace. Molly reached up and ran her hand across the mantle. Her tears blurred the dust trail. Zack touched her shoulder. She winced.

"I'm sorry, Mol. I never meant for this to happen." His hand slid off her shoulder.

Molly looked up at the ceiling. She waited until she heard the last of his footsteps on the porch before turning around. Molly kicked the cleaning bucket once more. She saw a glimpse of his curly black hair as he disappeared by the trail. She could tell he was looking down. Molly sat on the bed as her legs grew heavy. Her knees shook, and she let a levy of tears break free. She felt them drizzle down and dangle from her chin before falling into her lap. She didn't reach for a towel or bother to wipe her face. Molly let her head hang and let a stream of tears run wild. While the tears started for Zack, they soon morphed into unleashing anger at Kenny, and her father. All three led her to believe life would and should be one way. They led her to feel safe and comfortable across from each of them. Each, in his own way, loved her and had been loved by her. Their protection was her safe zone. Her father was supposed to care for her above all others, above himself and his demons. Her husband was supposed to guard her heart, grow old only wanting to be with her. Zack was the one who made her feel the resort was home again and she could have the fresh start she needed and deserved. She sat on the edge of the bed, feeling the years of disappointment leave her eyes and roll down her face. Each man, each love, had left her crushed, alone, and feeling helpless. The hardest part was the realization that she let it happen. Molly let them leave her like this. She wanted the future she pictured for herself there with Zack, Emerson, and Hannah. She wanted those nights in rocking chairs on the porch watching guests relax and chat. She wanted those nights in his arms or under him in the sand. She wanted to make memories that would replace the ones that haunted her. It was all ripped away when he disappeared down the trail.

She pounded her fist on the bed. Molly let out a scream before hitting the top of the mantle with her fists. She instantly felt pain radiating from her wrist up to her arm. She didn't care. She hit it again. Her hands were stinging. A picture fell off. It was of the pond at sunset. Molly looked around and saw the lamp on the table next to the love seat. She grabbed it by the base and threw it at the fireplace. Glass, ceramic, and pieces of plastic scattered through the air and then the floor. Molly felt a sting on her leg. She saw blood and realized a piece of the glass cut her right below the knee. Enough, she thought. Enough. Molly sank down and sat on the floor in front of the mess she had made. The pieces were everywhere, even on the bed. She exhaled and looked up at the quilts. Her shoulders slumped once she realized she just added to her workload. Molly looked at the bucket on the floor. The cleaner was leaking. The rags were strewn across the wood floors. She reached over broken glass and ceramic to grab a rag and small garbage bag. This was the only mess in her life she could take care of in one swoop. It was the only mess she felt she could clean up at all.

She sat back on her feet and wiped her face with her forearm. Molly glanced at every corner of the cabin. She could see the flowers in the flower box outside peak up in front of the windows. They were pink petunias planted by Zack. She wondered if Hannah hadn't been in an accident, would he had left her another time? Would she have woken up to a note one day? Would she have walked in and found him in front of a nurse, waitress, or delivery girl one day? Not Zack, she thought. But, even if he would've never deliberately hurt her like Kenny the Philanderer did, she knew he would've hurt her all the same. It would've been a matter of time before he slipped back into loving

Melissa or quietly slipped out of loving her. She shook her head. It was for the best, she thought. At least he left before she missed any chance to sell and move on. At least she still had Plan A.

Molly picked herself up and carried the bag of broken pieces to the bucket. She walked over and sniffed the quilts once more. She ran her hand over the mantle and checked the bathroom. All was clean. All was perfect again in time for an unsuspecting couple to begin a marriage. She smirked and wondered what awaited that innocent couple, untouched by disappointment, pain, and betrayal. Maybe they'd be lucky and live blissfully ever after? Maybe they'd waltz through life's pain, arm in arm, and never waiver? Maybe he'd leave her for an ex-girlfriend he reconnected with on a business trip, or maybe she'd become an alcoholic? Whatever awaited them as they started their journey together, Molly knew one thing—their first night would be perfect and clean. There'd be no dust, dirt, or clutter. There'd be a clean place to relish in their love and fresh quilts to cover their exhausted, intertwined bodies. There would be no trace of her or her mother's scent. No one's past would sully the cabin. The newly married couple wouldn't drown in the river of tears Molly had just unleashed. She just needed to replace the lamp.

She stepped outside with the bucket and walked to the trail. Molly stopped at the sign with an arrow pointing to the lodge, and one pointed to the lake. She placed the bucket on the ground and walked toward the lake. The trail was clear, the branches pushed to the sides guided the way, and birds sang in the background. She could see a glimpse of the water. The trail she and Zack worked to clear became wider. The sand became softer. Her shoes started to sink some. She could hear one of the family's at the resort coming down a trail that ran parallel. They must've hiked the radius of the lake, she thought. Molly walked within ten feet of the water. It looked clear even though it had rained the night before. A fish swam past, rippling the water behind it. Molly sank to her knees. She replayed the first time she made love to Zack over in her head. The feel of the sand absorbing them under her back, her shoulders as he laid on top of her. She bit her lip as the rush of tears reemerged. Her hands shook harder than they had when she threw the lamp and pounded the mantle. She balled her fists and looked up at the sky. The clouds passed overhead in a hurry to make it past the tree line.

"Dammit, Molly. Dammit," she said to the sky. "What the hell were you thinking?" She sunk further into the ground. The weight of the last few months and what to do now pressed down on her shoulders. "I give up, okay?" she muttered to no one. "I'm waving the white flag here." Molly glanced at the sky again. She thought of her parents. She wondered if they could hear her. "I tried. I tried." She felt as if her entire world was once again slipping away from her grasp as she unclenched her fists and let the sand fall back to the ground. Everything she ran from all those years ago had pulled her back in. Now, it spit her back out. "I'm just so damned tired."

The water of Moose Pond glistened just as it did every time she jumped in. Molly could almost feel it on her body. Part of her wanted to jump in, cleanse the day off her skin. Cleanse the last few months, years, off her skin, too. Molly stood up and ambled to the water's edge. She tossed off her sneakers and walked in. The water lapped up further on her legs as she went in deeper. The initial chill and goosebumps subsided quickly. Molly let the water tease the edge of her jean shorts. Then, without thought or care, she bent her legs and lowered her body. The water was up to her shoulders. She pushed off the soft murkiness below her feet and lunged forward, completely immersing herself. Molly let the water swish into her ears and nose. She closed her eyes and let her body sink slightly. The world was silent. The pain in her fist, the sting of the cut on her leg, her broken heart, all dissipated. She was cleansed. Molly slowly let her face, shoulders, and arms emerge back into the air, the world. She felt heavy again. She felt pain again. She wanted to dive back under and stay. She wanted to let the pond absorb her wholly and keep her forever. But, there was work to do.

As she stood and drew in a breath, she let it all back in-- the pain of her failed marriage, her lost chance at having her father, or at least getting to know him as an adult, and being left by Zack. While their relationship was short-lived, it had engulfed her. Molly let herself not just fall for him, but also the possibility of a real life there with him. She fell asleep each night thinking about the two of them running the resort. It was only a season, but it was love. He fixed everything, including her. Molly rolled into the resort with a broken heart and somehow ended up with another. Even though he was only one man, Molly knew Zack was one hell of a man, the kind that doesn't come along more than once in a lifetime. The craving to run away again was all she could taste. Molly walked back onto the beach. The water ran down her body and her clothes stuck to her tiny frame. She once again wiped her face with her forearm. When she was sure the hiking family was far from her part of the trail, she started the walk back to the lodge, her home for now.

The pines swayed above her, causing the sunlight to hide and reveal itself in waves. Molly let those waves wash over her. She kicked at the sand as she schlepped along. She wanted to be sure Zack was gone before making it to the opening of the trail. Molly knew Zack needed awhile to give Dustin the instructions for the arrangements since he wouldn't be back for the wedding. She kicked a few pinecones out of the way. Her hands still stung as she wondered if she'd have to explain bruises to the wedding party or Emerson. Shit, Emerson, she thought. She let Emerson get close to Zack. News of another breakup would only make things harder for Emerson. Molly stopped and stood in the middle of the trail she and Zack had cleared together. Her fit of rage in the cabin and wallowing at in the pond led to wet strands stuck around her face. She wiped them away from her eyes. Telling Emerson could wait until after the wedding, she decided. She'd also have to tell Emerson they'd be back to Plan A, selling and getting the hell out of Great Pines.

Molly picked up the pace as the long list of chores and wedding details displaced her anger toward Zack and Melissa. The tail end of the bartender's car came into view. Without hesitation, Molly accepted the fact that a night at the lounge might be on the agenda after she changed into dry clothes.

Once inside, Molly called Maxine as she melted into the couch. She usually stayed off the lobby furniture when she was covered in dirt or wet, but she was too exhausted, mentally and physically, to adhere to any of her own rules. As soon as Molly heard Maxine's voice, she unleashed another endless stream of tears. Molly felt lighter as she told Maxine about the accident, vague texts, the breakup, and the fit alone in the honeymoon cabin. She told Maxine about screaming and throwing the lamp. Saying it all out loud helped unleash some of the rage. It was still on the verge of boiling over again. Her gut felt like a volcano gearing up for another eruption. Her cheeks grew hot all over again. Molly sat straight up and exhaled loudly. She used her free arm to wipe away tears and sweat.

"Dammit, Maxine. I gotta pull it together before these people get here tomorrow for this wedding. I just have to. It's got to go off without a hitch."

"It will. It will. At least he hadn't moved in or anything too crazy, you know? Just keep perspective," Maxine said.

"I'm trying. It just hit me harder than the divorce from Kenny did on some level. I don't know why. I mean, it was only a few months. But, hearing him say they were gonna give it another shot was like getting punched in the face. You should see my hands, wrist, from punching that mantle. I'm an idiot. Now, I'm a bruised idiot." She said with a laugh. "Seriously though, I don't know what to do now. I gotta talk to Emerson about signing those papers after this wedding. I gotta get out of here."

"Well, do what ya gotta do, of course. But listen, don't you dare leave town this time without saying goodbye. You hear me?" Maxine said. Molly felt a twinge in her heart. All the pain she caused Maxine and Maxine's explosion over it at dinner came back to her.

"I won't. I promise. Maxine, I'll never hurt you like that again." She said. Molly sunk back into the couch and blew the few strands of dry hair out of her face.

"I know you won't, Mol. Just let me know what you plan to do, or when you plan to leave, okay? I'll run over to say goodbye. We aren't losing each other again, not after all these years."

"Nope, we won't. I gotta go, but I'll talk to you later. Thanks for talking me down a little." Molly said.

"That's what I'm here for. Now get over that beat-up and broken ex-football player and move on already."

Molly laughed and nodded as they said goodbye. She looked up at the antlers above her as the phone fell silent. Molly went to the desk in the office and pulled out the papers for the sale. She placed them on top of the other papers needing her attention. Molly scanned the offer, the numbers, and the dates. "Later," she muttered. She shoved the stack back in the drawer and closed her eyes. "Focus on this wedding, then sign your ticket out of here." She said to herself.

After a quick shower and change of clothes, Molly went about her usual routine in a haze as the rest of the day unfolded. In an instant, she had gone from blissfully happy at the resort, planning a future with Zack, to drained of tears and painting on a fake smile when she encountered current guests. The couples and families filtered in and out for extra towels, snacks, and to lounge in the air conditioning as the humidity weighed down on northern Maine. She watched them in awe. They were unscathed, unaware that her world had fallen apart and her plans had dissipated. She envied their obliviousness, their happiness. The resort that felt like home again had slipped back into a foreign entity, one she needed to deal with before moving on. She grunted at the thought of moving on again, and whatever that meant next for her. Molly took her phone from her pocket and set a reminder to call Mr. Castille in the morning to let the interested corporation know she planned the sign the papers after the wedding.

As dinner was rolled out, Emerson played in the kitchen with the head cooks. They sat at the stainless-steel counter playing cards each night as the guests ate. The sound of Emerson laughing and slapping her hand on the stack of cards was the only thing that brought a genuine smile to Molly's face. She rubbed the purple and reddish bruise on the side of her hand. It hurt to touch. Everything was starting to hurt. Her temples throbbed as she helped clear tables and her forced smile became harder to flash at guests. The wait staff buzzed around her and Molly could feel their glances of concern as they all saw Zack leave earlier. She wanted to grab a few of the girls by the arm and warn them to never fall in love, never think a man will stay or be there when you need him most. She wanted to stand on a table and scream to them all that Zack was gone for good. Any childish dream of her and Zack running the place, being a family, was just a stupid dream that meant nothing in reality. She picked up dirty glasses and walked to the kitchen, set them on the counter, and hid her face, afraid she'd break into tears all over again. She needed to keep it together for a few more days. The bride and groom would be there the next day.

As the sun set, guests left the porch. Molly rearranged the rocking chairs and turned on the lights of the gazebo for the kids. She saw a few guests enter the lounge. While her responsible side told her to wrap up her hostess duties and get a good night sleep so she could be fresh for the wedding party tomorrow, her broken heart screamed for relief. She reached up and re-tied her mangled mane. Molly darted into her bathroom to wipe her face and put on some fresh lipstick. She pulled her sweaty t-shirt off and grabbed a clean one from the back of the bathroom door, her third change of clothes that day. Molly looked at herself in the mirror before darting back outside. She felt broken inside, but she could still flash a smile. She practiced. Her eyes started to well up again. "No," she told herself. There would be plenty of time to cry in a few days. She looked down at her phone on the counter and fought the urge to dial Zack's number. She wanted to hear his voice again, see his floppy black hair fall over his forehead when he laid down on top of her. She wanted to feel him breathe on the back of her neck in bed together. She wanted it to work. Molly wanted to go back to the honeymoon cabin and beg him to give them a chance. She wanted to go back and outline all the reasons they'd be incredible together. She wanted to redo every moment with him. Her heart started to pound harder, and her cheeks grew red again. The eruption was bubbling. Molly quickly ran a brush through her hair and darted out of the bathroom. She knew another minute staring in the mirror would cause her to unleash a puddle of new tears on the floor and Emerson would eventually find her. She needed to escape Zack and the space he had taken up in her heart. Molly needed to escape the afternoon that spiraled into another failure. She went straight to the lounge.

She slipped behind the bar as she had done on other nights. Carl flashed her a smile and tossed her a rag.

"Ain't you got other things to do tonight before this whole wedding thing goes down?" He said as he rubbed his gray goatee.

"Yeah, but I figure you could use the help, too."

"Or, you figured you could use a drink. Am I right?" Carl said. Molly felt a pang in her gut. She didn't want him to be right.

"Maybe. You know, to calm my nerves over this wedding madness. Chairs and stuff come tomorrow. Dustin brings all the flowers bright and early, too."

"Dustin? Zack's helper? What about Zack?" Carl said. He poured a beer for a guest across from him, a guy from upstate New York looking to explore the Appalachian Trail in the next year or so.

"He's got other things going on. You know, his daughter's rehab and all."

"Oh yeah. Poor guy. Cute kid. I'm so glad she's getting better at least. You going down to see them once the wedding is done?"

"Maybe, something like that, I guess."

"Can I get a white wine spritzer?" the woman with the beer drinker asked overtop Molly and Carl's conversation. She wore a sun visor. She pulled it back to reveal bright blue eyes. Molly raised her eyebrows.

"Of course, Janice, right? From upstate New York along with this guy?"

"Yes, exactly." She smiled. Molly slipped back into hostess mode. As she poured the spritzer, she tried to imagine how this couple got together, who they were away from the resort. Suddenly, the whole world seemed to be in a successful, healthy, and happy relationship.

Carl came up behind her and reached for a wine glass for another guest. He leaned over and whispered to Molly. "Whatever is going on, you know drinking the night away ain't gonna fix it, right?" Molly's shoulders tensed. She nodded 'yes' without turning around. Her fake smile got more challenging to keep in place. As Carl went back to his side of the bar, Molly followed.

"I'm not my father," she said through gritted teeth and a clenched jaw.

"Oh, I know. I'm not saying you are, kid. Just making conversation."

"Well, you don't have to worry about me. I sure as hell won't end up dead on the floor reeking of bourbon and rotting for three days." Molly said. She heard a gasp. Janice's eyes widened as she sipped her drink.

"Who died on the floor?" Janice said in a low tone.

"Nice, Molly. Nice." Carl said. Molly rolled her eyes. "You know what, kid? Your father certainly never thought he'd end up that way either. I'm just trying to look out for you." Carl said. He slammed down a rag on the counter. Janice flinched. Molly put her hands on her hips.

"No one needs to look out for me. I can handle myself. Been doing just fine so far."

"Yeah, real fine." Carl nudged his head at the side of her hand.

"I'm fine, Carl. Just fine." Molly shot a smile at Janice. "Janice, please disregard the ramblings of a bartender and a tired single mom." Janice's eyes widened again.

"Maine sure is interesting." Janice said as she raised her eyebrows and sipped again. Molly shot Carl a stern look and he shot one right back. While she knew he was only looking out for her and cared deeply about her father, Molly was exhausted by the interference of others who had her best interest in mind. As much as she wished for another chance with her father, she didn't have any desire for another man to act like one.

Once the last of the guests left the lounge, Emerson came in to say goodnight.

"Okay, honey. I'm just gonna help Carl cleanup. You get to bed so we can be up bright and early for the wedding guests tomorrow." Molly said as she bent down to kiss Em's forehead. "My God, you're getting so big this summer. Your dad will hardly recognize you when he sees you." Emerson smiled at her mother. "I love you so much, Em."

"Love you, too, Mom. Can I watch a movie in bed?"

"Yeah, just don't stay up late." Molly knew she'd have to tell Emerson about Zack no longer coming around once they woke. She watched her daughter bounce out of the lounge. Molly noticed Emerson was slimming down, also. The swims, hiking, and helping around the lodge was having a positive effect on her weight issues. The fresh food made for the guests as compared to the fast food Molly relied on in Nashville also helped. For the first time in a long time, Molly saw herself in Emerson's outline. The way she bounced toward the door was exactly how Molly would bounce out after saying goodnight to her father in the lounge. Molly looked over at Carl who was doing the dishes. Maybe she was more like her father than she wanted to admit. She glanced at the clock and knew no one else would be coming in. Molly reached up and took a highball glass from the top shelf. It was still damp from Carl's washing. She grabbed a bottle from the counter and poured herself some bourbon with one hand as she reached under the bar and grabbed two ice cubes. She saw Carl glance over.

"Zack broke up with me, okay? I think I deserve a drink." She shot at him before he could say anything. He shrugged. And wiped the bar.

"Yeah, well once you sober up tomorrow, you'll still be broken up," he said.

Molly put the lid back on the bourbon. She drew the glass to her lips and sipped. The smell burned her nose for a moment. She realized it had been awhile since she tasted bourbon. Molly felt Carl's eyes on her as he rinsed out the rag.

"I'm fine, Carl. Can't a girl just enjoy a drink to take the edge off a miserable ass day? Seriously. I deserve it."

"You deserve more than that, Molly. Any edge that drink takes off will still be there tomorrow."

"Dammit, I know that. I just...I just need to relax and forget for tonight. I'll get it together tomorrow. After this wedding, I'm moving on anyways."

"Really? Yeah, cause that'll fix it all. Won't it? Just run off again." Carl said. Molly slammed down her drink. Some of the bourbon splattered on the bar. "Jesus, girl. I just wiped that off."

"Sorry," she said. "I didn't say I was running off, necessarily. I'm just moving on. It's for the best, for Emerson and me, you know?"

"One thing goes wrong, and you hit the road?"

"It's more than one thing, and you know it. I wasn't meant to run this place. It's not my home anymore."

"Says who? Seems like the only home you've got." Carl said. He walked to the other side of the bar and toward the door. "For what it's worth, even if you sell tomorrow, you can chalk this all up to a success. I mean, what you've done here, you've done good. Shame you're just running off again instead of enjoying what you helped to create." Carl reached for the door.

"Thanks, Carl. And I'm not running off. I'm moving on." Molly said. She watched him walk out. As his shadow crossed over the lounge door light, Molly thought how she'd miss him. She'd miss everyone there. But, moving on from Great Pines was the only way she could move on at all.

Molly sipped more and poured more. She sat down on a stool and looked at herself in the mirror behind the bar. Her hair was still a mess. She ran her fingers through it. Molly noticed she had sunburn on her cheeks, or the after-effect of bourbon, she wasn't sure. She let that all too familiar warmth cascade down her windpipe and into her belly. Molly knew a few more sips would render relief from the heartache and headache she had from crying. She also knew Carl was right. It would all still hurt in the morning. After another glass, Molly didn't care.

She talked to her father as she sipped more and added more ice. Molly told him she was sorry for not coming sooner and not calling more. She told Mason she loved him despite the eye-rolling and arguing she did whenever he visited Nashville. Molly apologized for not keeping the resort in the family. "I just need a new start, Dad. Somewhere, somehow and selling this place is the only way I'm gonna find it." She said into the night. "I gotta go and sell this place. Move on. Just move on." Molly started to tear up again. "Nope, not gonna cry again over all this. I love this place, Dad. I do. God, do I. Remember dancing with me in here? Just me and you." Molly felt her eyes getting heavy. The initial buzz progressed to cloudiness. Her tongue felt thick as she sipped more. The warmth was a constant, not just when she sipped. The short conversation with Zack replayed in her mind. She shook her head trying to remember exactly what she did say as opposed to what she wished she'd said. Molly knew things were getting foggy, but she didn't care.

Molly decided to let go. As the glass landed on the bar with the thud of emptiness, she unleashed the tears. She was starting to realize there was no end to the well that built up inside her. Her gut seized as she fought to catch her breath. Molly caught a glimpse of herself in the mirror again. She saw her father standing behind her. His sandy hair and crooked smile floated above the mess that was her reflection. Molly blinked through the onslaught of saltwater escaping her body. She squinted at the mirror trying to focus on what she saw.

"Dad? I lost you. I sat my ass back in Nashville and let myself lose you. I lost everything. I won't be surprised at this point if I don't lose Em." Molly let the rest of her daughter's name linger on her tongue. "Is this it, Dad? Is this rock bottom? God, please tell me this is the bottom."

"Only if you want it to be, Molly-girl. You have to want it to be rock bottom." She heard in a whisper. Molly widened her eyes at the mirror. He was gone. No one was there but her. She exhaled and glanced around for an explanation for the voice. It was her father. She was sure of it. He was still there with her when she needed him to be. She exhaled and whispered, "I do, Dad. I want this to be the bottom. I need it to be. I need to find a better way. Help me find a better way."

Chapter 11

You are a child of the universe, no less than the trees and the stars; you have a right to be here—Desiderata

The low buzz of the alarm pierced through Molly's brain. She instinctively reached out her left arm to grab the phone. She felt nothing but the blanket. She reached out her right arm and felt the phone. She was laying at the foot of her bed in her clothes. The stench of old, spilled bourbon filled her nose as she tried to sit up. Her brain felt swollen; her head heavy. Molly fought to open her eyes, which were swollen shut from crying. Emerson flashed through her mind, then the wedding. She tried to focus on her last memory of the night before. Molly knew she was in the lounge. She knew she had bourbon, lots of bourbon. "God," she thought, "I hope I didn't wake up Em." Molly slid her legs over the edge of the bed and felt the blood gush down to her ankles. She was dehydrated and dizzy. She reached for a glass half-filled water that had been on her nightstand for a few days. Molly let the water hit her lips and slide down her throat. It was metallic tasting, as the well water always got when it sat for extended periods of time. She winced and squinted again. The sun was mocking her pain as it bolted through the blinds. Clouds outside rolled over the brightness to give her a few minutes of relief. Molly stood and let the dizziness subside as the headache increased. The throbbing was the most intense she had felt in recent memory. For a brief moment, Molly wondered if she hit her head on something. She hadn't. Once again, as she glanced at herself in the mirror above her mother's dresser, Molly saw a hungover shell of a woman. She saw her father. The memory of his voice in the bar last night rushed from her heart straight to her throbbing head. The dead still July heat only made it worse.

Molly walked to the shower and let the steam fill the room. She didn't want to see herself in the mirror. She stepped in and once again let the water wash away her disappointment in herself. She wanted to wash away any traces of bourbon and feelings of failure. Molly stood there piecing together the jagged and disjointed memories of last night. Part of her wanted to piece together the full picture, while another part of her wanted to forget again. She couldn't forget his voice.

As she stepped out to get ready for the long day ahead, she made a mental list of everything that needed to be checked off that day. The wedding couple, Allie and Jonah, would be arriving before dinner. They would stay in separate cabins for the two nights before the wedding, then be together in the honeymoon cabin. Today, they would approve the details, such as table linens, décor, and flowers around the gazebo. Tomorrow, they would greet their families, relax in canoes, hike, have the rehearsal and dinner, then retire early for the wedding day. While Molly had already tended to nearly every detail, she was still a nervous wreck about meeting them in person. She spent hours on the phone with Allie in May and June. She felt like they already knew each other. Molly understood the details and extras would make it special and everything Allie and Jonah had envisioned. As Molly put the finishing touches on her eye makeup, she was sure she didn't look as hungover as she felt. She also wondered just how her parents put on numerous weddings in the summer and fall when one had her nerves frazzled. Part of her nervousness and need to pull off the perfect wedding was selfish. She was convinced a successful event would give her a bit of leverage in negotiating a selling price for the resort. However, she also knew she needed to hide her desperation and the fact that a newly broken heart made her a motivated seller.

Over breakfast, Molly probed Emerson about when she fell asleep in hopes of quelling any fears that Em saw her mother blindly drunk. Molly drew in a sigh of relief when she realized Em never saw her stumble to bed. She was also sure Emerson was blissfully unaware of Molly's headache and confusion in general about the night before. Emerson rattled off which details she wanted for her own wedding someday. Molly couldn't help but smile listening to her talk about rose petals lining a path, lights twinkling from high atop a tree at sunset, and her ideas for a pale pink dress that barely brushed the grass as she walked. Molly let the image of Emerson as a young woman in love and getting married fill her mind. She closed her eyes. Her head started to throb some more. Molly shook her head as she remembered the times her father had forgotten their conversations or fights. As her daughter's dreams poured over her ears and muffled her headache, Molly swore to get herself in check and avoid the lounge, once again. She told herself she'd hold off on drinking until maybe the day the resort sold, and she'd hold off bourbon for a hell of a lot longer. She had to make this day a new start, a real new beginning for her sake and Emerson's.

Molly and Emerson buzzed around the resort cleaning, tying white covers over the chairs, and sweeping the porches and gazebos before the bride and groom arrived. As Molly swept a pile of needles off the bottom step of the grand front porch, Zack's truck came up the driveway. Her heart sank as she realized Dustin was behind the wheel. He hopped out as the engine settled and sputtered for another few seconds. Molly wondered how that old truck made multiple trips to town every day.

"Hey there, Molly. I got the last of the flowers for the wedding in the back and a box inside the truck. The florist said to put the boxes in the fridge to keep 'em fresh till Saturday. But, these ones in the back can go on the cabin porches now if you want." Dustin said. He opened the back door and pulled out cardboard boxes, which he delicately stacked high over his own head. Molly let the broom fall into the mulch so she could grab a few.

"Thanks so much, Dustin. I'm sure they're gorgeous. The bride and groom will be here this afternoon to see them."

"Oh great. Well, just shoot me a message if they want anything else done to them and I'll be back up to deliver whatever they need. You want those pots on the steps or on either side of the door." Dustin said as he lowered the boxes on the top step.

"Oh, the gazebo flowers, too right?" Molly said.

"Yep. I got them all in the bed."

"Great, Dustin. I can't thank you enough."

"Don't thank me. Thank Zack. He put the finishing touches on all this yesterday and last night."

Molly looked down at the pile of pine needles she swept into the driveway. "Where's he at now, anyway?" She asked without looking up at Dustin. He shoved his hands in his pockets and walked back toward the bed of the truck.

"He headed back to Portland this morning. I don't think he'll be back for a while."

"Yeah, I figured. I just thought I'd ask. I just, well I kinda got used to seeing him every day." Molly walked to the bed of the truck behind Dustin. He opened the tailgate and turned to look at her. Molly slid a piece of hair from her eyes and looked up at the tall kid in front of her. Dustin was no more than 19 but well over six feet.

"Listen, for what's it worth, I hadn't seen him that happy in a long time, Molly. I think he really did love being out here, helping get this place in order, and stuff. You know?"

"I know, I guess. I'm sorry. You don't owe me explanations at all and I don't mean to put you in this at all. I really appreciate all you've done and all the extra you're doing since he had to take off and all."

"Thanks. For what it's worth, too, Melissa is a good person. They both really love that little girl. I mean, not that it helps or is my business, but she isn't some evil person. They were pretty good together a few years ago." Dustin said. He turned around and grabbed two of the large pots filled with blooming white roses.

"No, Dustin. I don't think that helps much. But, I appreciate you trying." Molly said with a smirk. She wanted to hate Melissa or hate Zack. But truth be told, she didn't hate them, either of them. Molly reached into the truck bed and slid out two smaller pots of red roses. "These are gorgeous. I think I'll put these on the steps of the gazebo. They'll match the white petunias in the boxes." She needed a change in subject and in scenery. Soon she hoped to have both.

When Dustin was done with the delivery and pulled away, Molly watched the truck fade away. She realized it might be the last time she ever saw that truck. The ache from yesterday started to gurgle in her gut again. She glanced at her watch. Molly had two hours to finish everything and greet the bride and groom with open arms and clean cabins. One of the cleaning girls came from the trail and assured her everything was perfect and dust-free. Fresh towels, soaps, and quilts were awaiting everyone coming today and tomorrow. Relief replaced that gurgle and Molly reached down for the broom. There was more sweeping to be done.

Just as her headache faded and the final pots were arranged on the gazebo steps, a car pulled in. Both doors opened at the same time. A tall, dark-haired waif of a woman sprang from the passenger side. Her over-sized sunglasses hid her eyes, and her broad smile took up what was visible of her face. Her skin was a deep, rich brown. Molly thought she looked as if she had spent her entire life on a deserted island, not downtown Boston. From the driver's side, an equally slender man appeared. He was shorter compared to the statuesque passenger and half a dozen shades paler. The woman spotted Molly on the gazebo steps as she closed the door to their Volvo. She waved frantically as if she had seen an old friend.

"Oh my God! You must be Molly." She said. "It's me, Allie. Allie Cappelletti." She slid her sunglasses off and bounced toward Molly.

"Of course, you are. It's so exciting to finally meet you." Molly said as she tried to match her enthusiasm. Before she could reach the last step, Allie had already embraced her and pulled her in tight. Her brown arms were strong and showed Allie to the be the type of woman who never let go of a hug first. Molly gasped for air as Allie drew her in even tighter.

"Oh lord, I'm sorry, hon. I'm just so excited. This place is everything I expected and more, and I'm still in the front." Allie said as she let Molly go and glanced around. Molly tried to regain her balance. Allie's energy was dizzying. It was also infectious. Her slight southern accent was even more noticeable in person. For the first time in over 24 hours, Molly genuinely felt excited and hopeful. There was a warmth, a familiarity, about Allie that hadn't come through on the phone. As Molly got lost in her eyes, Jonah came from behind. He extended a hand, in stark contrast to the hug from Allie.

"Hello, I'm Jonah. Jonah Parker. Sorry for the attack. She's been bursting at the seams since we crossed over the Maine line."

"It's fine, really. Nice to meet you. If you guys want, I can show you around and then take you to your cabins, or you can relax on your own for a bit?" Molly said to them both. Allie shrugged her shoulders.

"What do you think, Jonah? I'm up for checking out the wedding stuff then seeing our cabin, but whatever you feel like."

"Trust me, Molly, she isn't always this agreeable," Jonah said with a smile. He blew an air-kiss to his soon-to-be bride. A twinge went through Molly. She remembered that kind of playfulness in the early years with Kenny the Philanderer. She looked Jonah up and down. Molly didn't peg him as the type who'd break this girl like Kenny broke her. Allie reached up and pulled her long, shiny black hair behind her and away from her face. "Well, maybe freshen up first, then see the wedding stuff?" She said back to Jonah.

As they agreed to see their separate cabins, Molly dashed inside to get the keys. They drove slowly down the trail and over the bridge to the cabins to unload their stuff. Normally, Molly's father made a point of hand-carrying guests luggage to cabins, but Molly let people drive to drop off and then park in the main parking lot. The last thing she wanted to do was drag someone's wedding dress down the path and over a bridge. Her klutzy nature wouldn't allow for successfully handling the treasured items of others. Molly waited by the car as Allie and Jonah checked out their separate spaces and unloaded their car. Allie bounced off the cabin porch and leaned next to Molly against the side of the vehicle.

"He always takes longer than me. Always." She said with a laugh. Molly laughed back.

"Yeah, most guys do and never realize it. So, how do you like your cabin? The honeymoon cabin is bigger and has a fireplace."

"I love it. It's quaint, rustic, but not too rustic, if you know what I mean," she said. "I think my parents will love it, too. I haven't seen them in months. I'm so excited for them to get here tomorrow."

"How about Jonah's parents and the wedding party? Will the cabins suit their needs?"

"Oh, I'm sure they'll all be fine. Well, Jonah's parents might be a little out of their element, but they'll just have to deal. City folk through and through. If you know what I mean. I don't think they've ever set foot in the woods unless you count the Public Garden in the middle of the city." Allie fingered a necklace that dangled close to her belly button. Her fingers were long and nimble. Piano fingers, Molly's mom would call them. "The quilts inside? Gorgeous. You make them?"

"No, no. My mom made them all years ago. I have some in every cabin and our rooms in the main lodge. She passed away when I was thirteen." Molly found herself wanting to grab back the words. Allie reached over and put her hand on Molly's.

"I can't imagine. I'm so sorry."

"It's okay. It was a long time ago."

"And now you run this place? Keeping up the family tradition kind of thing?"

"Well, not necessarily. My father passed away in March, and I came back from Nashville to take it over, fix it up, and sell it soon."

"Sell it? Oh my, why? It's gorgeous here. In today's society, this kind of place is a gem. People will pay good money to get away from it all, technology, work, all that and come out here in the middle of nowhere. It has to be profitable, I'd assume. I mean, look at our wedding. That's certainly costing a good bit here. No offense. It's worth it, but why would you let this place go? It's gotta be a goldmine."

"It's a lot more complicated than making a profit. Trust me. I just got divorced. I'm a single mom, and my dad left this place to me. It's my chance to start over. And, well, I never wanted it really." Molly said. She realized she rattled off more personal details than necessary.

"Hey, well it's not my business, but if you never wanted all this, what do you want? I know, not my business, but that never stops me from asking questions. Seriously though, starting over somewhere else seems like just as much work as starting over right here. Is there someone out there to start over with or something?" Allie said.

"Nah, not at all. I kinda started over with someone here, an old friend from high school. But, that ended."

"Oh. Now I see. You aren't running toward a new start. You're running away. I get it."

"No, no, it's not—"

"Hey, it's none of my business. Like I said though, starting over somewhere else is just as much work," Allie said.

Just as Molly searched her mind for more excuses and reasons she needed to sell, Jonah emerged from his cabin. Allie leaned up from the car and reached for his hand and slid her sunglasses back over her eyes. She turned and winked at Molly. "Just think though, running toward something, running away from something, it's all running all the same. That'll get exhausting. Trust me."

"Huh?" Jonah said as he opened the car door for Allie and then for Molly.

"Nothing. Just dishing out life advice to our wedding planner, honey." Allie said as she slid into the passenger seat. Her movements were fluid, slow, yet deliberate. She wove her way through the air around Molly as Molly wished she could move with such confidence and purpose. Jonah kissed Allie's hand just as he started the car. New love, Molly thought. There was a freshness to them, a spontaneity. She remembered stopping to kiss Zack on the bridge as the car slowly crossed it. She had that freshness with Zack even if it was tempered with the heaviness of her divorce, the stress of adjusting to single-motherhood, and constant anxiety over the resort and her financial future. His small gestures, and grand gestures such as surprise lobster dinner and wine on the porch, were all still so vivid in her mind and heart. She shoved them further into the recesses of her gut and averted her eyes from the bridge as they made it to the end.

"So, what do you want to see first? The main lodge where the reception will be or the plans for seating for the ceremony at the gazebo? Or, the cake? It's your call." Molly said in an attempt to distract herself from her own reality.

"I think the lodge, then the other stuff. What do you think, Jonah?" Allie answered.

"Whichever. As long as it all ends with me getting time alone with this lady after it's all over, I don't care."

"Oh, stop it, Jonah. You care more about the cake and seating than I do, and you know it." Allie said with a laugh as she tried to corral her long hair blowing out the window.

"True. I won't lie. The seating has to be perfect, or my parents will be miserable. Or, I should say, they'll make everyone else miserable." Allie turned around in the seat just as the main lodge came into view. She flashed her wide smile to Molly and widened her eyes.

"Jonah's mom and dad are a hoot. They are bound to hate something, so don't take it personally. God knows I haven't in the last three years."

"Oh quit. They aren't *that* bad." Jonah said as he let her hand go and playfully squeezed her thigh. She winked at Molly.

"I'll just be happy to be done with formalities myself, so I can bum around and take pictures of these fabulous trees and the lake. You don't mind if I wander around later, do you?"

"No, not at all. I forgot. You're a photographer, right?" Molly said.

"Best the Boston Herald ever had," Jonah said.

"Ah, I don't know about best, but I've got an eye if I do say so myself—mostly for nature. However, they stick me with boring city events and crime scenes more than anything. Hate that aspect of it, but it's a paycheck." Allie said as the car came to a stop. Emerson ran from the lodge steps to the car to greet Molly and the couple. She beamed as Allie got out of the car.

As Molly and Emerson showed them around, Molly couldn't help but notice how entranced Emerson was by Allie's sheer presence. Molly wondered if it was that obvious that she was just as enamored with the bride-to-be. Molly saw Allie as everything she thought she wanted to be or at least thought she was at some point in her youth. She radiated confidence, humor, and floated above everyone else. Partial credit for that was due to her six-foot-tall frame. Allie gushed about Emerson's hair and southern accent, which Molly appreciated. She also gushed about the resort, woodwork, stone walls, and the trees. Allie grew up in rural Georgia, and while she only had a trace of her southern accent, she hadn't lost her love of massive willows and pines. She hated that there was no moss swaying from the trees in New England, but she loved the trees nonetheless. She told Molly the trail, the lake, and views all reminded her of home, a home she hadn't seen in years.

After dinner, Allie asked Molly to walk one of the trails with her so she could find the best spot for sunset pictures. As they meandered down the main trail and left the lodge's view, Allie fiddled with her camera. Emerson trailed behind. Allie craned her neck to look as far up as possible.

"Those pines, right there. Perfect with the sunlight." She said as she pointed to some of the tallest white pines. "How old are these trees anyways?"

"I have no idea. I guess I never thought about it. Just seems these woods were always here. But, now that you point it out, I can definitely see a difference in the size compared to when I was a kid. That was twenty-five, thirty years ago, of course," Molly said. She raised her hand to her forehead to block the sun enough to see the treetops. "I guess they've grown a ton since then."

Allie crouched down close to the ground. She drew her elbow up to her knee and balanced her camera. She twisted the lens and peered through the view finder. Even crouched down, she was still more than half Emerson's height. Molly admired her sense of balance.

"That's the thing about trees, guys. They grow more than people think. Funny thing is that people think it's just time, sunlight, and water that gets them close to the heavens." Allie said as she snapped pictures and tilted her wrist and face more to get a different angle. "It's not, you know? It's more than that."

"What do you mean?" Emerson said.

"It's love."

"Really?" Said Molly.

"Yeah. Love. Like with people, trees know when they're loved. Both will grow accordingly. Love makes everything grow." Allie looked up from her camera and winked at Emerson just as she had done with Molly.

"I like that idea, Allie," Emerson said. She craned her neck to look at the treetops, too.

"These trees, these woods, were very loved by someone. That's for sure. And, they love you back." Allie said. Molly let her eyes scan the rest of the tree as the sun bounced off the tops. As Allie started to walk further up the trail and Emerson followed close behind her, Molly noticed more just how much those woods had indeed grown since she was a kid. She glanced at the trail's edges and saw small, newborn pines peeking through the edges, surrounded by needles. The piles of needles were shed to make room for new, sturdier, healthier needles, she thought. Molly contemplated the idea that love affected those trees, all of them, young and old. Had her love of those woods spawned some of those now-massive pines? Had her absence stunted some? Had her father's love and care encouraged the overgrowth she and Zack had to cut back? Maybe Allie was right. Those trees, like everything else, fed off love. Those woods absorbed and grew from the laughter of hundreds of guests. It grew from the love that was made in its presence on the beaches of the pond. Maybe, she thought, the brief love between her and Zack fueled growth of something, somewhere in those woods. It might have been short-lived, but that love mattered. Molly was comforted by the thought that their brief love affair fed those woods somehow. It fed her when she needed it most. The lake, the lodge, those dusty moose antlers anchoring the entire place had also loved her back. She smiled and quickened her pace to catch up to Em and Allie. As she ran to catch up, Molly felt those old needles break free from inside her to make room for healthier and sturdier needles.

Once the sun set and the whirlwind of a day wound to a close, Molly showed Allie and Jonah the lounge. Her mouth watered when she walked in. Carl shot her a stern look. Molly had put a noticeable dent in the open bourbon bottle, and she knew he knew it. Molly cringed at the thought of a lecture from Carl in front of Allie and Jonah, in front of anyone. On the other hand, she knew if he did, it was well-deserved. She exhaled as he walked to the other end of the bar to wait on the couple from Rhode Island. They all yelled 'congratulations' to Allie and Jonah as they made their way to the two side stools on the opposite side of the bar.

"Thank you so much," Allie yelled back to them. "This bar is phenomenal, Molly. This wood, the décor, it's all so mountain cabin-chic, like an old movie or something. It's everything I pictured when I was scrolling the internet to find the perfect place." She said to Molly as Molly tied a white apron around her waist and washed her hands.

"Thank you. It was all my father's doing. The wood, all of it. Built with his own two hands." Molly said. Carl cleared his throat and looked her way. "Oh yes, Carl here helped some, too."

"Helped? I'm the one who planed the wood for this bar. Dragged it out of the woods myself." He said as he rubbed his wrinkled and calloused hands over the polyurethaned slab of pine. Molly smiled at him.

"Yes, you did. You and my dad were a great team." Molly said to him. "He loved you very much." Carl looked down at the ground and then up at the ceiling.

"I miss him every day. It's just not the same without him. But, having you here, well, that makes it a little easier."

"Thanks, Carl. It makes it a little easier on me to have you here, too." Molly said.

Carl walked over and kissed her forehead as he scooted past to get to the bottle opener. Molly turned to him and then turned back around to the other side of the bar. The incident with her father's voice the night before was on the tip of her tongue. She swallowed the words and thought it was best to keep to herself. It was a lesson she needed to absorb alone, not one to be shared. She let those words play over in her head as she poured beers for Allie and Jonah. Rock bottom. Could last night really be her rock bottom if she wanted it to be? Could it be that easy to just decide, yes, last night was it, the worst it will ever get? Is she strong enough to make that decision, to stop and let last night be the real turning point? She swallowed hard as she glanced at the row of bottles. Perhaps she was strong enough. And, maybe it wasn't something she needed to do alone. Molly knew after last night, she still had her dad with her whether she stayed at Moose Pond Lodge or not. Molly told herself that once she sold, it would all be much easier anyway. Everything would.

A few hours later, Jonah kissed Allie goodnight and said he was heading to his cabin. Molly promised to walk Allie to hers and be sure both of them got an early morning wake-up call. They both seemed to itch with anticipation of seeing their parents and the rest of the wedding party the next day. Allie vowed just one more beer as Jonah shot them both a smile and walked out the door. As the screen door to the parking lot slammed shut, Molly asked Allie how they met. Allie told her they met three years ago when Jonah worked for an ad firm that did work for the Herald. The first thing she noticed was that he was shorter than the rest of the team. The second thing she noticed was that his personality was bigger. After two years of dating, he proposed in the Public Garden during a picnic under the willows. She was mid-shot with her camera as a duck swam past when he just blurted out "Let's get married." He didn't have a ring, a plan, or anything. Allie said he just knew in that instant that they were meant to marry. He told her he couldn't picture a day in his future that made sense without her in it.

"And quite honestly, Molly, I couldn't either. I mean, I wasn't as sure as he was. But, hell, I love him. I'm not sure how our worlds will mesh in the future, but they will. They can't *not* mesh." Allie said as she sipped the last of her beer. Molly sighed and untied her apron.

"That's beautiful. I think you guys make an adorable couple."

"How about you? You said Em's dad lives in Nashville. You guys just got divorced recently, right? And, this high school guy came back in the picture?"

"Well, I wouldn't say he came back in the picture. He was never really in the picture before. I had a mad crush on him, but he didn't know me. But, yeah, my divorce is in the final stages right now. Once I sell this place, I'll probably go back near Nashville with Em, make it easier for her to see him and stuff."

"Easier on her or you?" Allie asked.

"Oh her, definitely. I don't need to be around him, trust me. There's nothing there." Molly said. She took Allie's glass.

"One more, please. Just one more." Allie asked. Molly raised her eyebrows.

"Are you sure? You have a long day tomorrow and the rehearsal dinner and stuff." She said as the irony of asking someone if they really wanted another sunk in. Allie nodded yes and motioned for Molly to get another bottle. Molly poured her another and slid the glass to her.

"So, if there's nothing there with the ex, are you leaving here to run from the high school guy then?" Allie asked with raised eyebrows as she sipped the foam from the top of the glass.

"No, not really. Well, maybe a little. I thought we had something real and it fell apart very quickly, just yesterday, actually." Molly said. "He helped me get this place in order this spring, helped me get Em adjusted, and just helped me feel good about this place again. Then, boom, it was over. So, I guess, yeah. I want to just get away from it all. I need to start over."

"Didn't you come here to do that to begin with?"

"Yeah."

"Well," Allie said.

"Well, what?"

"So, you're just gonna sell, leave, and start over again?"

"I guess," Molly said.

"Molly, I know I don't know you very well, but let me tell you something. I felt lost for a few years. Long story, bad breakup, all that. I left. I mean I physically left. I packed up after college in Athens, Georgia. I headed out west. I started over. I was doing fine for a while." Allie said. She sipped her beer. "Good stuff, by the way. Local, right?" Molly nodded. "Anyways. I got my heart broke again. Then headed to the mid-west for a bit. I basically headed out cross-country and fell madly in love again with a grad student from Illinois. It went to hell after a year, so I left again. I thought a change of scenery again would fix it all. I really did. I just ran, really—ran from it all. I ran straight to Boston."

"Yeah, but all that running brought you to Jonah, right?" Molly said. She folded her arms and leaned on the bar across from Allie.

"No, Molly. I got my heart slashed up, torn up, set on fire in Boston, too, by a cop I met in a bar. We lived together for two years, and he bought me a ring, the whole works. Then, he tore my heart out and left so easily I thought I'd die. I couldn't breathe when I saw him get in his best friend's truck and leave our apartment." Allie looked down for a minute. "But, that time I didn't run away. I knew running wasn't going to fix it. Running wasn't helping me find myself, the right guy, or anything else. Staying did. Staying is what led me to find what I needed to find, right when I needed to find it. I stopped running, and that's when I met Jonah." Allie said as she sipped more. "Listen, whatever problem you had with the ex, or with this guy who lives here, you'll have anywhere else you end up running to. Running isn't going fix it. It'll just change the scenery when it happens again.

Get your heart broke here, there, anywhere. It'll still be just as broke." She sipped more. Molly stood back up and unfolded her arms. She blinked away a tear.

"Come on. You need to get to bed. You have to look fabulous tomorrow." She said as she took the near-empty glass and put it in the sink. Molly grabbed a flashlight from under the bar and took Allie by the arm. Allie leaned on her. Molly hadn't realized just how much taller Allie was than her. She moved Allie's falling black hair from her face and guided her to the door.

"Just think about, Molly. Just think before you sell this beautiful place. You can fix yourself here just as good as you could anywhere else." Allie repeated. Molly could tell she was on the verge of slurring.

"I'll think about it. I promise."

Molly woke up in the morning smiling at the thought of not having a hangover. While she had gone several days in a row without drinking at all since returning to the resort, this morning felt different. It felt like a fresh start. She stretched and let the to-do list for the wedding unfold in her mind. Instead of feeling overwhelmed or anxiety-ridden over the thought of pulling it all together, Molly let the excitement of the occasion fill her up. She wanted everything to be perfect for Allie and Jonah as if they were old friends, not simply paying guests. As she pulled back the quilt and wandered to the shower, she looked back at the bed. Yes, perfect, she thought. She would dig out a quilt from the linen closet to give as a wedding present. She had never given away any of her mother's quilts before, but for some reason, it seemed like the perfect time to start.

Molly woke Emerson and nearly skipped to the cabins with fresh flowers in hand. She knocked on Jonah's cabin door to find no answer. She tried Allie's next. Molly heard them both stir about and Allie giggle.

"We're up, Molly. Thank you." Allie said with a laugh.

"What happened to staying separate before the wedding?" Molly asked as she placed the flowers on the table in between the rocking chairs on the porch.

"We'll have to tonight once the family is here. I just couldn't be without my Jonah." Allie shouted out to her.

"Well, you still have to pay for two cabins, you know?" Molly said.

"Only fair." Jonah laughed back. Emerson laughed, too. "Oh jeez, we've gone and corrupted the kid, huh?"

"No, not at all," Molly said as they started back down the porch. She wanted to yell back that Em has seen worse just in jest. But, Molly stopped herself when she remembered that Emerson had truly seen worse only a few short months ago. On the way back to the lodge, Molly found herself wondering how that image of her father and nurse would affect Emerson in the long run. They had never really talked about it. Molly sure knew Kenny hadn't bothered to talk to Emerson about it. Of all the balls she and Kenny had dropped while raising Emerson, this one might be the biggest, Molly thought. 'I'll do better,' Molly said to herself as they walked back up the trail. She noticed Emerson was almost up to her shoulders. She had grown since they left Nashville and Molly was startled by how much at that moment. Molly realized how quickly Emerson's childhood was passing her by. She saw a taller, slimmer, more vibrant and aware girl walking beside her compared to the chubby and confused kid who stumbled from the backseat a few months earlier. Emerson no longer sulked around with slumped shoulders and ill-timed eye rolls. Molly knew today had to be a new beginning that would last. She felt one step above rock bottom and up was the only direction she could let herself go from here on out. She wasn't going to have too many more chances to get it right with Emerson or with herself. Emerson reached for Molly's hand.

"Thanks, Mom," Emerson said as she swung Molly's arm.

"For what?"

"All this. This summer. Showing me this and letting us live here this summer. It's cool." Emerson said. Molly smiled and drew her daughter's hand up to kiss it. Just then, Emerson jerked her hand away.

"Race ya!" she yelled as she bolted ahead of Molly. Molly yelled and chased after her. She barely caught Emerson before they hit the parking lot. As she caught her breath, she looked around at the lodge, the gazebo, the perfectly mulched shrubs. She smiled. It was all beautiful. Molly was thankful that her daughter got to experience it and that she got to experience it again herself. She knew if she signed those papers, Molly could end up anywhere, but at least she had given Emerson those memories.

The parents, wedding party, and other guests arrived in droves throughout the day. The finishing touches, embarrassing stories from older relatives, and endless hugs filled the lodge and gazebo. Molly watched Allie from afar as she was swarmed by each new arrival. Molly watched Jonah stand tall and confident as he anxiously awaited to be Allie's husband. He beamed when she brushed past him. Molly saw Allie wink at him every time they came into each other's view. She could feel their happiness, their excitement to start this new chapter together. She felt grateful to be a part of it in a small way.

As Molly tied up the last of the lanterns around the top of the gazebo, she saw one more car pull in. Maxine hopped out of the driver's side. Molly's heart jumped.

"Hey, girl. What are you doing here?" Molly said as she stepped down from the ladder.

"I came to see if you needed help decorating. I know you suck at it alone." Maxine said as she slid sunglasses off her face and up past her forehead. Molly laughed. "Plus, I wasn't taking any chances of you bolting out of town without saying goodbye once you signed those papers."

"I told you I wouldn't do that," Molly said. She knew she deserved the jab.

"I know. It's just an excuse to come out."

"You don't need an excuse. But, I'm glad you're here to help." Molly said. She hugged her oldest friend. Molly thought having Maxine by her side was making this self-proclaimed new beginning even better than it had been so far.

The rehearsal dinner went as planned as Molly, Emerson, Maxine, and the kitchen staff burst through the swinging doors in rapid succession. Sheer excitement and adrenaline kept Molly going as the last of the dishes were cleared, and toasts were made. She listened to more childhood stories from the side wall and found herself laughing along with the family. While she noticed Jonah's parents looked slightly out of place and rigid, their pride in their son was palpable. They came up to Molly numerous times to thank her for the extra amenities in their room, the extra quilts, and for sweeping off their cabin porch just one more time. The sight of pine needles in the corners was apparently too much of a reminder that they were in the woods. Molly realized she spent a great deal of the day ensuring they weren't subjected to too much nature in a 48-hour period. While it would've annoyed her any other time and from any other guests, she was happy to do it since it alleviated some of the stress carried by Jonah. Once the crowd moved to the lounge, Maxine pulled Molly aside.

"Do you need me tomorrow? I'm free. Josh is taking the kids to the ocean tomorrow." Maxie asked.

"Nah, I think it's all taken care of," Molly said as she hugged her friend. "But, thanks so much for helping today."

"How about the lounge? Are you okay handling that on your own? Do you want me to stay?"

"I won't be alone. Carl will be there until eleven." Molly said as they let go of each other.

"You know what I mean," Maxine said. Her face turned serious. Molly understood what she was asking.

"Yeah, I'm fine. I'll be fine. Don't worry about me, Max. I think this time, I've got it. Today is a new start for me. I mean it." Molly brushed her hair back behind her ears. "Tomorrow will be just as great as today. I've got this. I really do." Maxine smiled and mouthed okay. As she left, Molly followed the few stragglers into the lounge where more toasts to Jonah and Allie were already underway. Her mouth didn't water. She knew there was nothing she could drink away, nothing she needed to drink away. She squeezed past the best man and his girlfriend to get behind the bar with Carl. She flashed him a smile, and he flashed one back. Her night would end sober, and she was excited to awaken feeling just as refreshed as she had today.

The wedding day was born and blessed with a cloudless sky. The sun streaked through Molly's window and made her squint before she fully opened her eyes. Molly had fresh flowers to deliver to the cabins and breakfast in bed for Allie. She also had chair pads to tie and a cake to guard with her life. Her stomach fluttered as she stepped in the shower. She briefly thought of her own wedding day. She was hungover that morning and the next day, too. It wasn't until the last few months at Moose Pond Lodge that she realized how much she drank in Nashville, too. It had been her crutch through more than she realized. It numbed her to the truth about Kenny for longer than she cared to admit. Ironically, it numbed her to her father's problems, too. Molly washed those little revelations away and reverted her attention to the wedding and anticipation of another day and night without too much bourbon clouding her mind.

After she woke Emerson for breakfast and made her stops at the cabins, Molly started back towards the lodge. She stopped dead in her tracks and turned around. Despite the long list of to-dos, Molly had the urge to walk to the pond. She wasn't sure how many more chances she'd have to sneak off to that pond. She quickened her pace as the water came into view. Molly stopped a few feet before the water. She slipped off her shoes. She rolled up her shorts a little more. Molly stepped in. The sand unfolded and curved around her bare feet. Molly let herself sink a little. The water gently lapped at her calves, then her knees. It was cold, but not icy. It woke her mind more than her morning coffee. She went in a little further. The water caressed her thighs, and she let her hands drop in. It embraced her. She let it completely envelop her and sway her from side to side. Molly let her feet sink a little deeper into the sand below. She could no longer see her feet as the sand swirled her legs in murky brown. The slight shock of the cold subsided. Molly and the water were one body, one being. The sun bounced off and she ran her hands along the top, parting the pond. Needles floated around and drifted to the sides of her legs. Those discarded needles had clung to trees along the water's edge for years, only to fall and float mere feet from where they were born. She inhaled that pine air, the cleanest air she'd ever known. Molly closed her eyes and let the water lead her slightly deeper inside. She felt protected by that pond. She felt loved by it, all of it. Every drop of that water was part of her. Each needle, tree, and grain of sandy shore was part of who she was. She grew from it just as much as it grew from her and her family. Molly opened her eyes and turned her body back towards the shore. She moved her legs slowly and emerged. She hadn't realized she went in almost to her hips until her body was fully out of the water. This time, she didn't feel heavy or pained coming out. She picked up her shoes and started up the trail. Before she left it all behind, Molly turned back and looked at the pond. She could once again hear her own laughter as her father slung her into a canoe, as her mother splashed her back in the water, as she ran into that pond with her first boyfriend, then with Zack, too. Her heart pounded as those memories flooded her mind. Molly smiled and turned back toward the lodge. Allie was right, she thought. It was all fed from love, and it had loved her back.

Molly and Emerson dressed up for the wedding once the details were all set. They took their spots in the back as the ceremony got underway. Allie emerged from the lodge doors and graced the porch before walking to the gazebo with her father. Her path was lined with flowers. Her dress was straight ivory silk and flirted with the blades of grass. There was no lace or inlays. There was merely a layer of silk flowing over her long body. Her every curve was accentuated on full display. It was a bold choice, yet it suited Allie. The ivory lit up next up Allie's dark skin and hair. Molly gasped as the sun hit Allie from behind. She swore she heard Jonah gasp, too. The pair held hands, exchanged vows, and exchanged private, intimate glances. Molly admired how private they seemed to keep their love, their thoughts about each other. As they kissed, and guests cheered, Molly found herself clapping and wiping away a tear.

"What's wrong, Mom? You thinking about dad?" Emerson whispered.

"No, honey. I'm just happy for them. I'm just happy about all of this." The happiness of the guests, Allie and Jonah, and even the staff rippled through the air. Molly thought to herself that there were so few perfect days in life. But this day was one of them. She wanted more like it.

The crowd ate, cheered, posed for pictures in the grass, and fawned over the newlyweds. The celebrating moved from the lodge, the porch, the grass and back to the porch. Drinks clanked, and kisses were sloppily slathered on Allie and Jonah, both. Molly saw Jonah's mother cry as she refilled her wine glass. She saw Jonah's dad's cheeks reddened as he drank more, too. Both seemed to forget their aversion to nature as they sat on the gazebo steps and blew bubbles with the kids. Molly's heart was full as she absorbed the happiness of these families and guests. She grabbed a tray of more pieces of cake to distribute to the guests on the porch. Molly let her body fall back against the wall and laugh as Jonah lifted Allie over his shoulder to carry her back to the gazebo for another dance. The music grew louder than it had before. She saw the best man grab Allie's equally slender mother and twirl her around. As the day started to slip into night, Molly lit candles around the porch. Allie had collapsed in a rocking chair and sipped a beer. Despite playing with kids, taking endless pictures, and making her way through every inch of the resort, her dress was still perfect. Molly sat in the chair next to her.

"So, was it everything you wanted?" Molly asked Allie. Jonah snuck up and kissed Allie's cheek. She giggled and took a sip.

"It was more, Molly. It was so much more." Allie reached over and took Molly's hand. She squeezed it. "I see Emerson loves my cousin's kids, huh? They've been playing all day." Allie pointed to the yard off the side of the gazebo.

"Yeah, she's loving this. She loves it here." Molly said. "We've loved hosting this wedding. Your families are awesome, Allie."

"Thanks. Some of them are a little more awesome than others," she said with a wink.

"That's every family, I think," Molly said. They both laughed.

"Seriously, Molly. This has been perfect. All of it. I've never been happier."

"Good. I'm so glad to hear it."

"Jonah and I already decided, we talked. We want to come back for our first anniversary. He wants to fish some more. I want to dance on the gazebo. We want to sit on this porch and watch the sunset. This place, it's, well, it's magic."

"That's wonderful. I'm so glad you see how special this place is." Molly said. She let go of Allie's hand and folded hers in her lap. Molly started to rock in the chair as Allie sipped her beer.

"Will you be here, Molly? Next year? Say you'll be here." Allie said. "You're not still gonna run, are you?"

Molly sighed. She glanced around. She rocked. She saw Emerson run past laughing louder than she had ever heard before. Emerson was bursting with joy. The gazebo lights came on and Jonah's mother brushed past with a flower in her hair and piece of cake in her hand.

"Molly? Will you be here?" Allie asked again.

Molly sighed and let the sights, sounds, and smells of the resort and that night engulf her.

"Yeah, Allie. I'll be here next year. This is my home, my daughter's home. It's where I'm loved. It's where I have my roots and—"

"It's where you'll find your wings," Allie said. She winked at Molly and sipped some more.

"I hope you're right," Molly said as she peeled herself from the rocking chair. "I'll be back, okay?" Allie nodded and then laughed as her bride's maid stumbled up the last step of the porch with another drink.

Molly walked into the lodge and glanced at the antlers at the top of the stone fireplace. She looked over at the photo albums on the shelf and the stool by the desk, the same stool she climbed as a kid. She walked to the office which was flanked in thank you cards from guests. Molly went to the desk and opened the drawer. She took out the offer awaiting her signature. Molly tore the stack in two. Then, she tore it some more. The sound of ripping paper was freeing. She looked around at what had been her father's office. The pictures of her on his shoulders and pictures with her mother were exactly where they had been since she was a kid. She looked at the baby pictures of Emerson tacked to the bulletin board. They were crinkled and worn. Her entire past was in that office tacked to the walls.

Molly realized the memories of her father, in that place, tacked to those walls and in those albums, were all memories she wanted to keep. The memories she ran from, the ones that kept her away for years, were residing in her head. She couldn't get rid of those lingering bad memories by selling and running away, again. She could replace them. She could stay, love the resort and the woods, and help it grow even more. She could grow there, too. As for Zack and the ache in her heart, he helped her fix the resort and fix herself, but she had done her part to repair what was broken inside and around her, too. She would keep fixing herself, keep working to be better. Molly had scrubbed away the pain of her father's death and her divorce. She could scrub away the pain of losing Zack, also.

As for the lure of the lounge to fix her pain, Molly spent months cleaning the resort and knew she could clean herself up, too. Besides, any demons she fought in that lounge would follow her if she left anyway. There would be a lounge tempting her somewhere else. Molly had no choice now but to be strong enough to fight that temptation regardless of where she called home. There was no need to run, no desire to walk away from what she created. She was finally tired of running. Molly smirked when she realized she ran so fast from her past that she ended up right back where she started—Moose Pond Lodge.

A picture of Molly with her father swayed on the bulletin board. Molly wasn't there when he needed her. He wasn't there when she needed him. She might not have been home when others were there for him, But, she was home now. Molly knew in her heart that her father would consider that good enough. Moose Pond Lodge needed her now, and as she looked at walls of the office and the torn pieces of paper on the desk, she knew she needed it, too.

Molly got up and walked to the porch, her porch. She took a seat next to Allie's bride's maid and laughed as she told stories about Allie in college. Molly craned her neck to see Emerson running through the gazebo with the other kids. The echoes of laughs, the smell of cake and candles burning, and the coolness of the night air embraced her and flooded her senses. She sat back and let it roll over her. Just as she was about to close her eyes and rock in her chair, Molly heard the all too familiar sound of a pickup truck over the laughter on the porch. She leaned up and caught a glimpse of Zack in the driver's seat. He smiled at her and shrugged his shoulders as the engine settled. Molly smiled back at him. It felt natural and easy to smile his way despite what had happened. He slid out of the truck without taking his eyes off her. He put his hands in his pockets and started to make his way through the crowd of wedding guests. Molly's heart fluttered, as it had every time her eyes met his. But this time, she felt light knowing that whatever he was there to tell her or whatever he wanted, she could handle. She was content, strong, and had a future of her own planned. He could still add to it, but he certainly didn't have the power to take anything away from it. That porch, that lodge, and even the lounge was her and her daughter's future. Yep, Molly thought to herself, she was home, and she was going to stay there. There was no time to dwell on defeat, heartache, or regrets. Molly had a resort to run and a daughter to raise. She couldn't wait to see what the next day and next season would bring to Moose Pond Lodge.

Nature is not a place to visit. It is home—Gary Snyder

Acknowledgements

Moose Pond Lodge is a story about loss, love, motherhood, divorce, and the complex relationships all women have with themselves and those they love. Women try, women fail, and women get back up and try again—every single day.

Molly is a combination of many strong, flawed, and complicated women I've known over the years. She is a woman in transition, a woman who's trying to find herself and a sense of home while she brings so much emotional baggage along for the ride. She is a woman like many middle-aged women I know and love—scattered, floundering, clumsy, haunted, fiercely loving, unsure of where she's going, and one who wears her heart on her sleeve. No one woman has it all figured out and glides from one stage of life into another unscathed. Few women get it right the first time, or, for some, even the second time. Every woman has regrets, makes mistakes, and often turns to something unhealthy to deal with pain or loss, or to get over those messy missteps. However, most women keep trying to get better, choose better, and help other women along the way. This novel is for those women, that tribe that keeps rooting for us as we venture into the next chapter, even if we have no idea what the hell that next chapter may bring.

Moose Pond Lodge is also a love letter to the beauty that is Maine. The essence of the resort came about as I drove to Bethel, Maine. The trees, the silence of the woods and mountains, and the tiny resort cabins that peppered the way inspired the setting. As the state slogan suggest, Maine is Vacationland. It's wild, remote, breath-taking, and has the most miles of jagged coastline in the country. It's where others come to get back to nature, to find refuge from the noise and chaos of life elsewhere. There's a certain clarity that comes about when surrounded by nature, by the woods. A long walk in the Maine woods can fix nearly everyone and everything, or least reveal a better perspective. It's where I find peace every time I walk through my woods and listen to the whispers of the white pines swaying above me. It's my home.

**If you enjoyed Moose Pond Lodge, you'll love Book 2 in the series. Book 2 will reveal more about Allie and Jonah Parker as their young marriage is tested. As they travel back to Moose Pond Lodge for their first anniversary and on subsequent visits, Allie and Jonah find themselves facing challenges they never anticipated and evolving as a couple and as individuals, proving love takes constant work to grow as tall and strong as the pines they love to explore in the woods of Maine.

61972688R10130

Made in the USA
Middletown, DE
17 January 2018